Are You There, God?

Are You There, God?

Theresa A. Campbell

www.urbanchristianonline.com

Urban Books, LLC
97 N18th Street
Wyandanch, NY 11798

ISBN 13: 978-1-60162-720-9
ISBN 10: 1-60162-720-3

First Printing January 2014
Printed in the United States of America

10 9 8 7 6 5 4 3 2 1

Distributed by Kensington Corp.
Submit Wholesale Orders to:
Kensington Publishing Corp.
C/O Penguin Group (USA) Inc.
Attention: Order Processing
405 Murray Hill Parkway
East Rutherford, NJ 07073-2316
Phone: 1-800-526-0275
Fax: 1-800-227-9604

This book is dedicated to my four guardian angels (in order of their sunsets).

Mr. Sydney Allen: Grandfather (October 1995)

Mrs. Celestina Allen: Grandmother (January 1997)

Mr. Stanford Allen: Uncle (October 2006)

Mrs. Barbara Robinson-Jenkins: Sister in my heart (February 2013)

"Wherever you are in heaven, tell God I say you deserve a pair of wings."

Acknowledgments

Thank you, Lord, for the many blessings that you have given me. It's not because of my goodness, but your mercy. I'm still in awe of everything that you are doing in my life. Who would have thought that this day would come? But now I know, if I am says I am, then I am!

Heartfelt thanks to my mother, Maxine Allen, for showing me that with God on my side, victory is always mine. Your strength, dedication, and courage are a constant inspiration to me. May God bless you always!

To my brother, Warren Osbourne, thank you for always supporting me. Remember with God, if the mind conceives it, you can achieve it!

To my editor, Mrs. Joylynn M. Ross, now I see why you are the best at what you do! Thank you for allowing the Lord to use you to make my dream come true.

To my agent, Dr. Maxine Thompson, thank you for the wealth of knowledge you shared with me and for believing in my work.

To the reader, thank you for taking the time to read my book. I hope that you will be inspired and you will always remember that God is always there for you.

Prologue

"I am going to kill you!" he roared. "Not even the vultures will find you when I'm done with you!"

His trunk-like arms around her neck tightened their hold and her small mouth popped opened like a drowning man as she gurgled, struggling unsuccessfully to suck some much-needed oxygen into her lungs. With her tiny arms flapping around wildly and her feet hovering above the ground, she kicked frantically as she fought against her own demise.

Two enlarged pools of tears connected with his two fiery eyes, pleadingly, but the vise grip only clamped down harder, crushing her trachea. Aunt Madge always said, "Whatsoever sweet you will sour you," and she was admittedly right as always.

She felt her strength creeping away and his grip tightening as she realized now that it was all a lie. Everything was a lie.

Earlier that day, the sea of green, white, and khaki uniforms spilled through the wide-open classroom doors and the front gate of the high school in triumph as if they were escaping from prison and feared recapture. Talking, laughing, and screaming voices collided with each other as hurried feet zigzagged in every direction. After five days of hard work, the anticipation of the upcoming weekend was contagious and explosive. And she was no exception.

She hustled her way through the tight-meshed bodies, stepping on toes, excusing herself, slightly running, and waving to familiar faces. She was on the clock and it was ticking faster than she wanted. Her brown eyes sparkled and her head bobbed softly back and forth, to and fro as she hummed a tune, grinning and giggling as she rushed home. She needed to complete her chores as soon as possible before sneaking out to meet her baby. Tonight she would tell him the good news, she thought excitedly.

A few minutes later as she sprinted down the small, narrow dirt-paved track to her house, her head snapped back sharply as her body collided with a falling heap of flesh and bones. Recovering quickly, she reached out and grabbed Mother Sassy's arm before she hit the ground. Too wrapped up in her thoughts, she failed to see the older woman coming toward her.

"I'm so, so, sorry," she apologized, her cheeks flushed with embarrassment.

"Your head is certainly in the clouds today," was Mother Sassy's curt response. "Chile, you just too young to be running around like a chicken with its head cut off. But after a long day at school, I guess you are a little distracted."

She smiled awkwardly without making eye contact and tried to carefully maneuver around Mother Sassy, but she grabbed on to her arms.

"What is this, dear Father? Girl, is that belly you have there?" Mother Sassy exclaimed. Her hands flew to her mouth and her eyes widened in shock, already answering her own question instead of waiting for a response.

"Oh, no, no, ma'am," she stuttered in fright. "I just put on a little weight. That's all."

"That's all my foot! I know a bun in the oven when I see one. I done have me eight chil'ren, so you can't fool little ol' me."

She knew she was in trouble now. Mother Sassy and Aunt Madge had been going to the same church for years and became very close after Mother Sassy took a younger Aunt Madge under her wing. Mother Sassy was also the "mouth-a-masse" for spreading other people's business, and she knew many people in her community would see her as an outcast once her secret was exposed.

"I don't know what you are talking about," she responded, her words chipped in ice, and she quickly walked away.

With her mind running a hundred miles per hour, she pondered her situation. *But what if he isn't happy with what I am about to tell him? After all, he is a well-respected man in the community and his reputation means the world to him.* She felt a sense of uncertainty nestled in her gut.

Later that night her breathing echoed around her with every fast exhale and weary inhale. Worry was etched across her face as she stared into the darkness of the night through the broken, dirty classroom window. Frantically pacing the uneven concrete floor, she wrapped her little arms around her body in a futile attempt to ward off the cold draft that crept into the already-chilly room. Muttering words of comfort, she sighed impatiently as she went again to sneak another peek outside.

The pitch-black classroom lit up for a few seconds from headlight beams of the approaching vehicle as it passed through the gates of the high school. With a renewed burst of energy, she shot to her feet. By now she knew the routine very well and as if she were programmed to do so, she went into action. She quickly pulled her well-worn dress over her head and slipped off her underwear. After spreading an old, thin sheet on top of the shaking, metal table, she gingerly lay down, staring up at the ceiling, and waited in silence.

Soon his presence filled the room, and to her he seemed larger than life itself. He rubbed in hands in glee and smiled in anticipation when he saw her waiting for him. He was in a hurry to get home that night so he knew he had to get out of there fast. The usually insignificant sound of his belt opening seemed to reverberate loudly off the walls. With her eyelids tightly closed, creating a barrier for the unshed tears, lips firmly folded, she trembled uncontrollably. She wasn't sure if it was fear or anxiety but her mind was too numb then to figure it out. It took a minute for him to undress and without saying a word to interrupt the haunting silence of the night, he went to her.

It was a brief encounter but to her it felt like forever. Feeling fully satisfied with himself and not the least bit concerned with his despicable behavior, he slowly raised himself up and began to pull away from her. But she wrapped her small arms around his neck and forcibly held on to him. She knew she couldn't allow him to leave until she told him her news. With her eyes still closed in fright, she stuttered as she tried to speak but no words came. Now impatient and frustrated with her actions, he reached behind to unclasp her hands from around his neck and was surprised at her strength as she held on.

Still visibly shaking but determined to be heard, in a small but clear voice she whispered softly in his ear, "I think I am pregnant."

He froze in shock as he saw his entire life flash before his eyes. He was as good as dead, for surely his wife was going to kill him.

"You are what?" he shouted. "You can't be pregnant. Weren't you on the pill?" he asked.

She looked at him blankly; she had no idea what he was talking about.

He stared down at the naïve, naked girl and felt sick to his stomach. It had just dawned on him that he had been abusing this young girl for a few weeks now. And to make matters worse he never took the necessary precaution to protect them both. Now here she was, a child who was going to have a child: his child. He knew he might as well just kill himself because his wife, her parents, or his were going to do it anyway, and if not, then he was going to prison for a long, long time. But maybe, just maybe, there was a way out of this awful situation.

"You can't have this baby. I will give you the money to go to Kingston and get an abortion. No one has to even know you were ever pregnant."

She looked at him as if he had lost his mind. Her mother had lost her life to give her life and she would rather die herself than kill her baby.

"I am not killing my baby," she screamed. Her anger gave her the courage to go against his wishes. And then it happened. He snapped and changed into a terrifying animal right before her eyes.

In a flash he jumped to his feet and reached over and grabbed her by the neck, lifting her small, naked body like a rag doll into the air.

"Oh, yes, you will," he growled. "One or both of you will have to go, someway, somehow, and I am going to make sure of it."

Then he began to squeeze the life out of her, literally.

"I'm going to die now," she thought as she kicked wildly and scratched at his face.

As the room spun around and around, Officer Gregg's grip on her neck tightened. She felt lightheaded and knew she was about to lose consciousness. Suddenly her head seemed to explode as she was flung roughly into the wall where she bounced off like a ball before landing face down on the dirty concrete ground. Pain exploded in every available artery in her body. Choking and coughing, she desperately sucked some much-needed air into her burning lungs. Tears poured from her red eyes as she whimpered weakly, folding her aching body into a protective ball. She wasn't sure why he didn't kill her, but she knew she needed to get away from him quickly before he changed his mind and finished the job. But she was hurting too much and was too weak to move.

She felt her aching head jerk back as Officer Gregg grabbed a handful of hair and snapped her head off the floor. She felt the cold metal of the gun pressing in her neck and screamed in terror.

"Please, don't kill me," She pleaded. "I'm sorry. Please."

"You better not call my name to anyone," Officer Gregg screamed into her ringing ears, spit flying out his mouth. "If you do, I will come back and kill you. In fact, I will kill your precious aunt Madge first. You wouldn't want anything to happen to her now, would you?" he threatened.

She shivered in fear.

"Would you?" Officer Greg growled.

She shook her head and winced at the pain. He waited a few seconds before he loosened his tight hold on her hair and stood up, before hurriedly pulling on his clothes. He then stormed out the classroom without a backward glance at the wounded young girl he had almost killed.

She breathed a sigh of relief after the rackety door slammed shut. Pain like she had never known before pierced her body from head to toe but she found the strength to roll over onto her back and then into a sitting position. Even her shallow, labored breathing sent arrows of piercing agony through her body, but down on all fours she slowly crawled to an old metal chair close by. Feebly hanging on to its unsteady legs, she painfully stood up and wobbled over to a window that overlooked the tall bushes where he usually parked. Trembling in fear, she peeked outside, noticed his vehicle was gone, and breathed a sigh of relief.

Staring aimlessly, hurting physically and dying mentally, the small flicker of something bright in the distance caught her squinting eyes as she gazed into pure blackness. The haunting shadows of the large pine trees at the back of the old high school made the dim light even more obscure, but she knew what it was and strained her eyes to get a glimpse of the big old cross on top of the church. Most of the lights were broken, forming an I instead of the usual T, but she knew what it was, and instantly Tiny felt her shame and loneliness choking the life out of her, again.

Chapter One

Brown focused eyes hardened into small slits. Her nostrils flared open and her teeth locked tight behind folded lips as she held her head high and walked swiftly but steadily down the noisy school corridor. Dupree knew she needed to get away from them fast. She refused to give in to her anger or reveal the pain their ugly words were inflicting. *Whoever said "sticks and stones will break your bones but words will never hurt you" was a big fat liar,* she thought.

"Dupree is ugly like duppy."

"Dupree is as black as night."

"Dupree is an awful sight."

Those were just some of the hateful words ricocheting off Dupree's back as she hurried down a flight of stairs. But her haste never deterred the bullies who ran behind her singing their new Dupree rhymes, giggling, laughing, and jeering as they hurled bullets of venom words at her back.

Eyes burning from unshed tears, Dupree flew across the schoolyard, trying to avoid a collision with the many students and teachers who seemed oblivious to her distress. Finally breaking out into a sprint, she zoomed through the school gate, briefly glancing back to see that her tormentors had fallen behind. But she kept running like a bat from hell, until she got to the privacy of the narrow dirt track leading to her house.

It was only then that Dupree allowed the floodgates to open. With her back pressed firmly against a tall breadfruit tree for support, she deeply sucked some much-needed air into her dry lungs as she sobbed uncontrollably. Her woeful, wet eyes looked over the top of the trees in the farm below and stared at the flowing body of water in the distance.

"I can't do this anymore," Dupree whispered. "I'm so tired of this."

Thirteen-year-old Dupree lived with her grandaunt on the outskirts of Falmouth Trelawny, in Jamaica. Her mother, Tiny, was only fifteen years old when she got pregnant with Dupree and dropped out of high school. She told everyone that she didn't know who Dupree's father was, and no one volunteered for the job, so it was left to Aunt Madge to take care of Dupree.

One week after Dupree's birth, Tiny took off for bright lights and fast action in Kingston and was never to be heard from again. Aunt Madge, who didn't have any biological children and had raised Tiny like her own after her sister Ellen died, was heartbroken when she left. Now she had another young baby to take care of and she took Dupree like her own daughter. Many people who didn't know their history actually thought she was.

Later that night the crickets could be heard whispering to each other, the trees cast their shadows on the ground, and the stillness of the dark night hugged the small board houses in the closeness of its arms. It seemed as if everyone was on a sleeping journey far into a place filled with snores and steady breathing. Everyone, that was, except for Dupree, who lay curled up in a fetal position under her little metal bunk bed. The tears flowed freely down her face as she cried softly into her tiny arms. Her small body shook in agony as the pain in her heart became just too much for her to bear. She felt she was ugly because of her deep dark-chocolate complexion and her bullies at school did enough to hammer it into her head and her heart.

As Dupree cried, she prayed quietly, hiccupping between words, knocking on heaven's door for a much-needed miracle. "Are you there, God? It's me, Dupree, again, dear Father. Can you hear me, Lord? Please, God, I am begging you to make me into a pretty girl. I don't want to be ugly no more, God. Please, please, God, I am begging you from the bottom of my heart."

But as she wept, Dupree knew in her heart that God would not hear her prayer, because she had been praying every night for over four years now and nothing had changed.

"Juicy oranges! Fresh corns! Barbie yam, yellow yam, sweet grapefruits! Come and get it! For a small price, we have it!" Dupree's small voice struggled to win the shouting match of numerous altos, sopranos, and tenor sale pitches and sale bargains of the many sellers and buyers, scattered all over the confined space like ants seeking fat.

There were dozens and dozens of wooden stalls that created a market maze. Some were leaned to one side in protest and others were piled so high they defied the law of gravity. Anxious sellers desperately in need of a sale screamed out offers at the top of their lungs. Some daring enough grabbed the arms of potential customers, pulling them in one direction, while another competitor pulled in another. Frustrated losers protested the freedom of choice, resulting in cussing sessions, some very embarrassing to Dupree and Aunt Madge.

It was a buyer-seller circus and Dupree and Aunt Madge were a part of the act, desperate to lose their goods in exchange for some much-needed cash—goods that were planted by Aunt Madge's own hands.

Their little stall was rainbowed with neatly arranged fruits and produce of every color and variety, such as yam, bananas, sweet potatoes, breadfruits, sweet corn, ackees, oranges, mangoes, and grapefruits. It was like a guppy in a school of sharks. But what they lacked in quantity was made up by the high quality.

"Business is good," Aunt Madge said as she watched their goods flying off the stall.

Aunt Madge was a small-time farmer who planted most of the food they ate and all they sold. She also raised a few chickens and a pig now and then. So Dupree was never hungry because she could always have found something to eat, even if it was an orange or a mango.

By society's standards Aunt Madge and Dupree were very poor, but if you asked Aunt Madge she would tell you that she was one of the richest women on earth. Oh, yes, she was a child of God and her Father was the King of all kings. Aunt Madge was a very religious woman and she instilled these values in Dupree.

Then it happened.

When you think it's peace and safety, it's sudden destruction, came to Aunt Madge a few mornings later, her face drenched in sweat as pins and needles poked into every available pore. Her hands and feet lay lifeless on the bed as the unbearable pain fought to rip her apart, making it impossible to move. She was as sick as a dog.

Not hearing the familiar banging and knocking of Aunt Madge's pots and pans in the outside kitchen before she left for the field, Dupree, who had just awoken, quickly jumped off her bed across the room from her aunt's and in four quick steps was leaning over her in concern.

"Aunt Madge, are you okay?" she asked nervously as she picked up a lifeless hand, staring into her agonizing eyes. The only responses were deep groans and moans.

As she watched her giant crumble right before her eyes, Dupree wept deep heartbreaking, soul-wrenching sobs.

It is said that when it rains it pours, because Aunt Madge's condition went from bad to worse.

Dupree, assisted by Sister Nadine, took Aunt Madge to the hospital, and was told that she was suffering from a neurological disorder that gave her a stroke. However, without health insurance and little money, there wasn't much done for her. She was given some pain medication and basically sent home to pray for a miracle.

As one sorrowful day dragged into the next, the life seemed to slowly drain from Aunt Madge. Her legs were like two stiff pieces of board, while her tongue stayed frozen in one place. She was unable to walk or talk, and was eventually bedridden. Now thirteen-year-old Dupree had to take care of herself and her aunt.

Ducking under low-limbed trees that grabbed at her face, Dupree waddled through the rough knee-high bushes, trampling on slippery, stained grasses, skipping over sharp rocks and swatting biting, annoying insects as she ran back and forth, huffing and puffing, collecting dry wood as the afternoon sun rained down mercilessly.

When her pile was high enough, she pulled both ends of the rope under the wood together and tied a tight knot. Groaning under the weight, she lifted her heavy load onto her head and gingerly made her way back home. This was a routine she did every few days and knew the woods around her house like the back of her hand.

They needed the dry wood for cooking because they could not afford a gas stove or the money to purchase coal from Mr. Weather down the road.

Once she arrived back home, over and over again Dupree raised the big machete over her head, and then brought it down hard, slicing through the big pieces of wood, creating a much larger pile of smaller pieces to fit under the cooking pot.

But it only took one missed second. As the machete sliced through the air rhythmically, when lowered, it missed the piece of wood intended and instead connected with Dupree's big left toe. Blood spurted out like a sprinkler and quickly covered the surrounding area like a thick red blanket.

Grinding her teeth in agony, Dupree fell to the ground and wrapped her fingers around the throbbing piece of flesh. Unshed tears burned her eyes and her lips trembled uncontrollably but she willed herself not to cry. As the shock of the accident washed over her body, she struggled to stand up and hopped into the house to retrieve a clean old shirt. Ripping off a piece, she wrapped the cloth tightly around her injured toe, stopping the flow of blood and warding off an unwelcome infection. But as the pain wreaked havoc on her body, Dupree fought against it and went back to make dinner for Aunt Madge.

Rough, uneven boards held together by long, sharp nails and a few naked sheets of zinc on the roof, was the small outside kitchen. On a rainy day, the pouring water danced right on in, turning the dirt-covered flooring into a slippery, muddy slop.

Standing on two cement blocks, Dupree added a few inches to her shorter stature to reach the height of the fireplace. As she peered into the big cooking pot, thick clouds of smoke quickly filled the small space, wrapping itself around her and lashing out angrily at her eyes, drawing a constant flow of tears as if she was crying. But using the clean towel she kept around her neck, Dupree wiped her face without losing concentration on the dinner she prepared.

Dupree tried to cook everything from stew pork and jerk chicken to red pea soup. That evening the delicious aroma from the chicken soup perfumed the air. Balancing a steaming bowl in her hand, Dupree slowly made her way up the shaky board steps inside the house to feed Aunt Madge dinner.

With great effort she lifted Aunt Madge into a sitting position and while one hand unsteadily kept her from falling, the other awkwardly placed two pillows behind her back to keep her upright. Perched on the edge of the bed, Dupree repeatedly blew cool air on a spoonful of the hot liquid before putting it to Aunt Madge's slightly open, unmoving lips.

The long days turned into weeks and the exhausted weeks into months but there was no change. Was there a light at the end of the tunnel?

Chapter Two

The water rapidly spurted from the standpipe into the waiting big bucket that sat on rocks below. Filling quickly, it ran over the rim onto the street. Immediately Dupree sprung into action and hurriedly turned the tap off. Using dry interwoven banana leaves, she created a big, soft cushion called katta and placed it on her head.

Taking deep, even breaths, with bended knees almost swiping the ground, two small hands reached down and daintily lifted the heavy bucket of water. Grunting and slightly swaying under the pressure, she stood up slowly and placed the bucket on her head, trying carefully to keep the cushion in place. But it slipped off and the weighty container landed on her bare head. Millions of firecrackers exploded in her head as the bucket fell off, spilling all the water all over her, before rolling to a stop in the middle of the road.

"Grrrrrrrr!" Dupree growled through tightly clenched teeth. Holding back angry, pain-filled tears, a soaking wet Dupree hurriedly retrieved her bucket before it got run over by a passing vehicle.

Face hardened with determination, she refilled her bucket, ignoring the drills pounding away in her head. Once again the cushion was placed on her head and slowly and carefully she lifted the heavy bucket of water. Barely breathing, she held her aching head still and gently placed the bucket of water on the cushion. Her lips widened in a big, victorious grin and she headed home.

Dupree and Aunt Madge had no running water, so she fetched water from the standpipe a few miles close to town, day after day, rain or sunshine.

It was a hot, humid afternoon and small drops of water spilled from the big plastic bucket that lay askew on her head as she walked slowly alongside the road. Even though it was a frequent sight to behold, a few people still stopped and looked at the small girl with the heavy bucket of water that was almost bigger than her.

Dupree's head hurt terribly and her back felt like a piece of cedar wood as she occasionally swayed under the heavy load, but she kept her footing and held on to her bucket. Flipping and flopping, Aunt Madge's old, torn-up slippers were no match for the unpaved, gravel-covered road, and the stones rubbed harshly against her toes, causing painful blisters.

But Dupree never stopped.

The water was poured into the big water drum located in front of their house, and making a U-turn, with a hand on her narrow hip, she made another three-mile trip to the standpipe.

Grunting and groaning by the seventh trip, Dupree was a few feet from her house when the wet, soggy slippers slid off some uneven stones. Too tired to break her fall, Dupree and her bucket went rolling down a steep incline. The bucket was in first place, and then Dupree overtook it. But not to be outdone it reclaimed its lead but only for a short while as Dupree rolled past a few seconds later. Luckily landing in a thick shrub, Dupree lay still, with her eyes closed more from gratitude and fear than pain.

"Gosh, if only I could just go home and get in my bed," Dupree spoke softly into the air. "But the drum is not yet full and we need the water."

So, reluctantly she got up and noticed her faithful bucket had stopped a few inches away from her. With the bucket in one hand, she used the other to grab on to grass and bushes as she wearily pulled herself out of the ravine and up onto the track.

Briefly glancing down at her busted knees, Dupree looked at the complicated map of ugly scars that made trails all over her legs and knees: the result of the many falls and bruises she suffered, but also a testament to her willpower.

And Dupree never stopped until the water drum was filled to the top with water.

It was another school morning and Dupree was running late as usual. She quickly fed Aunt Madge a simple breakfast consisting of a thin slice of hard-dough bread that she dipped repeatedly in a cup of lime leaf tea, to make it softer. It wasn't very much or very nutritional but money was very scarce.

Things had gotten even more difficult for Dupree over the last few months. They had little food and no money because she wasn't a farmer like Aunt Madge. Her aunt never spoke of any other relative except Dupree's mother, Tiny, and no one knew where she was. Dupree felt all alone in the world and often wondered what would happen to her.

Rushing into her class a few minutes after the last bell had rung, Dupree was late again. Her teacher, who was in a deep discussion at the head of the class, stopped abruptly and gave her a stern look as everyone turned their attention to her. Deeply embarrassed, she crept to her desk in the far right corner.

"I'm so glad you could grace us with your presence, Dupree," Miss Scrabbie said loudly. "We are truly honored."

A few students snickered loudly and some giggled in amusement.

"I'm very sorry, Miss Scrabbie. I'll try not to let it happen again," she told her teacher humbly before taking her seat. Miss Scrabbie gave her a final warning look before she resumed her class discussion.

Dupree loved school despite the many obstacles she faced. In fact, if her bullies would let her be, it would have been one of her favorite places to spend her time. School for her represented knowledge and she grew up knowing that knowledge was power.

Dupree was twelve years old when she took the Common Entrance Examination. This was taken by children in Jamaica as part of the admissions process for academically selective high schools, usually at an average age of eleven. She passed with flying colors, claiming a spot at Falmouth High School. She still remembered the pride and joy in Aunt Madge's eyes as she congratulated her.

"From the second you were born, I knew you were special and would find favor in God's sight," Aunt Madge told her as she hugged her tightly. "My baby, always remember you are the head and not the tail," she imparted to Dupree. "You can be anything you want to be because you are very smart."

Tears clouded Dupree's eyes, and she rapidly blinked them away before Miss Scrabbie or any of her classmates saw her vulnerability.

Dupree was in one of the "bright" classes, which were filled with the most brilliant students, and she was very competitive in all her classes and exams. Though teased by some and isolated by others, her classmates and teachers had learned to recognize and appreciate her intelligence and ambition to succeed. Her life may have been spiraling out of control but Dupree was determined to get a good education.

I need to get a scholarship to a good college, Dupree thought as she tuned out Miss Scrabbie's voice. *And after college, I'll get a wonderful, high-paying job so Aunt Madge and I won't want for anything.*

Nodding her head absently to what was being said by Miss Scrabbie, she continued her internal plan for the future. *We will live in a nice house with running water and electricity, maybe get a big television and a VCR. I'll get some beautiful furniture and nice, new, fashionable clothes for Aunt Madge and me. I'll also get—*

"Ahem." The annoying sound interrupted Dupree's thoughts.

She glanced up guiltily and saw Miss Scrabbie standing over her desk as the entire class looked on in anticipation. *Let the show begin!*

"Are we still among the living, Dupree?" Miss Scrabbie asked smugly with a smirk on her face.

"Hmmm, yes, ma'am. I am, ma'am." Dupree was flustered.

"Good to know, my dear," was the sarcastic response. "Would you be so kind as to answer the question I asked you a lifetime ago?"

The entire class fell silent. Miss Scrabbie was showing her claws and poor Dupree was her prey.

"Hmmm, could you please repeat the question, ma'am?" Dupree asked softly. "I'm sorry for not paying as close attention as I should. It won't happen again, ma'am."

The one-sided fight seeped out of Miss Scrabbie like a punctured tire as she looked at the humble young girl before her. At a time when teachers were being abused physically and verbally by rude and obnoxious students, Dupree was a rare find.

"Please read chapter ten tonight and answer all the questions at the end of the chapter," she relented and stiffly walked away. Dupree breathed a sigh of relief as the bell rang and Miss Scrabbie dismissed the class. She had escaped, for now.

Chapter Three

Two years had passed since Aunt Madge took sick and life for Dupree was still a constant struggle.

"Dupree! Dupree!" shouted Deacon Livingston, a long-standing deacon at their church and a lifelong friend of Aunt Madge.

Dupree had just finished giving Aunt Madge her bath when she heard someone outside calling her. She looked through the small, dilapidated front window and realized it was Deacon Livingston and she got excited. She knew he was there to give her groceries and some money to get a few items for herself and Aunt Madge.

Deacon Livingston was a distinguished member of the community and owned the only mega supermarket in town. Really dapper in every sense, he enjoyed the finer things in life that his wealth afforded him. This was evident by his flashy vehicles, his bright pink- yellow- and red-colored expensive three-piece suits, matching felt hats, and the trailer load of mistresses. Of course, these were all sisters who needed prayer and counseling, or so he told his wife and the curious others.

A real creep in his own right, Deacon Livingston was nonetheless a very generous man. He was always giving a helping hand to the less fortunate people in the community who needed it and Dupree and Aunt Madge were now desperately in need.

His wife, Mrs. Livingston, was just as kindhearted and would send Dupree the clothes and shoes her two daughters no longer wanted. Dupree was very grateful for this because Aunt Madge could no longer make her clothes and she didn't have the money to buy new ones for herself.

Dupree hurriedly ran and met Deacon Livingston in the small dirt track that led from the main road to Aunt Madge's house. Deacon Livingston's eyes lit up when he saw Dupree. He remembered when she was just a baby and he used to help Aunt Madge with her after that no-good Tiny ran off. Now here she was, a very beautiful young lady with curves in all the right places. *God bless her soul!*

Deacon Livingston noticed Dupree's young, firm breasts under the thin, torn blouse she wore and the way her face radiated with the most beautiful smile he had ever seen. Instantly his breath quickened in excitement but he quickly got himself under control before Dupree could notice his perverted reaction to her. He was, after all, a respectable man of the community and a leader at Worship and Fellowship Church of God. He had a reputation to maintain, so he had to be careful and just bide his time for the harvest he was sure he would reap in the very near future.

Dupree looked up at Deacon Livingston adoringly. She thanked God every day for sending them such a generous man with an equally awesome family to help her and Aunt Madge. Sometimes Dupree wished that she was Deacon Livingston's daughter and Aunt Madge was his sister and they all lived in the big mansion in town. But Dupree was still very grateful for everything he was doing for them and often told him so.

"Nonsense," Deacon Livingston would respond in a humble voice. "The Lord said that we should love our neighbors as ourselves and I was blessed abundantly by the good Lord Almighty. It is my duty to give back to His people, as said the Lord."

That's something Dupree also admired about Deacon Livingston. He was such a strong man of God. "Thank you, Deacon Livingston, for the groceries and the money. I am going into town tomorrow to get Aunt Madge painkillers and some personal items for myself. May God continue to bless you for being so kind to us," Dupree said shyly as she hugged the big paper bag full of groceries to her bosom, her eyes fixated on the ground.

"Nonsense. You are like a daughter to me and I have known your aunt since we were in primary school," replied Deacon Livingston. "I love both of you with the love of the Lord and will always be available to help."

"God bless you, sir," Dupree said again and slowly lifted her head and gave him the biggest smile in the world.

Deacon Livingston's heart skipped a beat, literally, as the radiance of Dupree's smile hammered at his lustful heart. He stood as if in a trance as he gazed adoringly at the stunning fifteen-year-old girl.

"Deacon Livingston? Sir, are you okay?" Dupree asked with concern a few seconds later as he stood gawking at her.

"Oh, I'm okay, my child," Deacon Livingston quickly responded as he struggled to compose himself. "I was just breathing a quick word of prayer for you and Sister Madge. Hallelujah!" And he began to mutter some gibberish nonsense.

Dupree closed her eyes and bowed her head in reverence until the charade was over a very short time later.

"I'll be going now, my dear," Deacon Livingston said as he wiped his face with a silk handkerchief. He had worked up a sweat during his prayer. "Please tell your aunt I'll visit with her soon, as I have to get back to the store now." And he hurriedly walked away.

"Okay, sir," Dupree replied and headed the opposite direction with the big bag of groceries, oblivious to

Deacon Livingston, who had stopped and turned around to stare at her.

Dupree had no idea how beautiful she looked then, especially when she smiled. She was a stunning young lady standing approximately five feet seven inches tall, who weighed 115 pounds. Her breasts were firm, her waist was small, and her tummy was so flat even the bullies at school began to look at her in envy. But it was those hips that were beginning to draw attention to the long legs that seemed to go on forever. Her dark, blemish-free skin was smooth like molasses and would literally seem to glow in the sun. Dupree was a very beautiful young lady and was only getting more beautiful as each day passed. But was it a blessing or a curse for the vulnerable young girl? Only time would tell.

Chapter Four

"Oh, happy day. Oh, happy day."

With her head thrown back slightly and her face turned upward, Dupree eyes were tightly closed as she rocked side to side, the words of the song flowing smoothly from smiling lips.

It was Saturday night and Dupree was at choir practice rehearsing the song for church the next day. Dupree loved to sing praises to God. It uplifted her when she was going through all her trials and tribulations and it was an outlet for her pain and sadness. When she opened her mouth, Dupree felt as if God was sitting right there with a big, pleased smile on his face.

After choir practice Dupree walked home with Sister Nadine and Sister Carol. They talked about the song they would be singing at church the next day and how excited they were. The streets were very dark and lonely in the country at that time of night. Most of the streetlights were out and there was no moon and very few stars in the sky.

After a few miles, Sister Nadine and Sister Carol went one way and Dupree the other. She was the only one who had to get off the main road and cut through the old, abandon house to the small muddy track that led to her house. But Dupree had been doing this since she was a small child and had no concerns at all. She hummed a song as she slowly walked home, a big grin on her face.

Then she heard the sound! Dupree spun around and looked everywhere but saw no one. Her heart started to beat a little faster and her breathing became irregular from the fear she began to feel. This was the first time since going home alone that Dupree felt fear. She began to walk faster as she prayed. The tall trees created huge shadows that looked at her eerily, as the high, abandoned grass grabbed at her legs mockingly.

"Dear God, this is your daughter, Dupree. Lord, I am asking you to please protect me from all harm and danger. Please, God, send your angels to walk beside me so that I can reach home to Aunt Madge safe," she prayed quietly.

Dupree began to walk even faster, now almost a slow jog. Her breathing was sporadic as her heart hammered against her chest. She had an eerie feeling that someone was following her. She tried to tell herself that maybe she was feeling this way because she had just passed the two graves over by the old house, but she knew better. Someone was close by and it certainly wasn't a ghost.

Suddenly out of nowhere two hands grabbed her from behind. It happened so fast Dupree had no time to run. Her eyes grew wide in terror and she tried to scream but a large hand was already covering her mouth. Dupree struggled to free herself but she felt as if she was trapped by a brick wall. The person who held her was very tall and strong. Poor Dupree was no match for her attacker. She knew that she was about to be violated in the worst way and felt the sandwich she ate at church earlier that evening forcing its way back up. She was getting sick to her stomach.

Still kicking and struggling to break free, Dupree felt the grip loosen a little, and she spun around to face her attacker. Almost instantaneously she felt a hard, stinging sensation across her face as she was knocked to the ground. Her small back made a hard contact with the unpaved track that had a lot of loose, prodding, sharp stones and gravel. But she didn't feel the pain as she looked up and stared straight into the eyes of the devil standing a few inches away from her.

Her attacker wore a stocking mask over his face with only his wild eyes showing, and Dupree could have sworn that they were red. Who knew after spending all her life in church and reading about the devil that she would actually meet him? But here he was in the flesh and she just knew he was about to kill her.

Dupree's mind flashed to Aunt Madge. Who would help her now? Would Aunt Madge die of a broken heart after hearing of her rape and murder? Dupree felt the tears about to fall but willed herself not to cry. She remembered something Aunt Madge once told her: "It's not over until God said so."

Suddenly the story of Daniel who was thrown into the lion's den and came out without a scratch popped into Dupree's mind and her body began to relax. Dupree knew that Jesus was the same today as He was yesterday so she did what Daniel did: she prayed.

Dupree slowly rose to her knees and lifted her hands to the heavens, oblivious of her attacker who was drawing closer to her, and she prayed without ceasing. She called on the almighty God for protection, and praised and blessed His holy name.

"Precious Jesus, I know if you bring me to it then you can bring me through it. Lord, remember I am your daughter and you are my Father. Please keep me safe from the devil who is about to take my life. Please remember Aunt Madge needs me. I know I am not perfect and I have lost my faith in you so many times, but please forgive me for all my sins, dear Lord. Please do not let the devil win this battle tonight. Let us show him that you are the mighty warrior. Dear Father, I submit my life into your hands right now to do as you please, because your will must be done."

Dupree grew up praying. Aunt Madge taught her how to pray before she could barely talk and it was embedded in her. They spent many days and nights on their knees talking to the Lord.

"Prayer is our direct line to our Savior, my child," Aunt Madge had told her. "It's the telephone to Glory. Never forget that God is always on the line and you can talk to Him anytime."

The attacker sneered when he saw Dupree praying. "You are going to need more than prayer, honey bunch," he replied mockingly. "In fact, when I am through with you not even the Big Man above can help you."

The voice sounded vaguely familiar but Dupree was unable to place it. "Even though I walk through the valley of the shadow of death, I will fear no evil, for you are with me . . ." Dupree continued to pray aloud.

"Oh, you have no need to fear me, sugar plum. See, I'm a lover, not a fighter," he stated with a sick sense of humor. "I've been watching you for a minute now: the cute little skinny church girl who followed her aunt everywhere. But look at you now. The ugly duckling is now a beautiful swan and big papa will be plucking you tonight," he gloated, rubbing his hands together as he licked his long tongue.

His heart sped up in anticipation as he grinned nastily. Tonight was the night that he was going to have a taste of his first virgin. This he knew because he had been watching Dupree since she was just a toddler, and in his sick, twisted mind, protecting her from anyone else who wanted to beat him to the prize. Oh, happy day was here!

But Dupree was now unmindful of her attacker and her surroundings as the Holy Spirit gathered her up into His arms. She felt a sense of comfort and peace as she continued crying out to her God. Her tears were now of joy and not of fear because she knew that the Lord was with her. She slowly got to her feet, raised her hands to heaven, and started to sing and praise the Lord.

Her attacker was shocked at her behavior and wondered if the rumor he heard that she was crazy was really true. He reached out to pull her to him and realized that his feet seemed to be stuck to the ground and he was unable to move forward. His mouth opened in disbelief and his red haunted eyes widened in fright.

"What the heck is going on here?" he asked himself. He began to feel as if the strength was evaporating from his body. His arms grew as heavy as lead and his breathing became labored. As he felt himself getting weaker and weaker, the attacker looked at Dupree and saw the big smile on her face. He was puzzled at what was taking place. He didn't know what was happening but he sure as heck wasn't hanging around to find out.

So he took a step back, away from Dupree. By now he was scared as a mouse and looked like a rabbit caught in a trap. He realized that he could move away from Dupree but he did not have the power or the strength to move toward her. Fear took over and the attacker turned around and ran down the road as fast as his legs could carry him, screaming and waving his hands in the air as if he was the one being attacked by the demonic forces.

As if coming out of a trance, Dupree slowly looked around in amazement. The yells from her attacker shook her out of the faraway place where she was, back into reality. Instantly, Psalms 91 came to her mind and she quietly recited verses 5–7: "'Thou shalt not be afraid for the terror by night; nor for the arrow that flieth by day; nor for the pestilence that walketh in darkness; nor for the destruction that wasteth at noon day. A thousand shall fall at thy side, and ten thousand at thy right hand; but it shall not come nigh thee.'"

Dupree ran home, shouting and praising God for the miracle she had just experienced, knowing that He was always with her. But she just couldn't seem to get those haunting red eyes out of her head. Had she seen the last of the devil? Would that monster try to attack her again? Dupree shuddered at the thought.

Chapter Five

"Cock-a-doodle-doo."

Small glimmers of the dawn light crept through the windowpanes and flittered through the house, casting shadows on the walls. The bed squeaked as Dupree slowly rolled over on her back and stared sullenly and silently into the ceiling. Except for the blinking of her eyes, she lay as still as a mummy as her mind ran tracks in her head. A few minutes later she sluggishly got out of bed and stole a quick glance at Aunt Madge sleeping soundly across the room before tiptoeing into the bathroom.

After splashing cold water on her face, Dupree looked at her reflection in the small broken window above the face basin and gasped at her appearance. Big, fat pimples polka-dotted her once-flawless complexion, while her puffy red eyes struggled to peek out under heavy eyelids. She had been up all night crying into her pillow.

"I look a mess," Dupree sobbed into her open hand. "Oh, Lord, I don't know what to do." She sat on the edge of the bathtub and cried softly.

It was time for Dupree to take the Caribbean Examination Council Examinations (CXC). These examinations are usually taken by students after five years of secondary school to mark the end of it and for those who wished to continue their education at the tertiary level. Dupree wanted to take mathematics, English language, biology, and accounting, the cost of which was $1,000, and the deadline for payment was one day away. And that was the problem.

"I don't even have the first dollar," Dupree moaned. "Everything has been in vain."

A few minutes later, feeling worse instead of better, Dupree got up and rinsed off her face again, then brushed her teeth.

"I have a lot to do before school," Dupree reminded herself. "I need to get started or I'm going to be late." With a fake smile on her chapped lips, she walked out into the bedroom to begin her chores.

Dupree woke up at five-thirty every morning and cleaned the small one-bedroom house from top to bottom. She gave Aunt Madge her bath, then prepared and fed her breakfast, after which she went down to the river, where she washed the soiled bed linens she took from her aunt's bed and to have her morning bath. This left little time for her to get to school before her first class started, and as such she was often marked late.

"Dupree, do you have a minute?" Mrs. Patty asked gently as she walked up to Dupree's desk after the class was dismissed. Mrs. Patty was Dupree's English and form teacher.

Dupree stood up and slung her book bag over her shoulder. She quickly glanced around the classroom and realized it was empty except for her and Mrs. Patty.

"Yes, ma'am," Dupree muttered reluctantly. She knew Mrs. Patty was going to let her have it for always coming to school late.

"Why don't you go and close the door? I have a few minutes before my next class." Mrs. Patty walked back to her desk and took a seat behind it.

Dupree went and pulled the classroom door shut. Slowly she walked to the front of the room, dragging her feet and staring at the ground the entire way.

"Thank you for staying back," Mrs. Patty said and waved her hand toward a chair facing her desk. Her kind eyes swept over Dupree's disheveled appearance and instantly unshed tears filled them. This was so unlike Dupree, who was always neatly dressed and well put together.

Mrs. Patty was a very understanding Christian lady and she knew how difficult things were at home for Dupree. "Dupree, I don't want to make you uncomfortable," Mrs. Patty began softly and smiled at her. "I just want to help you."

Tears welled in Dupree's eyes. She hung her head and stared close-mouthed at the floor.

"You are worried about paying for your exams, aren't you?" Mrs. Patty addressed the big elephant in the room.

Dupree lowered her head into her lap and wept. Mrs. Patty saw her slim frame shake with each labored breath and noticed how her uniform hung loosely on her shallow frame.

She has lost so much weight, Mrs. Patty thought. *And she didn't have much to begin with.*

Mrs. Patty got up and walked over to Dupree. Reaching down she slowly pulled the troubled child to her feet and wrapped her into her arms, rocking gently, side to side. "It will all be okay," Mrs. Patty said as she slowly rubbed Dupree's back. "I wish I had the money to give you myself but God is going to make a way, my child."

"I worked so hard." Dupree's wet eyes held those of her teacher. "I need one thousand dollars and I don't have the money. What am I going to do?"

"That's easy," Mrs. Patty replied with a smile. "We are going to take it to the Lord in prayer because God didn't bring you all this way to turn His back on you now."

Dupree's eyes opened wide with acknowledgment. Her mind flashed back on her encounter with the devil and how he fled from her in fear when she armored herself in the Holy Spirit. Dupree started to cry and fell to her knees in shame. But Mrs. Patty wasn't going to have any pity party because she knew there was work to be done.

Mrs. Patty fell to her knees with Dupree and took hold of her hands. "We are going to pray right now," she said. "The Lord said that where two or more are gathered He is in the midst to bless them.

"Heavenly Father, we come to you now on behalf of your daughter, Dupree. We ask that you give her the strength to continue holding on to your unwavering hands knowing that no problem is too big for you. Right now she is in a financial bind but we loose it in the name of Jesus! We ask that you provide for her according to your riches in glory. And we declare and decree that Dupree will take all her exams and excel in all. We know it's already done and we receive it! In Jesus' name we pray. Amen."

"Amen," Dupree said with conviction. "Amen, Lord."

"Dupree, if you have faith like a mustard seed, you can move a mountain," Mrs. Patty said as she got to her feet and helped Dupree up. "It's now in the hands of the Lord."

"Tomorrow is the deadline to pay for my exams," Dupree said, "But I believe it's going to be all right."

Her pimpled face took nothing away from the big, bright smile. Giving Mrs. Patty a big hug, she rushed out of her office and skipped all the way home.

"Dupree, Dupree!" someone shouted from outside. Dupree ran to the window and almost fainted when she saw who it was.

It was Mrs. Livingston, all dressed up in a fabulous pink pantsuit and matching accessories, smiling from cheek to cheek. Even though Mrs. Livingston was a very wealthy woman, she was also very humble and often visited Aunt Madge when her busy schedule allowed.

"Yes, ma'am," Dupree replied with excitement.

"I would like to talk to you, sweetheart," Mrs. Livingston said as she slowly made her way down the small dirt track to the house.

Dupree ran and held her arm and assisted her inside the house. Mrs. Livingston went and kissed Aunt Madge on her cheek before she took her usual seat on the old wooden three-legged stool that was placed in a corner to keep it standing upright. Dupree sat by her feet.

Mrs. Livingston looked down at this beautiful young lady and her heart swelled with pride. She knew firsthand how hard life had been for Dupree, yet she never compromised her dignity.

"Dupree, I fasted yesterday and you kept showing up in my thoughts," Mrs. Livingston began. "Then this morning I overhead two of my customers at the supermarket complaining about the high cost of the CXC exams and I remembered that you were getting ready to take yours. I immediately wondered how you were going to pay for those exams. So it became obvious what the Lord wanted me to do," Mrs. Livingston told Dupree with a big smile on her face.

Mrs. Livingston reached into her handbag sitting on her lap and withdrew her purse. She opened it and took out a wad of money. "How much is it for your exams, sweetheart?" she asked a wide-eyed Dupree.

"Hmmm, one . . . one . . . one thousand dollars, ma'am," Dupree stuttered.

Mrs. Livingston counted out the money and handed it to Dupree. This was too much for Dupree. She wrapped her arms around Mrs. Livingston's legs as the tears ran down her face. She was overwhelmed with joy.

"Thank you, thank you, thank you," Dupree muttered over and over. "God bless you, ma'am, for all that you are doing for me. I promise you I am going to study real hard and pass all my exams. You won't be disappointed."

"I know you will make us all proud, sweetie," Mrs. Livingston responded cheerily as she glanced at Aunt Madge, who had heard everything she had said and done and was also crying.

Aunt Madge silently shouted praises to God as she thanked Him for coming through for her great-neice one more time.

Deeply touched by the level of appreciation shown by Dupree and Aunt Madge, Mrs. Livingston knelt down and gathered a crying Dupree in her arms. Her happy flow of tears joined the others as she stroked Dupree's hair, showering her with words of love and comfort.

The next day Dupree was the first in line at the bursar's office. She waited to pay for her exams with a big, toothy grin on her face. She knew she probably looked silly to some people, but they didn't really understand the joy in her heart. She was so delirious with happiness it was almost too overwhelming. After she received the receipt for her payment, she quickly went to find Mrs. Patty.

Mrs. Patty was walking toward her classroom when saw Dupree running to her at a fast pace. She was almost knocked off her feet when Dupree grabbed her in a big bear hug.

"I got it! I got it!" Dupree shouted, waving the receipt in the air. The look of exhilaration on her face was priceless.

"I knew you would, my dear. I knew that my God would keep His promise and come through for you. Oh, this is so wonderful!" Mrs. Patty rejoiced with Dupree. Everything was falling into place beautifully, or was it?

The little chicken was merry, but the hawk was near!

Chapter Six

Dupree was in full "exam preparation" mode. The last few months flew by like a kite. Her seventeenth birthday popped up for a quick hello and an almost instantaneously good-bye. But she was too busy to care. After all, there was a time and place for everything.

So every night like clockwork, Dupree sat at the small, lopsided kitchen table with the small flicker of light from the kerosene lamp and studied until the wee hours of the morning. Her eyes hurt from the dim light and her body ached from lack of sleep but this continued for the months leading up to exams. Dupree pressed on because she had her eyes on the prize.

The days ran into weeks as Dupree got very busy with preparing for and taking her exams. She got little sleep during the week because she had so much to do. She took care of Aunt Madge in the mornings, and then ran off to school to take an exam or to attend a final preparation class.

Finally Dupree completed all her exams and felt good about them all. Mathematics, her least favorite subject, was a challenge for her as always, but she gave it her best shot and could only hope for the best. In a few weeks, the results would speak for themselves.

Dupree was sitting on a bench under the big mango tree at the back of the school, wrapped up in a fascinating novel when Silvia and Monique came and sat beside her. They were a part of the clique of bullies who had been trying to make Dupree's life at school a living hell.

"Hey, girl, I tried on my dress this morning and it was the bomb!" loud-mouth Silvia boasted to Monique.

"I am going to get my hair and nails done at Maxine Hair and Beauty Salon in Montego Bay. I am so excited!" squealed obnoxious Monique.

Rudely ignoring Dupree, they babbled on and on, hoping to make her jealous. They were taking a break from practice for the graduation ceremony that was in three weeks, and the girls were talking about the dance to be held after. Practice was mandatory for all students who were graduating, so Dupree went. However, she knew she would not be going to the graduation ceremony or the dance because she just could not afford it.

So she sat and watched the excitement on the other students' faces. Most of girls were talking about their clothes, dates for the dance, and their summer vacation plans before they left for college. Dupree did not even have a date for the dance because no one had asked her.

Dupree actually saw it as a blessing because she did not have the money to get a dress, the shoes, and all the necessities for the dance. In fact, she could not even afford to pay for the graduation gown

The cost to rent the gown was one hundred dollars and her only pair of black shoes, which Mrs. Livingston had given her a few months ago, was already bursting out at the sides. Dupree was thankful they carried her through the school year but knew they would not hold up for the graduation.

As Dupree stared into obliviousness, the unrestrained sadness stained her eyes against her will.

I won't be missing much anyway. She tried unsuccessfully to comfort her spirit. *Aunt Madge is too sick to*

attend and I have no other relatives to see me graduate. Yes, it is a good thing I'm not going to that stupid graduation and dance.

If only her heart would be convinced just as easily.

Dupree swayed in perfect rhythm to the upbeat worship song as she lifted her hands in praise. The bright Sunday morning sunshine streamed through the opened church windows and washed over her exuberant face. She was really feeling the presence of the Holy Spirit that day and was just thankful that He was there with her.

A light tap on Dupree's shoulder interrupted her flow. She spun around to see a smiling usher standing beside her. He handed her a note before walking away as silently as he had appeared.

Dupree opened the note and gasped in surprise to see it was from Pastor Pallen and First Lady Pallen. The note asked her to meet them in the pastor's office after church.

Dupree wondered why they wanted to meet with her. Dupree chewed on her bottom lip nervously. She had a great relationship with her pastor and his wife and they always looked out for her and Aunt Madge.

After church, Dupree hurried around to the back to the pastor's office, greeting church members along the way. The door was opened and she walked in to find her pastor and first lady sitting on the couch waiting for her.

"So how are you doing today, Dupree?" Pastor Pallen asked as he stood and walked over to embrace her.

"I am feeling blessed, Pastor, thank you," Dupree replied and returned the warm hug. "Your message was very inspiring today."

"Thank God for His word," Pastor Pallen responded as he stepped back so Lady Pallen could receive her hug.

"So how were your exams?" Sister Pallen asked with a pleasant smile on her face.

"I think they went well, ma'am. I did the best I could and I am trusting God that I passed them all."

"That's good, because you know that only our best is good enough. I would like you to know that Pastor and I are so proud of you. We've had the privilege to watch you grow up, and what a wonderful young lady you have become."

Dupree blushed and hung down her head. She suddenly became fascinated with the zigzag pattern of the tiles on the floor.

"Look at me, Dupree," Pastor Pallen commanded gently. "Sister Pallen is right. I wish many more young girls could be like you."

The tears ran down Dupree's face as she listened to her pastor and first lady. It felt awesome that these people, whom she loved and respected so much, could say all those wonderful things about her.

"We would like to give you an early graduation gift." Lady Pallen beamed as she handed Dupree an envelope. Dupree looked at her in astonishment as she took it. She didn't know what to say or do.

"Go ahead and open it now," Pastor Pallen instructed her.

Dupree opened the envelope to reveal the most beautiful congratulatory card she had ever seen. It shook slightly as her tear-filled eyes ran over the wonderful words in print. She then pressed it firmly to her chest after she was finished, looking back forth between the two people who had made her so happy.

Then she leaped into her pastor's arms and gave him a big hug. After he released her, she grabbed Sister Pallen and hugged and kissed her on the cheeks.

"Thank you both so much," Dupree gushed tearfully. "You have no idea how happy you make me."

"Hey, there is more. Look farther down in the envelope," said Pastor Pallen with a big grin on his handsome face.

Dupree looked and saw that there was some money inside. She was so anxious to read the card that she never noticed it. She quickly pulled it out and counted it. *One thousand dollars!* She felt her knees wobble under her, and grabbed on to the edge of the pastor's desk to keep herself upright. Her mouth opened wide but no word came out. The tears ran freely as she stared at her pastor and first lady in amazement.

Her weakened knees slowly sank to the floor and Dupree lifted her hands to heaven and thanked God. Both Pastor and Sister Pallen stood there crying as well. "Hmmm, there is more," Pastor said and helped Dupree off the floor.

Dupree, still feeling overwhelmed, could not think of anything else that she needed then.

"Sister Pallen, the kids, and I will be at your graduation. We want to see you accepting your high school diploma because no one worked as hard and deserves it more than you. In fact, we also contracted with Mr. Greedy to take your photographs."

To say Dupree was ecstatic was an understatement. Mr. Greedy was the only professional photographer in town, and if you asked many people, they would tell you that his name described him well.

"It's a crying shame how expensive that man is," complained Mother Sassy on numerous occasions. "The only thing he is good for is to rob poor people."

Mother Sassy was over eighty years old and was a long-standing member of the church. Most people secretly called her Mother "Spirit" because she was always catching the Spirit: at church, on the bus, at the supermarket, on the road, at the clinic, wherever she was. Last year Dupree heard that Mother Sassy was home and was using the outside bathroom, known as a pit toilet, and she caught the Spirit while in there and fell in head first! Luckily, she grabbed on to something inside and this broke her fall. Her older grandson was passing by and heard the muffled scream and went to investigate. He saw his grandmother's two legs sticking up in the air, kicking like a wild horse. He quickly pulled her up and Mother Sassy came up breathing hard and screaming in fright with feces all over her.

Her husband heard the commotion and slowly made his way outside to see what was going on. He was shocked when he saw his wife and quickly stepped back when the foul smell hit his nose.

"Woman, how many times I done tell you to watch where you get that Spirit, huh? You see what happen now, the Spirit almost killed you!" he shouted feebly.

A humiliated Mother Sassy just cut her eyes at him and sucked her teeth before she wobbled down to the river close by to wash herself. She knew her husband was right but she wasn't going to admit that to him. However, she made a vow to herself that she had to watch where she got the Spirit because that Spirit thing was getting too dangerous for her!

"We are so, so proud of you, darling," Sister Pallen said and that brought Dupree's attention back to her and Pastor Pallen. "I am going to scream so loud for you; I hope I won't embarrass you," she said jokingly.

All Dupree could have done at that moment was gather her pastor and first lady in a group hug and thank them immensely. God was just too good to her. Really, He was.

"Good morning, ma'am. My name is Dupree and I would like to pay for my graduation gown, please." Dupree smiled brightly as she stood waiting patiently.

Mrs. Scott stared up over her glasses, which sat on her nose, at the beautiful young lady standing before her in her office. She was the head bursar at the high school and it was one of her duties to collect all monies for the graduation gowns. However, the deadline ended last week Friday and there was no exception to the rule. But here stood this disobedient child, waving around her measly one hundred dollars, asking to pay for her graduation gown.

"Are you aware that the deadline was last Friday, young lady?" Mrs. Scott asked in a loud, stern voice.

"Yes, ma'am," Dupree replied in a very meek voice. "But I didn't have the money last week. My pastor and first lady just gave me the money yesterday at church. I know I am late but if you could please make an exception, I would appreciate it very much, ma'am."

Mrs. Scott was astonished at how well spoken Dupree was and the respect she showed her. Some of these kids were so rude and out of order. If you asked her, she thought what they needed was a good old-fashioned whooping. But here was Dupree humbled before her and she really appreciated it.

"Old Granny" was the name Mrs. Scott was often called by some of the students, and the brave ones even had the nerve to call her that to her face. She had been working at the high school for almost twenty years and felt like it was her school. No one could tell her what to do, not even Principal Williams. Ever since her husband was ripped out of her life by the arms of death, Mrs. Scott spent most of her time at the school. She was known to be a tough woman and was hell-bent on enforcing the rules. One would probably have better luck reasoning with the devil than Mrs. Scott.

So Mrs. Scott stood there and looked at Dupree for a long time. She noted the desperation on her face, but her heart wasn't moved. *Rules were not meant to be broken,* she thought. Even though Dupree was respectful and seemed remorseful for her tardiness in meeting the deadline, Mrs. Scott just could not go against everything she believed in.

"I am sorry, my dear, but I can't help you," she finally replied.

Dupree was shocked at the cold-heartedness of Mrs. Scott. She felt the anger rising in her like a volcano and was tempted to curse her out but she could not. The God in her would not allow her to be disrespectful to this lady who reminded her so much of Aunt Madge.

"Thank you, Mrs. Scott. I am very disappointed with your decision, but I respect it. I guess it was never God's will for me to attend this graduation. Again, thank you and have a blessed day."

Mrs. Scott was in shock. She was bracing herself for the verbal assault she expected from Dupree but never in her wildest dream could she believe the words that came out of this young girl's mouth. She stood there unable to move until she heard her office door close softly. As if she were slowly getting out of a trance, it took a minute for Mrs. Scott to realize that Dupree had left her office.

Dupree felt as if a sumo wrestler were sitting on her shoulders. Her eyes were burning as she tried to hold the tears at bay.

"I will not cry, I will not," she repeated to herself over and over. "I know if God wanted me to attend graduation, He would have touched Mrs. Scott's heart and she would have helped me. So I guess it was not meant to be."

With that, Dupree trudged home to cuddle up with Aunt Madge. Her heart was crushed.

Chapter Seven

"You have to show these kids who is the boss around here," Mrs. Scott muttered as she sat in her office. "I make the rules and I will not break them for anyone, not even Jesus himself."

Mrs. Scott went about the rest of her day, or at least she tried to, but had no success doing so as her every thought was filled with the distraught young lady who left her office earlier. So she decided to get some lunch from the cafeteria.

After receiving her lunch Mrs. Scott looked around for somewhere to sit in the staff lounge. Then she noticed Mrs. Patty sitting by herself in the back of the room. She decided to sit with Mrs. Patty and headed her way.

"So, how are you doing today, Mrs. Scott?" Mrs. Patty greeted Mrs. Scott.

"I am doing very well, thank you," Mrs. Scott responded as she sat down across from her.

"It shows, because you look great. Let's give God thanks for His blessings."

Mrs. Patty could tell Mrs. Scott was uncomfortable with the remark she made and she smiled sweetly at the lady who seemed so weak, even though she acted so tough.

"It's okay, Mrs. Scott. We all need someone to talk to sometimes, and as a child of God, I can assure you that I am here if you ever feel like talking. I know we are not friends but you are my sister in the Lord and I will always be available for you if you ever need me."

Mrs. Scott was leery of Mrs. Patty words and looked at her suspiciously. But as she looked into her eyes, she saw that she was genuine and meant every word she said. For the life of her she could not imagine why this woman would be so kind to her; but she suddenly felt the need to talk to someone about the young lady who was haunting her every thought, and so she decided to talk to Mrs. Patty.

"Some of these kids have no respect for rules and regulations," she began. "The deadline to pay for graduation gowns was last Friday. Letters were sent to the parents of all the graduates; it was posted up all over the school and announced every morning in devotion. Everyone was well informed and therefore they have no excuse to be late with their payment."

Mrs. Patty looked at her and said nothing but waited for her to continue.

"Then earlier this young lady came in my office with the biggest smile on her face, waving around her hundred dollars, asking if she could pay for her gown now. Can you imagine the nerve she got?"

"Is the name of this young lady Dupree?" Mrs. Patty asked with dread.

"Why, yes, it is. Is she one of your students?"

"She is more than that to me. Dupree is a special young lady who will always have a place in my heart."

"Oh, really? Why is that?"

"Dupree is a very bright young lady who is determined to beat the odds at all cost. She lives with her elderly aunt who is very sick and bedridden. Dupree takes care of her while attending school and is in the top of her class. But most importantly, she is a child of God. She knows the Lord up close and personal."

Mrs. Scott sat with her mouth wide open in shock. She knew there was something different about Dupree, but her heart was too cold to make an exception for her. Suddenly she began to feel very bad about what she did to Dupree.

"Please rent her a gown for me, Mrs. Scott," Mrs. Patty begged. "I can assure you if she had the money before the deadline she would have paid it. This young lady is very respectful of people's time and rules. She would never have broken the rule without a good cause."

Mrs. Patty reached for her handbag and took out her wallet. She then removed a hundred dollar bill and offered it to Mrs. Scott. "Please let me pay for the gown. Dupree had worked so hard to stay in school she deserves to attend her graduation. Please help her. The Lord will bless you."

"Put away your money," Mrs. Scott said.

Mrs. Patty's heart fell to her stomach and her head started to hurt instantly. She didn't know what to expect. "I will pay for the gown," Mrs. Scott stated.

"What?"

"I think I was too hard on that young lady. I could tell there was something different about her, but I refused to listen to my heart. Please let me pay for her graduation gown to help make amends for my thoughtlessness."

Mrs. Patty sat there in stunned silence. She knew she was supposed to say something but words failed her for a minute. So she sat and looked at the woman whom many referred to as being callous and cold-hearted. She knew that there was no one who had such a tough exterior that the Lord could not break through.

"Thank you," Mrs. Patty said finally. "I will come by your office to get the gown and then I will take it to her."

"Where does she live?"

"She lives very close to the school, just a small walk away. It's one of the reasons why it's possible for her to go home during her lunch break to see to her ailing aunt."

Mrs. Scott felt like the lowest of worms creeping around on its belly. "I'll take it to her," she said and surprised herself and Mrs. Patty again.

"Are you sure?"

"Yes, I'm sure," she said with more conviction. "I would like to do this for such a wonderful young lady and also ask her forgiveness for being so insensitive earlier."

Mrs. Patty looked at Mrs. Scott and knew she meant what she said. "Okay then, please tell Dupree that I will come and visit her and Aunt Madge soon."

On her way home that afternoon, Mrs. Patty was elated at how God just continued to work in mysterious ways. She had been serving Him for over twenty years and He had never failed her yet.

Chapter Eight

As Mrs. Scott walked gingerly along the narrowed path, lugging the large bag over her shoulder, she wished she had changed her pair of low-heeled mules for her sneakers. The ground was uneven and full of stones. This made walking for her difficult, but she refused to turn back. She knew she had to do this for her peace of mind.

Slipping and sliding, Mrs. Scott finally saw the little board house with a thick, dark cloud of smoke coming from around the back and her compassion rose for Dupree. She lived in a big, beautiful house in Arcadia. It was very beautifully furnished with all the luxury she could afford.

"Hello, anyone home?" Mrs. Scott called as she got closer to the house. She didn't know if they had dogs and she wasn't about to try to find out the hard way. So she stood at the top of the little hill and called out again. "Hello, Dupree?"

Dupree was inside, deep in concentration as she stood in the kitchen finishing up the red pea soup for their dinner. Her eyes and nose were running from the smoke that filled the small kitchen. She thought she heard someone outside calling but shrugged it off. She told herself that her mind was just playing tricks on her, but then she heard her name. She suddenly stopped what she was doing, took the pot of cooked soup off the fire, and went around to the front of the house to see who was there. Dupree was shocked when she saw Mrs. Scott. Her eyes opened wide in recognition and she felt herself trembling. She wanted to move but was unable to.

Mrs. Scott noticed Dupree's expression and felt even worse than she had before. She knew that she was the last person Dupree expected to see standing outside her house, but she could only hope that she would listen to what she had to say and accept her apology.

"Hi, Dupree," she said meekly as she walked the final few steps to stand in front of Dupree.

"Hello, ma'am," Dupree responded humbly as she finally found her voice to acknowledge Mrs. Scott. "I'm sorry for staring so rudely and not responding when you first called, ma'am, but I was just so surprised to see you," Dupree added.

"Oh, my dear, there is no need to apologize. I am the one who should be apologizing and that is why I came here. I spoke to your teacher, Mrs. Patty, and she told me where you lived. I hope you don't mind."

"No, ma'am." Dupree was confused about what was going on but she decided to wait for Mrs. Scott to explain her unexpected visit to her home.

"Can I come in and talk to you for a while? You seem busy so I won't take up much of your time."

Dupree hesitated a little. She wondered if Mrs. Scott would feel comfortable in their small home. She knew she was a woman of wealth and class and was used to the finer things in life. But, as if she was reading her mind, Mrs. Scott took a hold of Dupree's hand and led her toward the house.

There was a boarded gate that was hanging on one hinge; the others were broken off. The yard was uneven with stone, lumps of dirt, and wild grass but it was obvious that it was swept clean. There were five lopsided steps where eight should have been leading up to the house, but these too were sparkling as the sun made connection with red polish on them. Mrs. Scott took her time and carefully went up the steps and into the small house.

The first thing she noticed was how clean and neat everything inside was. The small table in the living room leaned to the side as if it were in pain, but there was an old, cracked vase on it with some of the most beautiful wild flowers Mrs. Scott had ever seen. She glanced down and saw her reflection looking back at her through the red shined wood floor. And as the cool breeze caressed the old, clean, tattered curtains at the windows, she smelled the freshness and cleanness that permeated the air. She instantly felt comfortable in a home that could not be compared even to the kennel she had made for her babies: her two beautiful Rottweiler dogs.

Dupree stood silently watching Mrs. Scott's reaction to her home.

"Your home looks very comfortable," Mrs. Scott said with a smile. "It's so homely."

Dupree was pleased with the compliment and relaxed.

Mrs. Scott went and sat on the stool by Aunt Madge's bed. "Hello. You must be the lady responsible for raising such an outstanding young lady," she greeted her.

Aunt Madge gave her a wet, lopsided smile.

Mrs. Scott looked at the woman who was unable to move by her own free will but had the biggest smile she could manage on her face. She wondered what she had to be so happy about when her situation seemed so dismal.

What Mrs. Scott didn't know was that Aunt Madge had a joy that surpassed all understanding. She woke up every morning with a heart of thanksgiving and a silent voice of praise. Her body may have failed her but she knew her God had never failed her yet.

Dupree went and sat on the floor beside Mrs. Scott. She was now very anxious to hear what she had to say. She glanced at Aunt Madge and noticed that her face too was lit up in anticipation. Dupree had shared with her what happened in Mrs. Scott's office and Aunt Madge knew that her Lord was on the case once again.

"Dupree, I must apologize to you for my behavior earlier in my office. I should have listened to why you were late with your payment for your graduation gown and shown some compassion, but I didn't. I was so set in my ways to always enforce the rules, it never dawned on me that due to circumstances beyond one's control there should be some exceptions to the rules."

Aunt Madge made some unrecognizable sound as she blinked her eyes rapidly in happiness and Dupree stared up at Mrs. Scott with her megawatt smile.

"Believe it or not, my behavior bothered me so much that I was unable to get any work done. So I went to lunch, saw Mrs. Patty, and sat with her. I really needed to talk to someone about what was troubling me, so I began to tell her. She knew instantly it was you I was talking about and immediately explained your situation to me. She begged me to let you have the gown and offered to pay for it, but I said no."

Dupree felt as if someone threw a bucket of cold water over her head. She turned to look at Aunt Madge, whose eyes became wide as saucers.

"I decided to pay for it myself and bring it to you," Mrs. Scott said with a big grin on her face and pointed to the big bag resting by her feet.

Dupree bent her knees up toward her chest, rested her head on them and wept. Aunt Madge was so overcome with joy that tears rained down her cheeks with a life of their own.

Mrs. Scott noticed their reactions and felt like she'd won the lottery. It was a very gratifying feeling to help someone in need. Her heart swelled with pleasure and joy.

Mrs. Scott reached down and took the gown out of the bag and handed it to Dupree. "Here is your graduation gown, Dupree. Why don't you try it on for me and Miss Madge?"

Dupree wanted to say so much to Mrs. Scott but she could only smile as she timidly took the graduation gown from her hand. She put the gown over her head and tried unsuccessfully to pull it over completely because her hands were shaking so much.

"Here, let me help you," Mrs. Scott offered and helped her into the gown. Even standing in the small room, barefoot with her wild hair all over her head, Dupree looked absolutely beautiful. Mrs. Scott looked on in admiration and Aunt Madge in pride. It was a very special moment for everyone present.

"Words can't explain how grateful Aunt Madge and I are for your kindness, ma'am," Dupree told Mrs. Scott after she took off her gown and hung it up behind the bathroom door. They didn't have a closet but that was okay; the gown would be perfectly fine where it was. "I knew that the Lord would work it out for me as usual and He did. I just had to keep my faith in Him. And please believe me when I tell you that He will bless you richly for your act of kindness toward me. I will never forget this and will keep you in my prayers always," she concluded.

"You are welcome, my dear," Mrs. Scott responded, ignoring Dupree's comment about the Lord, as she had nothing to do with Him anymore. In fact, she hadn't in a very, very long time and she would have liked it to remain so. "I have to go now. I have a few stops to make before it gets dark," Mrs. Scott stated hurriedly. All this God talk was making her very angry and uneasy.

"It was very nice to meet you, Miss Madge," Mrs. Scott said to Aunt Madge as she held her hand. "Good-bye."

Aunt Madge blinked her eyes and gave her the lopsided smile.

"Good-bye, Dupree. Have a great time at the graduation."

"Thank you, ma'am, for everything. God bless you."

Dupree was very happy about what the Lord had done again for her, while Mrs. Scott was pissed off that Dupree thought it was the Lord who had done it. All He did was take all the praise and glory for Himself and He knew darn well He didn't do anything for anyone. She knew this from personal experience. He could fool Dupree, Aunt Madge, and all the other stupid people out there who worshipped Him, but she would never again get suckered in by Him. For as long as she lived, she wanted nothing to do with God and He couldn't do a darn thing about it! Or so she thought.

Chapter Nine

Saturday morning, bright and early, Dupree went into town on a "graduation preparation" mission. She browsed various stores and outdoor stalls before finally decided on laced-front, black patent leather shoes with a fashionable low heel and a black medium-sized stylish clutch, decorated all over with small embroidered rhinestones. She also treated herself to a small bottle of perfume.

Next stop was Miss Sam: "the poor people's hairdresser," as she was referred to by many. Miss Sam lived on the outskirts of town in a small boarded house that had a tendency to slightly dance with the wind. One really had to have the heart of a lion to sit on her veranda without fear that the whole structure would give way anytime soon. However, Dupree and many women from near and far were brave enough to do so because the result of her talent and expertise was well worth the risk.

With a big smile that reflected her warm personality, Miss Sam plump arms engulfed Dupree affectionately as they greeted each other.

"So what are we getting done today, Miss Graduate?" Miss Sam asked Dupree in a friendly voice.

"I would like you to straighten my hair for me and wrap it," Dupree replied excitedly. She had only gotten her hair straightened once and that was a few years ago when Aunt Madge sent her on a school trip to Pantomime in Kingston. She still vividly remembered how pretty she felt and that was a rarity for her.

"Okay, sweetie. When I am through with you, tomorrow everyone is going to wonder who this fashion model is," Miss Sam said and went to work.

Dupree smiled politely before she took her seat on a stool on the veranda. Beside it was a small coal stove that was brightly lit red with an iron comb placed in it to be heated. She had washed her hair that morning by the river so it was clean, but tangled up. Miss Sam used a big-tooth comb to help do the trick of detangling Dupree's thick mane of hair. She then used hair oil to grease her scalp and softened her hair.

Dupree gave a small yelp and flinched when the scorching heat from the hot iron comb came a little too close to her ear for comfort. She was a little scared at first but the excitement won out. The strong smell of burnt hair and grease permeated the air as Miss Sam parted Dupree's hair into very small sections, the heated comb weaving through it slowly but immaculately. The iron comb was frequently returned to the stove to be heated again and again and the process continued until it was all completed. To a very anxious Dupree it seemed like forever but the experienced Miss Sam only took about two hours.

"Wow, wow, wow," Dupree said as she looked at herself in the mirror Miss Sam offered her. Her shiny, straightened hair hung down her back like a black velvet cloth. Strands as smooth as silk caressed her fingers as she gently ran her hands through it. She was just elated!

"You are such a beauty!" Miss Sam gushed. "A real knockout."

Dupree turned away from the mirror and hung her head in embarrassment.

Miss Sam expertly wrapped Dupree's gorgeous mane of hair and tied a hair scarf around it to keep it in place for the big day tomorrow.

Gently pulling Dupree into her arms, Miss Sam held her tightly. "Don't ever let anyone put you down or undermine your worth. Always remember you are a very beautiful young lady and you have the power to rule your destiny," she whispered in her ear.

An emotional Dupree swallowed the big lump in her throat and nodded her head in acknowledgment before she left for home.

A few quick contrasting minutes later, with her head hung low, her lifeless eyes fastened on the hilly track. Putting one leaded foot before the other, Dupree was submerged in a cloud of uncertainty as she pondered what tomorrow would bring. What would her tormentors say when they saw her? Would they finally think she was beautiful or would they ridicule her in front of everyone? Would they ruin this important day for her? But better yet, would she allow them?

Tomorrow would speak for itself.

That morning Dupree had woken up before sunrise, as she had gotten barely any sleep. Standing by the small, broken front window, her glowing eyes gazed up at the still-dark sky as she willed her overloaded mind to predict the happenings of the upcoming day. She drew a blank. Of course, she was not worried because she knew she had already overcome the odds; but there was a gnawing feeling fluttering around in her gut that hinted of something spectacular to come.

Humming softly, an exhilarated Dupree gave a grin-ning Aunt Madge her bath, washed and combed her hair, then prepared a quick breakfast. After breakfast, with fingers snapping, head rhythmically bobbing and feet skanking, Dupree grooved to a song in her head as she cleaned the house and swept the yard. She then skipped over the sharp rocks, glided over the small hills, and boogied as she walked the exiguous roads, making the ten trips carrying water to fill the water drum look like a breeze. After all her chores were completed, she actually felt rejuvenated instead of being exhausted.

Tired of bathing out of the bath pan, Dupree went to the naturally jade colored, smooth-flowing Rio Minho River to have her bath. As she hid behind some dense growth of bush that adorned the massive riverbed, she closed her eyes in deep pleasure as the cool, fresh water washed over her body in a soft caress. Finally, feeling clean and revitalized, she reluctantly got out of the water and dried herself off before heading back home to finish getting herself ready.

Like a beautiful silk curtain, her hair slowly danced in the air and softly whipped around her pretty, grinning face as Dupree daintily twirled around for Aunt Madge's approval, releasing the soft, exotic fragrance of her perfume that wafted through the tiny house. Her uniform was clean and crispy ironed and her new shoes shone brightly. She was a stupendous sight to behold.

Chapter Ten

Dupree kissed Aunt Madge, grabbed her handbag and gown, and set off for the school. This was it.

The crowd was electrifying with beautifully dressed people moving back and forth, talking and laughing. The road leading to the school was blocked with vehicles parked on both sides of the street. Vendors were out in full force selling hot dogs, ice cream, boiled corn, goat head soup known as "mannish water," jerked chicken, and other delicacies. There was a certain excitement and expectancy in the air and Dupree felt it.

As she slowly made her way into the noisy students' lounge, where they would put on their gowns and march from into the auditorium, Dupree felt astonished eyes gawking at her. For the first time in a very long time, she felt good about herself and had decided she would not let anyone ruin her day. So she flashed her megawatt smile and went to find her space in the long line. But the troublemakers were staring because they were flabbergasted at Dupree's beauty: her hair, her shoes, her handbag, and the tantalizing scent from her perfume that tickled their jealous nostrils as she floated by. In their eyes the ugly duckling had turned into a beautiful swan, but the truth be told, Dupree was always a beautiful girl. It only took superficial material stuff for her beauty to be seen by ignorant people.

After all the students were lined up, the marching song began to play and they were off to the auditorium.

Families and friends screamed and cheered as they saw their loved one enter the auditorium.

As Dupree made her way into the crowded building, a deafening cheer went up from a large section of the upper balcony. Pastor, Sister Pallen, their children, and almost the entire church body of Worship and Fellowship Church of God screamed her name with exuberant joy and happiness. A surprised Dupree looked up at the number of people who came out to see her graduate and tears sprung to her eyes. Suddenly, a bright light flashed across her upturned face, momentarily blinding her as she turned around to see Mr. Greedy standing before her, snapping away with his camera.

As she took her seat, Dupree noticed a graduation program on her seat. She opened it to read and was again rendered shocked at what she saw. The program fell from her trembling hand and she slowly reached down and picked it up almost as if in a trance. Some students were being honored for outstanding performances in various subjects, and under the prizes section of the program, Dupree saw her name listed five times!

"And the prize for outstanding academic performance in biology goes to no other than . . . Dupree!" the over-zealous principal screamed into the microphone, his booming voice echoing around the huge building.

Thunderous applause, high-pitched screams, and loud finger whistles pierced the air like flying bullets as a blushing Dupree gently made her way to the podium on rubbery legs. Happy tears clouded her vision, but with her head held as high as a peacock, her bright smile masked her nervousness as she proudly received her prize, holding it up in the air for everyone to see. Mr. Greedy, busy at work, took advantage of the heartfelt moment.

"And the prize for outstanding performance in ac-counting goes to Dupree!"

"Again, it's Dupree for outstanding performance in English language!"

"For the best performance in physics, the prize goes to Dupree!"

As the now-familiar name Dupree rang out repeatedly, the crowd cheered loudly, her own cheering squad being the loudest.

Then it was time for her to receive her last prize. A hush went over the crowd as Dupree made her way to the podium for the fifth time. Her disheartened bullies looked on in envy, rolling their eyes, sucking their teeth, and grumbling under their breath, their disgruntled parents and friends also hating. But many students, teachers, staff, classmates, and acquaintances were overjoyed for her. She got a standing ovation as she received her award. Cameras flashed from left, right, and center as everyone wanted to capture the moment. This was really history in the making. Without even trying, Dupree had stolen the show and no one deserved it more. The Lord had indeed blessed her richly.

After all the graduates went and received their high school diplomas, the graduation ceremony was over. Dupree ran over to her church family who had made this day possible and hugged and kissed everyone. Sister Pallen and Miss Sam were crying tears of joy.

"Chile, you mash up the place!" Mother Sassy screamed, pinning Dupree's face to her bosom affectionately. "We need a trailer to carry home all those presents you just won."

The crowd that gathered around Dupree laughed merrily in agreement.

"Baby girl, you sure you don't want to be a model?" Miss Sam asked Dupree, planting a big kiss on her forehead.

"Beauty and brains, you can't beat that!" Pastor Pallen, who overheard the comment shouted, pumping his fist wildly in the air.

Dupree's fans howled! If Dupree were light skinned, her face would have been crimson bright.

"So are we ready to party?" Sister Pallen shouted, putting both hands to each side of her mouth like a megaphone.

"Ready like Freddy!" the crowd responded.

What party? Dupree pondered, looking around at the amused faces.

Pastor Pallen grabbed hold of a confused Dupree's hand, pulling her toward the auditorium exit, the enthusiastic crowd following, talking and laughing jovially.

Stepping outside, Dupree halted sharply, causing Sister Nadine who was walking closely behind her to bump into her back. Salty puddles poured from dilated eyes as her trembling hands provided a cover for her wide-open mouth. Her ability to speak instantly evaporated like a puff of smoke.

Standing out like sore thumbs in the middle of the chaotic schoolyard were two large buses. Pastor Pallen gently urged Dupree toward one, her feet felt like two planks of cement, one plodding before the other. Could this day get any better?

Chapter Eleven

The buses pulled up in front of Jimmy's Restaurant, located in the heart of town. The restaurant was owned and operated by Mr. Jim and his wife, Shauna. It was an upscale restaurant patronized by people from near and far for the mouthwatering food.

As she stepped through the door of the restaurant, Dupree's breath caught in her throat; her heart flip-flopped in her already-fluttering stomach. Her enlarged eyes meticulously travelled around the empty restaurant, taking in the big banner in the center of the room that read Congratulations Graduate. Dozens of big, colorful balloons were suspended from the high ceiling, and the bright rainbow-colored electric lights danced around the room. Multicolored confetti that drizzled over windows decorated chairs and tables as the velvety voice of the popular Jamaican gospel group The Grace Thrillers gushed from hidden speakers, "Ain't No Giving Up."

Dupree covered her face with trembling hands. She had gotten her own private celebration party.

The buffet-styled table was burdened down with so much food that Dupree was confused by what to choose. She ultimately settled for some spicy jerk chicken, rich gungo peas and rice, and a big, tasty steamed parrot fish.

The clatter of forks and knives swiping across plates, passionate chewing, and heavy slurping created an appetizing ambiance as the flavorous aroma snaked itself around the room and its animated occupants.

After dinner, the real party began. Tables and chairs were cleared away, creating a dance floor in the center of the room, which was filled almost instantly with jiggling bodies. The dancers dipped and fell back, shook and flashed, arms flying wildly in the air and feet pumping and kicking as onlookers clapped and cheered them on.

Dupree shyly stayed on the sidelines, watching and giggling in amusement. Her eyes bugged when she saw Mother Sassy leading the train of dancers. Her flared skirt was tied at one end on the bottom, her eyes glazed over in pleasure as her small mouth pouted in deep concentration. Sweat poured down her greasy face and her auburn wig was now sitting on her forehead.

A gasp went up when Mother Sassy dipped, her knees bent in opposite direction as her bottom swiped the floor. Her hips ground to the beat as her tongue hung out the side of her mouth in absolute delight.

"What is this, dear Father?" Miss Sam muttered, her eyes filled with fear.

"Have mercy, Lord," Pastor Pallen prayed, his brows knitted together in concern.

"I bet you a million dollars she can't get back up," someone whispered.

"I think we should get an ambulance on standby," was the soft response.

No one noticed Brother Shawn as he inched closer and closer to Mother Sassy.

Now in her element, Mother Sassy was the center of attention as some amused spectators egged her on. The louder they shouted, the faster the aged hips tried to move. Her body was now soaked from head to toe, her breathing deep and short, her frail body trembling under the pressure, the energy slowing but surely creeping away. It was now time to get back on her feet. With one hand on her hip and the other still waving in the air,

Mother Sassy tried pulsating her way back up, but her arthritic knees protested and finally gave way to gravity, sending her flying forward.

Brother Shawn leaped after her, his arms outstretched, but he was a few inches short of a grab. Mother Sassy landed face down on the plush carpeted floor with her bony butt sticking up in the air. Her wig sailed in one direction and her dentures the other.

For a few seconds, no one breathed. Mr. Jim, who witnessed the incident, had quickly turned the music off. The room was arrested by the stunned silence.

Suddenly, Brother Shawn ran to her, followed by other concerned people. He effortlessly lifted Mother Sassy in his arms while Pastor Pallen screamed for the pushing crowd to step back, making a way for him to the back of room.

A few giggles filtered through but stopped abruptly when Pastor Pallen furiously scanned the room for the insensitive culprits.

Mother Sassy was placed in a chair as some of the members fussed over her, poking and squeezing, searching for broken bones or disjointed body parts. Thankfully everything seemed intact. The only thing that was seriously hurt was her pride.

Sister Louise placed the wig back on Mother Sassy's head and guided her hand to slip her dentures back in.

"Honey, here is a glass of water," Mother Blossom said as she held the glass to Mother Sassy's mouth.

Mother Sassy drank greedily, emptying the glass in a few seconds. Now fully composed, she slowly looked around at the concerned faces staring at her. "Who in heaven's name turned the music off?" Mother Sassy shouted. The room erupted in laughter. Yup, Mother Sassy was fine.

***

With their hands filled with packed leftovers, everyone dragged their stuffed, exhausted bodies to the bus. Dupree was given four big plastic bags bursting at the seams with food. Inside she smiled. She had enough food to feed her and Aunt Madge for a few days.

As soon as she entered the house, Dupree gave a small wail and jumped on Aunt Madge's bed, laughing and talking so fast her words ran into each other. Even though she didn't hear most of what was said, Aunt Madge took one look at the joy radiating from her grand-niece's face and knew it had been a great day for her. Her prayer was answered.

After she settled down, Dupree fed Aunt Madge some ice cream before it melted, and, slowly this time, relayed everything about her fabulous day from beginning to end. Aunt Madge cried with joy as she listened to her happy daughter. She knew it would have been a special day for Dupree but she had no idea how special. To God be the glory for the things He had done.

Everything was falling perfectly into place for Dupree, or so they thought. But the devil is like a roaring lion, seeking whom he may devour.

Chapter Twelve

"Hello, Pree, how are you?"

Dupree heard the deep voice close to her ear and her body stiffened like a piece of granite.

"Is it okay if I sit beside you?" he asked.

Now she knew he wasn't going away anytime soon. Robotically, she slowly turned and looked at the handsome young man leaning over her and could only stare. She finally smiled shyly, nodded her head, and moved over on the church bench to make room for him. They were about to watch the play *Little Baby Jesus,* which was being dramatized by the younger kids from the Daily Vocational Bible School (DVBS).

Dupree knew who he was. His parents and grandparents were long-standing members of her church. They were about the same age, attended and graduated from the same high school, but they never officially met before.

Summer had swept in with a bang and gone viral! School was out and overzealous children were enjoying adventurous summer camps, loud neighborhood barbeques, boisterous house parties, competitive soccer matches, bush cooking by the river, lively street dances, and any other form of entertainment that presented itself.

Dupree was also having a blast at the DVBS, where she taught Monday through Friday. Her excitement hung on the opportunity to share her Bible knowledge with the younger kids, the fellowship with her church brothers and sisters, the biblical plays, Bible quizzes, games, prizes and giveaways, and the delicious food.

"Well, Pree, my name is Anthony Gregg Jr., but please call me Tony," he whispered in her ear, boomeranging her attention back to him.

"And mine is Dupree, not 'Pree,' so please call me Dupree," she replied testily.

Instead of being insulted, Tony threw his head back and laughed out in delight. A few people in the church turned toward them disapprovingly and Mother Sassy gave them the evil eye. They both took that as a cue to stay quiet, and watched the rest of the play in comfortable silence.

Dupree was nervous. She had felt his piercing eyes tracking her every moment like a laser beam gun over the last few days but she ignored him. She had never had a boyfriend. She was not a fool to believe that was going to change anytime soon.

After the play was over, Dupree got up to head home to Aunt Madge. She smiled politely at Tony and wished him a good evening but he wasn't having that.

"What do you say I give you a ride home?" he asked her, flashing those pearly whites of his, advertising that his mother was indeed a dentist. He was only seventeen years old but had gotten a new car for his graduation present from his parents.

Dupree was horrified. Her teeth gently gnawed on her bottom lip as she nervously rocked back and forth on the balls of her feet. "That's okay, but thanks anyway. I am not going far and it is still light out," she finally responded.

"But I don't mind really. Please let me give you a ride. I just want to talk to you some more and get to know you."

"Why?" Dupree asked. No boy had ever shown interest in her before, but here stood a handsome, rich, popular boy wanting to get to know her.

"You seem like a nice person and I just want to be your friend," Tony said sincerely.

"Let me tell you something, pal," Dupree began, pointing her finger at his face, "if this is some bet or game you and your obnoxious friends are trying to play with me, you better keep right on stepping because I am not that type of girl. Got that?"

"No, no, no, this is no game," Tony stammered, his eyes pleadingly interlocked with Dupree's fiery ones. "I have seen kids teasing and making fun of you at school but you never got in a fight with them. At first I thought you were just scared but then I realized that you were just taking the higher road. You behaved like a good Christian girl should and I think that makes you the bravest of them."

Dupree lowered her eyes to the ground as the anger slowly tiptoed away. She was at a loss for words.

"Perhaps some other time." Tony's smiling voice snapped Dupree's head up. She shyly smiled at him and nodded before she turned and walked away.

At first Dupree wasn't sure what to make of Tony, but she finally let her guard down and interacted with him more. They sat together at DVBS, watched the plays together, and laughed and talked about stupid things. Just kids being kids.

But someone else never saw it for what it was.

Chapter Thirteen

On Saturday morning, a few days later, Dupree was on her fourth trip back from the standpipe with a big bucket of water on her head. Her back and head hurt but she knew they needed the water to use. As she slowly walked along the main road to get to the track that led to her home, she heard a car pull up behind her. She began to walk faster and then someone called out to her.

"Pree, Pree, wait up!"

Only one person in the world insisted on calling her Pree. Dupree was so shocked that the bucket of water fell off her head and splashed all over her from head to toe. As she stood there soaking wet and embarrassed, she wished the ground would have opened up and took her right in.

"Oh, I'm so sorry I scared you, Pree," Tony said as he ran up to her. He had a handful of napkins in his hand that he used to get some of the water from her face and hair. Dupree took the unused ones from him and took over the task. She was still too embarrassed to speak to him.

"I'm really sorry," he repeated. "Why didn't you ask me yesterday to come and help you this morning? You knew I would have been glad to." Tony went and got the bucket from the side of the road where it fell. He told Dupree that he was going to refill the bucket and help her carry the water home, whether she wanted him to do so or not.

Dupree looked at him, saw the determination on his face, and knew she had lost this battle. Tony was finally going to see where she lived and she was not sure how she felt about that.

Tony parked his car on the side of the road because the small track to Dupree's house wasn't big enough for him to drive and they began to walk. Tony had the bucket of water on his head and Dupree saw his discomfort and knew he had never done anything like this before.

"Let me take that from you," she said, reaching for the bucket but Tony brushed her hand away.

"No, I got it," he replied in a strained voice, his face masked with determination. "It's not that heavy."

Dupree smiled knowingly. For Tony, the bucket of water probably felt like a ton of bricks.

Stealing a glance at Tony's face when her house came into view Dupree carefully watched his reaction to her home. But Tony showed no sign of disgust and this pleased Dupree very much.

They both made two more trips to the standpipe for water, Tony with one bucket and Dupree with another. After that task was completed, Dupree invited Tony inside to meet Aunt Madge.

"Hello, Aunt Madge," he greeted her as he leaned over the bed and kissed her on the cheek.

Aunt Madge giggled; her face brightened like a Christmas tree. Drool ran down the side of her open mouth when she responded incomprehensibly. Tony took a handkerchief from his pocket and gently wiped her mouth before reaching forward to hug her again.

Dupree had told Aunt Madge all about Tony and she was glad that he attended church. Aunt Madge knew that because of her sickness Dupree rarely got the opportunity to live life as a normal young girl. She had to grow up too fast and she became a woman too soon. She was glad that Dupree found a friend in Tony.

***

Dupree looked at the letter in her hand like it was a live snake. She saw her name printed clearly across the front but still thought the post office might have made a mistake.

It was a beautiful Wednesday afternoon and Dupree was hurriedly making her weekly trip into town. She had to hurry back and get everything done before Bible Studies later. As she sorted through the mail, she paused when she saw her name on one of the envelopes. Aunt Madge got a few letters on occasion but never had she. "Who would be writing me?" Dupree said aloud, glancing around as if the person was lurking nearby. Now very curious, she used her fingers and ripped the letter open to reveal a beautiful congratulations card from Deacon and Mrs. Livingston. There was also a brief note inside:

Congratulations on graduating high school. We are very proud of you and would like you to join us at our home for a special dinner in your honor on Wednesday at 8:30 p.m.

Dupree squealed in delight. She knew their children were away at summer camp but she looked forward to having dinner with these two people who had been so good to her. *I guess I'll be missing Bible Studies tonight,* Dupree thought blissfully.

After getting groceries, Dupree rushed home and swept through her chores like a vacuum, everything completed by nightfall. She had told Aunt Madge about her dinner invitation and she was also happy for her.

Dupree dressed with care that night, selecting a simple yellow sundress that fell to her knee and a matching pair of flip-flops, both given to her by Mrs. Livingston. She pulled her hair back in a tight bun and squirted some Charming perfume behind her ears.

At 8:00 p.m. Dupree wrapped her arms around Aunt Madge and they prayed together, her words loud and clear as Aunt Madge groaned deep in her throat, shaking her head uncontrollably as she covered her grand-niece under the blood of Jesus. When they were finished, Dupree kissed Aunt Madge on her leathery cheek, then grabbed her flashlight and headed out to dinner.

It was very dark in the small, narrow track from her house to the main road. Every since her encounter with the devil, Dupree used a flashlight the few occasions she had to walk there alone. She knew she would need it later that night when she returned home. Singing softly in contentment, she made her way to the Livingston property.

Dupree looked up at the big house perched at the top of the hill like a beautiful eagle with its wings reaching for the sky. Slowly walking up the long marble walkway illuminated by rows and rows of glittering lights, she paused briefly. Her widened eyes feasted on the exquisite garden of beautiful flowers that spanned both sides of the driveway, and rows of morning glories, kiss-me-over-the-garden-gates, hibiscuses, daisies, lignum vitaes, ferns, and poincianas. The property was a secluded paradise within itself, their closest neighbor over two miles away. A burst of giggles erupted from Dupree as she happily resumed her journey, skipping and hopping like a bunny rabbit, each excited step taking her closer and closer to a mind-boggling evening. Her life would never be the same again.

Chapter Fourteen

Taking a deep breath to calm her jittery nerves, Dupree's trembling index finger pressed down lightly on the doorbell. Its singing tone echoed throughout the big house. Dupree gave a small gasp and took a quick step back in surprise when the door popped opened and a grinning Deacon Livingston materialized a second later like Houdini.

"Hi, Dupree. I'm sorry I scared you, my dear. Please, come on in. I've been anxiously waiting for you."

"Thank you, sir. I'm so happy to be here. It's so nice of you and Mrs. Livingston to invite me to dinner," Dupree said as she stepped into the beautifully decorated house.

As she followed him into the living room, Dupree admired the expensive paintings that adorned the thick stucco-clad adobe wall. Deacon Livingston led her over to a soft white leather sofa and asked her to have a seat. He then offered her something to drink and she requested a glass of cold water and watched as he practically ran from the room to retrieve it. As the refracted light from the huge, sparkling chandelier that contained dozens of lamps and complex arrays of crystal prisms bathed Dupree in its glow, she wondered where Mrs. Livingston was.

"Where is Mrs. Livingston?" she asked Deacon Livingston when he returned with her water.

"Oh, she'll be down shortly. She is just running a little behind." Deacon Livingston handed her the water and sat on the sofa beside her, his leg brushing her thigh. Dupree quickly scooted away to the side, her free hand tugging at her dress.

"So, how have you been, darling?" Deacon Livingston asked as he leaned over to her, his minted breath fanning her face.

"Okay," Dupree mumbled and took a deep gulp of water.

"You are looking really beautiful tonight. But then again, you always do."

"Thank . . . thank you, sir." Dupree looked around frantically, her mind willing Mrs. Livingston to hurry on down.

"I love that scent on you," Deacon Livingston's breath tickled her ears. "You smell so delicious."

Now very uncomfortable, Dupree tried scooting over, but her leg was already pressed firmly against the side of the sofa. There was no more room.

"Hmmm, I think you should go and see what's holding up Mrs. Livingston," Dupree said. Then she felt Deacon Livingston's hand running up her leg and she jumped up, horrified. "What . . . what . . . what are you doing?" she stammered, her heart pounding in her chest. "Where is Mrs. Livingston? If she doesn't get down here right now I am going home."

"Relax, darling, she probably got held up in town. She'll be here soon."

Dupree winced at the term of endearment and suddenly realized what he'd just said. "I thought you said she was upstairs finishing up, but now she is in town?"

Deacon Livingston threw his head back and laughed out loud. "Upstairs, in town, who cares where she is? Baby, tonight it's just you and me."

His cold voice frightened Dupree and she knew she had to get out of there. "I'll be leaving now, Deacon Livingston," she said, with emphasis on the word "deacon." "Maybe we can do dinner another night." She tried to pass by him.

Deacon Livingston grabbed her by the arm and shoved her back down onto the sofa. A scream welled up in her throat, but her trembling hands covered her mouth, preventing its release. By now Dupree was horrified. She could not understand what was happening. This was Deacon Livingston, a man she loved and respected like a father. He was a friend to Aunt Madge, a wonderful husband, an awesome father, but, most importantly, he was a man of God. Certainly he had lost his mind. But whatever the reason for his weird behavior, Dupree knew she was in a lot of trouble.

She stood again and made another attempt to get around him, but this time he slapped her hard across the face. She screamed out in pain and backed away from him in fright.

"Please let me go, Deacon Livingston. Please, I am begging you, sir."

"You are not going anywhere until I say so. So stop trying to fight this and let's have some fun."

Tears ran down Dupree's face as she began to wail, her voice rising higher and higher in desperation. "I want to go home. Please let me go home, Deacon Livingston. I don't want to be here."

"Shut your mouth, now! I don't want to hurt you but I will if I have to!" he shouted. His cold, chilling voice rang out in the stillness of the night as he slowly advanced toward her. Dupree knew it was no longer Deacon Livingston standing in front of her. It was the devil himself.

As she looked into the wild, red eyes staring at her in anger and lust, she knew that she was looking at her devil. Oh, dear God, he came back for her again!

Deacon Livingston grinned nastily as he saw the look of recognition on Dupree's face. He knew she had recognized him now as her attacker that fateful night. But unlike that night, she would not be getting away tonight. He felt like a punk the way he ran away screaming like a girl that night and this had angered him for days. Well, he was about to show this little tramp who was the boss now. *All that voodoo crap she pulled that night isn't going to help her tonight,* he thought with glee.

It took him a few weeks to put his plan into motion. He knew that Dupree went into town every Wednesday to get groceries from his supermarket and would also stop at the post office for her mail. So Monday morning he got the postcard inviting her to dinner and dropped it in the outgoing mailbox. Choosing that day worked out perfectly because Mrs. Livingston attended Bible Study religiously every week, and he wasn't worried about Aunt Madge; after all, the woman was darn near comatose. All he had to do was convince Mrs. Livingston that he and another deacon would be visiting a sick church member at the hospital that night and he would not be able to attend Bible Study with her.

As Dupree backed away in fright from the devil, she knew that only the Lord could help her again. How did it come to this? The man she viewed as a father figure was trying to hurt her and she had never done him any wrong.

"What did I do to you, Deacon Livingston? Why are you trying to hurt me?" she cried as she pled with him for mercy. "Please let me go and I promise I won't tell anyone. Please, I am begging you, sir. I will go away from here and you will never see me again."

"Oh, you will be going away all right, but not 'til I'm finished with you. You are going to feel the loving of a real man tonight, honey," he replied and Dupree winced at the dreadful thought. "Now come here to big daddy and make this easy on the both of us."

Dupree screamed when he reached for her and quickly turned around, running toward the back door. Her heart was doing hopscotch in her chest as the tears from her eyes hugged the mucus from her nose and ran shamelessly down her face. Her breathing was short and shallow. She felt fainted and weak but she knew she had to get out of there. She grabbed the door handle and turned it, but to her dismay the door was locked. By now Deacon Livingston was slowly advancing toward her. The only way out was to get around him. She looked back at the six foot tall, 250-pound man and knew that was impossible. She was no match for this big beast. There was no way out and right then and there she knew what was about to happen to her. After everything she had fought so hard to accomplish, it would end right here tonight. She knew that monster was going to rape her but he would have to do so over her dead body! Anger as she had never known before swept over Dupree and she decided then that she would not go down without a fight.

She remembered Aunt Madge and more tears sprung to her eyes. Would the news of her death kill her aunt? Who would take care of her when she was gone? Unable to hold herself up any longer, Dupree crumbled to the floor and wept. She wept for her bedridden aunt who would be left at the mercy of strangers. She wept for the mother she never knew. She wept for Mrs. Livingston and her kids who had no knowledge of the monster they lived with, and finally she wept for herself. She just couldn't get a break in life. All she had were impossible dreams that were about to be ended at the hands of this madman.

"Where are you, my Lord? Are you there, God? Please do not forsake me now! Please I need you now more than ever! Have mercy upon me, Lord! Please, I'm begging you to have mercy!" she screamed out in distress, looking toward the heavens.

Mr. Livingston threw his head back and laughed out loud. He looked at Dupree on the floor praying but knew that prayer rubbish wouldn't work again. He got her right where he needed her this time.

He advanced toward her in anger and she tried crawling away from him but had nowhere to go. She leaned her back against the door and screamed with all her might. Her screams only seemed to excite the pervert more as he headed toward her.

"Keep screaming, baby. I like it when you do that. I'm about to make you scream for real now." He laughed mockingly.

Dupree folded her small hands into fists as she got ready to fight for her life, literally. Then she glanced down briefly and noticed a big seashell by the door that Mrs. Livingston used to keep the door open during the day. She slowly wiggled herself closer to it as the demon came for her. By now he was so excited that spit was dripping from his mouth; his eyes were wide open and lit up in excitement. He rubbed his hands together in glee and licked his big, long tongue in ecstasy. No one could say no to him and get away with it. He was about to teach Dupree a lesson that she would never forget.

As Deacon Livingston reached out to grab Dupree, she screamed as loud as she could in anger, swung the seashell with all her might, and watched as it connected with the side of the beast's head. Blood gushed out all over the living room as he went down screaming in pain. Dupree got up and tried to run around him again but she went flying through the air as her feet were kicked out from under her. She came crashing down in a mangled heap on her face between the sofa and the coffee table. The pain that ran through her body was so intense, she screamed out in agony. Too hurt and weak to move, she slowly turned over on her back and watched as Deacon Livingston came for her again. This time there was just pure hatred in his eyes as the blood continued running down his face.

"Now I am going to hurt you real, real bad," he growled. "All I wanted was to have a little fun with you, but now after I am finished with you, you are going to finally meet that Lord you are always praying to."

"Please, please, I'm sorry," Dupree begged in a weak, distressed voice. Her begging only seemed to infuriate him more. He grabbed her up like a rag doll and threw her across the room. She landed on her face again and tasted the blood in her mouth. Her right arm was twisted in an awkward position under her and her left leg lost all feeling in it. By now the pain was so excruciating she just wanted to die, and she knew she was about to when she felt her broken body being lifted up high into the air.

Mr. Bunny and his eldest son, John, were headed home after a long day on the farm. He was exhausted and hungry and just wanted to get home to have a bath, something to eat, and get some rest. As they passed the road that led to the Livingston's property, he paused briefly. He had borrowed some tools from Mr. Livingston last week but hadn't had a chance to take them back. Maybe he should just have John run up to the house and carry back the tools because this would definitely save him a trip tomorrow. But as he looked up toward the house, he noticed that the place was in darkness. Maybe the Livingstons were at Bible Studies, he thought. He knew how dedicated Deacon Livingston was to the work of the Lord. That was one God-fearing man and such a faithful servant of the Lord. He looked at the house again undecidedly and finally decided to wait until tomorrow to bring back the tools. No one was home anyway, he thought, as he slowly drove off down the road.

Glass went flying and some got embedded in Dupree's face and all over her body as she landed on the glass coffee table in the middle of the living room. She felt her back pop and watched as the darkness came down and wrapped itself around her like a warm blanket. Then she felt nothing.

The demon looked at Dupree lying motionless on the floor, bloodied and broken, and threw back his head and laughed out loud in victory. He had her at his mercy now and he was going to do with her as he darn well pleased. He quickly ran down the hall to the kitchen and grabbed a big cooking knife and headed back to the living room. He used the knife to cut Dupree's torn dress and her bra away from her body. His eyes always popped out of his head when he saw her small, young, firm breasts. He licked his tongue in anticipation as he continued to cut away her clothes. Finally the only piece of garment that remained was her underwear. This was actually the same underwear Dupree had bought for her graduation and kept for special occasions. She didn't have many, but Aunt Madge always told her that a young lady should have at least one good pair of panties.

The panties were cut away from her body and the sound echoed hauntingly throughout the house. Deacon Livingston felt faint as he looked at the perfection of Dupree's body. He had never seen anything like this in his life. Not even when Mrs. Livingston was younger did she have a body like this. His heart began to beat rapidly, sweat poured down his face, and his breathing got irregular. He stood up and quickly tore off his shirt, sending buttons flying. *There's no time to waste,* he thought as he almost tripped over his pants getting them off. These were followed by his underpants and finally he stood above Dupree as naked as a jaybird.

In his sick, twisted mind, Deacon Livingston could have sworn he heard the heavens open up and the angels singing a sweet melody of triumph. "This is it!" he shouted and kicked Dupree's legs open. Then suddenly he stopped, frozen into place, and slowly turned around. His eyes opened wide in terror at what he saw.

Chapter Fifteen

After Mr. Bunny drove away from the Livingston property headed to his home, John noticed something alongside the road a few miles down; it was Deacon Livingston's SUV parked in the dark behind a tree.

"Papa, isn't that Deacon Livingston's van over there?" John pointed.

Mr. Bunny squinted through the blackness of the night and gasped in surprise when he saw the vehicle. He quickly pulled over to the side of the road and they both got out and ran over to the van.

"I wonder why he parked all the way down here. That man got him a whole lot of land, plus a four-car garage," Mr. Bunny muttered, puzzled, as he and John peered through the window inside the vehicle and found it empty.

"Something is not right here, Papa. I smell a rat," John stated, his face twisted with deep concern.

"By God, you are right, my son. Come on, let's go and see what the devil is going on here."

The two men ran back to their truck and Mr. Bunny quickly made a U-turn in the road, his tires screeching out in protest. In the small, close-knit community where everyone knew each other, they all looked out for one another. Deacon Livingston was a wealthy man and they feared he was in deep trouble.

Mr. Bunny parked the truck down the road from the house. He grabbed his machete off the car floor, and then he and John proceeded on foot slowly up the driveway as quiet as mice. As they got closer to the house, they heard glass breaking and a scream that caused the hair on Mr. Bunny's head to stand up. Deacon Livingston was being attacked and he needed help immediately. They did not know how many culprits were inside and knew they needed backup, so Mr. Bunny took the truck keys and gave them to John to go and get the police.

John ran off as fast as lightning and Mr. Bunny crept around the side of the house to wait for the cops. He waited there for a few minutes but began to get restless. He knew that while he was waiting, Deacon Livingston could be dying inside. Not known for his patience, Mr. Bunny slowly made his way up the front steps to the veranda. He got on his stomach and crawled toward the front door leading to the living room, where he thought he heard the commotion earlier. He pushed the door gently and to his amazement it opened softly. Everything was quiet except for the heavy breathing.

As he slowly made his way across the room crawling on his stomach, Mr. Bunny stopped suddenly when his eyes came into contact with Deacon Livingston's bare buttocks. Blinking his eyes rapidly to clear his focus, Mr. Bunny glimpsed the body of an unmoving female between Deacon Livingston's legs. Deacon Livingston wasn't being attacked; he was the one attacking someone! Mr. Bunny stood up and tiptoed toward the big, naked man who was still oblivious to his presence. He knew something bad had happened, but nothing could have prepared him for what he saw. He gasped loudly and placed a trembling hand over his mouth in shock.

Deacon Livingston heard the sound and spun around to see Mr. Bunny standing there seethed in anger with his machete raised over his head. He looked like a mad bull with tears running down his face. Dupree's lifeless body lay exposed on the floor. Mr. Bunny felt sick to his stomach. If only he had stopped earlier.

"You disgusting piece of crap! What did you do to that baby there?" Mr. Bunny yelled, his booming voice ricocheting off the walls.

"I'm . . . I'm . . . I'm so sorry," Deacon Livingston stammered, his seedy eyes flickering around his head like an owl.

"Sorry! Sorry! That's all you have to say, huh?" Mr. Bunny growled as he inched closer to Deacon Livingston.

He had known Madge and her sister, Ellen, for years. They all lived in the same community and attended school together. He remembered when Ellen had Tiny, Dupree's mother, and he was there when Dupree was born. He could still vividly remember baby Dupree strapped to Madge's back as she planted those yams and corn in her farm. With the hot sun raining down on them, Madge labored away all day. She had no one to take care of Dupree after her mother ran away, so she carried the baby everywhere she went. He watched Dupree growing up with respect for herself and everyone. He knew how hard life had been for this young girl but yet she struggled on. He was there when Dupree graduated from high school and would forever remember the big smile on her face and how happy she looked. Now here she lay, dead. The pain was too much for Mr. Bunny and he screamed out in anguish as he advanced toward Deacon Livingston with the machete.

Deacon Livingston screamed in fright and backed away from the big, angry man as he came toward him. Earlier he had enough strength to brutalize a small, young, helpless girl but now that he had a worthy opponent he was quivering in fear. Where was the big bad wolf that howled in victory as he looked at Dupree's broken and bloodied body?

"You scared, huh? Were you scared when you were raping and killing that little baby there?" Mr. Bunny screamed in anger.

"Please, please, I'm sorry," Deacon Livingston said in a weak, terrified voice. The same words that Dupree had uttered to him earlier he found himself using now. But he didn't have any mercy on Dupree then, and Mr. Bunny certainly wasn't going to have any on him now.

"Whoop, whoop, whoop," echoed through the house as Mr. Bunny slapped Deacon Livingston repeatedly across the face with the machete. A few of his teeth went flying and blood ran down his face as he fell on some broken glass on the floor. He screamed out loud in pain and anguish as he scrambled to his knee, trying to creep away from Mr. Bunny.

"Where do you think you are going, you rapist? Where, where, you murderer? Did that little girl beg you for her life, huh? Did she try to get away from you, too?" Mr. Bunny was now shouting. He threw the machete to the floor and used his big fists to pound Deacon Livingston mercilessly. By now Deacon Livingston was bloodied and battered. The pain was so much that he silently prayed for death.

As if he could read his thoughts, Mr. Bunny bawled at him, "I bet you would like me to kill you, right? But you are not getting away so easy, pal. I am going to make sure you suffer like how this poor baby girl did." And he proceeded to beat Deacon Livingston within an inch of his life.

The door barged opened and two policemen followed by John rushed into the room. They stopped in shock as they looked at the sight before them. A naked Dupree lay lifeless on the floor. Deacon Livingston was on the ground, bloodied and barely breathing, as an angry Mr. Bunny with the machete again in his hands held in midair stood over him with sweat running down his face to make another connection.

"Please stop, Papa!" John shouted in alarm to his father. "It's okay now, the cops are here." He ran to his father and grabbed the hand holding the machete as the terrified two cops ran over to Dupree's body.

Try as he might, John could not get the machete from Mr. Bunny, who was still raving mad as a bull cow. As they struggled, Officer Dunn ran back over and grabbed Mr. Bunny around the waist and John seized the opportunity to wrestle the machete from his father before he could finish off Deacon Livingston.

Officer Gregg fell down on his knees beside Dupree and wept. "Lord, have mercy! Have mercy, dear Father! Not her, please not her!" he shrieked while pounding angry his fists on his chest. "Take me instead, Lord. She doesn't deserve to suffer for my sin! Please, take me instead!"

His haunting cries brought the other men's attention to him as they watched him take off his jacket and cover Dupree's nakedness as much as the small jacket could do. He then sat down on the floor, oblivious to the broken glass and blood, and placed her bloody head in his lap. Officer Gregg was crying so hard, his body shook with the anguish that was trapped inside.

"I'm sorry, baby girl. I'm so sorry for what I did to you," he muttered repeatedly.

The other men were puzzled by his behavior; they too were distraught by what had happened to Dupree but for Officer Gregg it was more personal, very personal. This was more than just pain. It was also the conscience of a guilt-ridden father as he held his daughter's broken, bruised body in his arms.

Chapter Sixteen

Officer Gregg was an outstanding citizen in the community. His grandfather and father were cops, so he knew from an early age that was what he wanted to do as well. He entered the police force right after high school and after graduating from the Jamaica Police Academy in Spanish Town, St. Catherine, he went back to Falmouth to serve his community. He got married to Beverly Johnson, the only dentist in the community. They bought a nice house in town and were members of the church where they both got saved and baptized. They had a wonderful life and everything was going great for Officer Gregg until he laid eyes on fifteen-year-old Tiny.

He was going home from work late one night and saw the young bootylicious girl walking home by herself in the dark. As a police officer, it was his duty to protect the citizens of his community, he had told himself, so he stopped and offered her a ride. Tiny gladly accepted when she looked at the handsome man sitting in the car. They struck up a conversation and Tiny flirted all the way before she got out the car. Officer Gregg knew what Tiny was doing and as a thirty-four-year old man he should have put a stop to it because she was only a child, but he felt flattered by the attention.

The next day Tiny went to the public phone in town and called Officer Gregg at the police station. She wanted him to meet her that night, and instead of putting Tiny in her place, he agreed to meet the young girl over by the high school.

"I'll just go and have a talk with her," he told himself. "The poor child looked as if she was going through a lot and probably just needs some fatherly advice."

But advice was the last thing on Tiny's mind he later found out that night. Tiny was inside an empty classroom, lying on the teacher's desk as naked as the day she was born.

"What in heaven's name are you doing, girl? You crazy or what?" he asked in surprise, as his wide eyes roamed hungrily over the Tiny's bare body.

"What do you think I'm doing, Officer?" Tiny replied as she winked and batted her long lashes at him flirtatiously.

"I'm leaving, now," Officer Greg whispered, still rooted to the same spot he stood, his eyes fixated on Tiny.

Officer Gregg knew he should have just turned around and gone home to his wife, but he became a victim of his lustful flesh as he stepped farther into the room and closed the squeaky door behind him. As he looked at Tiny's perfect, young body, he knew he just had to have her, and like a convict headed toward the electric chair, he went to her.

This sick, twisted affair continued for two months, where Officer Gregg would meet Tiny at the high school for their nightly sex sessions. He knew what he was doing was wrong and he could lose everything, including his wife. But most importantly, as an officer of the law, he knew what he was doing was statutory rape and he could get locked up with the criminals he himself locked away; but he couldn't stop himself. Tiny was like a drug and he was addicted to her.

One night shortly after they'd just had sex, Tiny whispered timidly in his ears, "I think I'm pregnant."

"You are what?" Officer Gregg shouted. "You can't be pregnant. Weren't you on the pill?" he asked.

"What pill?" Tiny looked at him blankly; she had no idea what he was talking about.

Officer Gregg looked at the child lying naked in front of him and felt sick to his stomach. It had just dawned on him that he had been abusing this young girl for a few months now. And to make matters worse, he never used any form of protection to protect them both. Now here was Tiny, a child who was going to have a child: his child. He knew he might as well just kill himself because his wife, her parents, or his were going to do it anyway. And if not, then he was going to prison for a long, long time.

"You can't have that baby. I will give you the money to go to Kingston and get an abortion. No one has to even know you were pregnant," Officer Gregg reasoned.

Tiny looked at him like he had lost his mind. Her anger gave her the courage to speak her mind. "My mother died in childbirth and I would rather die myself than kill my baby."

It was those words that almost turned the police officer into a murderer when something inside him snapped and he angrily choked Tiny within an inch of her life when she refused to have an abortion.

"You better not call my name to anyone," he screamed into her ringing ears before he released her, spit flying out his mouth. "If you do, I will come back and kill you. In fact, I will kill your precious Aunt Madge first. You wouldn't want anything to happen to her now, would you?" he threatened.

Tiny's young, immature mind was easily intimidated by the police officer and she believed he meant what he had said and so she promised not to reveal their secret. That was the last time Officer Gregg had any contact with Tiny. When he got home that night, he got another surprise of his life. His wife, Beverly, was waiting for him with the good news.

"Honey, I'm pregnant. We are going to have a baby!" she exclaimed with glee. Officer Gregg knew where his priorities lay and that was with his wife. He convinced himself that he had scared Tiny enough for her not to mention his name and he would just forget that she ever existed and that was what he did.

Over the next couple of months, even though Aunt Madge begged and pleaded with her, Tiny would not reveal who had gotten her pregnant. She stubbornly repeated that she did not know who it was. Aunt Madge was devastated. She wondered where she went wrong with Tiny and blamed herself. Maybe if she had gotten married and Tiny had a male figure in her life, this wouldn't have happened. But, despite her disappointment, she knew she had to be there for the young girl she loved like her own.

A few months after dropping out of high school, Tiny went into labor one night. Aunt Madge went and got Miss Mandy, the midwife, to deliver the baby because she knew she could not afford to take Tiny to the hospital. Miss Mandy was a good midwife and delivered many babies for the women in the community. After a few agonizing hours, in a small, dark boarded one-bedroom house, little Dupree came into the world at 10:30 p.m. on January 25.

While across town at the Falmouth Hospital, Mrs. Gregg was in labor with her dedicated husband right by her side, helping her along. Doctor Hanson, the best obstetrician in town, assisted by three nurses, was delivering the baby.

"Push, push, push, come on, baby, you can do this," Officer Gregg coached his wife. He was very anxious to see his first child and at exactly 10:30 p.m., Anthony Gregg Jr., aka Tony, was born. There was a big celebration at the hospital as the grandparents, relatives, and friends gathered around the newborn. Officer Gregg was filled with pride as he looked at his son; he was now a proud father—a father of two, unbeknownst to everyone except him, Tiny, and God, or so he thought.

Chapter Seventeen

John ran down the hall into the first bedroom where he saw and grabbed a sheet off the bed. He ran back and used the sheet to wrap around Dupree. Although it seemed as if it was too late, he knew they had to get her to the hospital immediately.

Meanwhile, Officer Dunn knelt down beside Dupree and tears came to his eyes as he saw the extent of her damages. He placed his finger on her wrist, trying to feel for a pulse, but he felt nothing. As he prayed, Officer Dunn cried openly like his partner, Officer Gregg. Officer Dunn was a Christian man and knew that only God could help Dupree now. Then he placed his finger at the pulse at her neck and shouted out in joy.

"She is alive, she is alive!" he shouted.

Mr. Bunny, John, and the two policemen all gathered around Dupree. It never dawned on Mr. Bunny that she might be alive because anyone who looked as she did could not have survived. But, lo and behold, he actually felt the low pulse himself. He was amazed at the strength and will of this young girl to survive.

The men hurriedly made their way through the pool of blood that enveloped the floor like a dirty bedspread, trapping sharp-edged pieces of broken glass.

"We have to get her to the hospital immediately."

"Here, grab her legs and I'll hold her head."

"Please be gentle. It feels like everything is broken."

"Oh my God, look at all this blood."

"How can she still be alive after all this?"

They were all talking at once, elated that Dupree was alive, even if just barely. Mr. Bunny decided to ride with Officer Gregg, who decided to take her to the hospital in his police car. He knew they would get there sooner with the police siren than to wait for an ambulance to arrive. As Mr. Bunny and Officer Gregg sped off, lights flashing and siren blazing, John went to help Officer Dunn get the pathetic Deacon Livingston to the police station.

The two men reached down and each one angrily grabbed hold of an arm, dragging Deacon Livingston's naked, battered body over the sharp pieces of broken glass toward the door. Bullets of pain pierced through his body and he screamed out in agony like a wounded fox caught in a snare.

"Shut up, you nasty piece of garbage!" Officer Dunn shouted, heatedly twisting Deacon Livingston's arm.

John stopped and furiously dropped the arm he held. He stepped to Deacon Livingston and began to kick him repeatedly all over his body. "You like to scream like a girl, huh? Okay, I'll give you something to scream about," he shouted, raining boot blows on Deacon Livingston. "Hold this old dog!"

Officer Dunn quickly rushed and held on to John as he kicked wildly in the air, yelling at Deacon Livingston, who was curled up in a ball, whimpering and moaning and groaning.

It took a few minutes for Officer Dunn to calm John down before they finally dragged Deacon Livingston outside to the vehicle.

They knew he was in a lot of pain and needed medical attention but they refused to take him to the hospital, at least not yet anyway. They decided that the animal needed to suffer some more for what he had done to Dupree.

"Please let me put my clothes on," Deacon Livingston begged, his face etched in anguish. "Please, please."

In response, Officer Dunn furiously tugged his hands behind his back, the click of the handcuffs surprisingly loud in the haunting night, before his bare behind was shoved into the back of the truck, his nakedness for the world to see.

The speeding, siren-wailing police car screeched up to the emergency ward at the hospital and Mr. Bunny jumped out before it came to a complete stop. Waving his arms frantically, his booming voice desperately shouted for help. Emergency personnel bolted to the car with a stretcher and carefully but hurriedly loaded Dupree's body on. They then rushed her off into the hospital, with the anxious doctor issuing instructions as he ran alongside the stretcher.

By now the news was all over the community about Dupree's attack and Deacon Livingston's arrest. Bible Study was in full force when Sister Jane burst through the doors screaming and shouting. Her husband was a police officer and he was on duty when Officer Dunn and John carried in a bloodied Deacon Livingston. He quickly called his wife with the juicy news after hearing what had happened to Dupree. Sister Jane left her kids with one of her neighbors and ran to tell Mrs. Livingston the news because she knew she always attended Bible Study. It never even occurred to her that she missed Bible Study but now found her way to church to gossip.

Pastor Pallen stepped down from the pulpit and quickly went to Sister Jane. "Sister Jane, what's the reason for disrupting my church?"

"Bad news, Pastor," Sister Jane replied breathlessly, sucking some much-needed air into her starved lungs before she continued. "Pastor, Deacon Livingston was just arrested. He raped and murdered Sister Madge's little girl, Dupree," she stated as if she was present and had all the facts. "Dupree is dead like a dog, Pastor."

A loud wail that could have raised the dead rang out in church before Mrs. Livingston fell over in a faint. The church erupted in chaos as some of the members ran to her aid and others who were close to Aunt Madge and Dupree rushed off to the hospital.

Back at the hospital, the doctors worked feverishly to save Dupree's life. It seemed as if she had bones broken just about everywhere on her body. Tears came to their eyes as they looked at the damage that was done to this poor little girl's body but they remained professional. The nurses, however, were another story. They cried openly at the sight. Dupree's back was broken, as well as her right leg and left arm. There was a deep cut in her head where a big piece of glass was embedded. Both of her eyes were swollen shut and her lips were busted. There were cuts all over her body from the broken glass and she had a concussion.

After a thorough examination, the doctors concluded that Dupree was not raped and surprisingly there was no internal bleeding as was expected with all the damage that had occurred. However, Dupree was in critical condition and needed a miracle real bad.

After reviving a devastated Mrs. Livingston and sending her home with some sisters from the church, Pastor and First Lady Pallen rushed to the hospital.

Officer Gregg sat in a corner of the waiting room, his head in the palms of his hands as he sobbed uncontrollably, oblivious to the chaos around him. Deep regret washed over his trembling body, his shame suffocating him.

Dupree had regained consciousness when she reached the hospital and the doctor quickly put her back under as they worked on her. After the X-ray and CAT scan were completed, she was rushed into surgery. There was no spinal injury but small bone chips and fragments were removed to avoid damage to the spinal cord over time. It took a few hours for the doctors to put Dupree back together, literally, and she was still sleeping when she was finally taken to her room. Dupree was in critical condition, but they had a good feeling about her prognosis. It would be a long, tedious journey to a full recovery, but anyone who went through what she did and was still alive would no doubt survive. Dupree was a fighter to the end.

Chapter Eighteen

Back at the police station was another problem. Angry citizens converged at the station like a swarm of hornets.

"We want justice!"

"Send out the bootleg deacon, now!"

"We burn fire on all rapists and child molesters!"

They screamed, shouted, and chanted as they demanded justice for Dupree. Some carried machetes, knives, and pickaxes. Others had pieces of big sticks, old iron pipes, and ropes. A few had some illegal guns hidden on their person. It was common knowledge that the people respected the police, but many also tried to help them do their jobs by administering a little vigilante justice if and when necessary. Well, tonight they deemed it was necessary. They wanted Deacon Livingston's head on a platter and they intended to have it, even if they had to break down the doors of the police station.

As the crowd got rowdy and out of control, Superintendent Chez called in all available off-duty police officers to report to work, and backup from the Runaway Bay Police Station in St. Ann.

He decided to move Deacon Livingston to the Runaway Bay Police Station, but first he needed to get him to the hospital as soon as possible, although he would like nothing else but to throw Deacon Livingston out to the people and let them rip him apart.

Superintendent Chez was a father to two beautiful girls, one almost the same age as Dupree. It angered him what had happened to her. However, he was also a police officer and he had to uphold the law as much as he hated to do so then.

Mrs. Scott was in her den relaxing when the animated voices of Miss Angie, her housekeeper, and the gardener reached her ears. She quickly jumped to her feet and went out to them on the veranda.

"What's going on?" she asked curiously.

"It's that poor baby, Dupree. We just heard that she was raped and killed by that slime ball, Deacon Livingston," Miss Angie replied between hiccups, tears pouring down her cheeks.

The glass of red wine fell from Mrs. Scott's hand and she backed away from Miss Angie in shock. "No, no, please tell me that's not so."

There was no way what she heard was true; not Dupree. Mrs. Scott had grown very fond of Dupree and had even attended her graduation and watched with pride as she collected her diploma. She ran inside and grabbed her car keys; she had to get to the hospital immediately.

Upon arrival at the hospital, Mrs. Scott saw a large crowd stretching from outside all the way into the waiting room. She forced her way through the bodies of mourning people until she got to the front where Pastor Pallen and his wife were. She could tell that Sister Pallen was crying, and briefly wondered if Dupree had really died. But when she asked the dreaded question, the pastor informed her that Dupree was not dead but in critical condition. Mrs. Scott breathed a sigh of relief.

The doctor finally came from behind the emergency room doors. He wanted to update everyone on Dupree's condition, but knew he needed some help to address the large number of people. He saw Pastor and Sister Pallen and asked them to follow him to his office. Pastor Pallen was well known and respected in the community.

As they followed the doctor to his office, Mrs. Scott slipped past the nurse's station into the first room she saw, searching for Dupree. She almost fainted when she saw the mummy-like figure lying on the bed. She moved slowly toward the bed and looked at the name on the chart in order to confirm if it was really Dupree lying in the bed. It was. A scream rose in her throat but she placed her hand over her mouth and held it back. She was horrified at the sight of the once-vibrant, beautiful girl. Dupree was connected to machines of all sizes, with tubes and wires running from one end of her body to the other. She was wrapped from head to toe with only her nose visible and a tube was connected to that as well. Mrs. Scott bowed her head and wept silently.

She remembered how Dupree had talked about and praised the Lord. What God would have allowed this to happen to his daughter? *Where was God when Dupree was being brutalized?* she thought angrily. If God could not protect people when they needed Him, then why were people wasting their lives trying to serve Him? These questions invaded Mrs. Scott's thoughts as she looked at a young girl who gave her life to the Lord, only to have Him fail her when she needed Him. She hoped when Dupree got better, if she did, she would realized her God for what He was and have nothing more to do with Him.

Mrs. Scott crept back into the waiting room just in time to hear Pastor Pallen's booming voice resonating around the raucous room: "May I have your attention, please?" Instantly all noises ceased. "I would just like to give you all an update on Sister Dupree. She is in critical condition but the doctor said her prognosis was good."

A loud cheer went up from the crowd.

"Also, I am pleased to announce that she was not raped." A deafening applause echoed around the room.

"Now, I am asking everyone to go home and get some rest as Dupree is doing right now. Please pray for her because she needs all the prayer she can get."

"I need to get someone to go and stay with Sister Madge," the pastor said to his wife. "She must be worried that Dupree isn't home as yet."

"I'll go and get her and she can stay at my house for a while," Mrs. Scott replied. "I met Aunt Madge once when I visited Dupree a few weeks ago and I have a profound respect for them both," she explained. "Also, I have a big house and my housekeeper and I are the only ones living there. If I could get two men to accompany me and help carry Miss Madge to my car, then I should be okay."

Pastor and Sister Pallen knew Mrs. Scott had been working at the high school for a long time and that she lived in a very big house in Arcadia. They also remembered that her husband had passed away shortly after she moved to the parish but that was all they knew about her. She never attended church and it was obvious that she was a wealthy woman, but they briefly wondered if she was the right person to help Aunt Madge.

Mrs. Scott knew what they were thinking and quickly tried to put their minds at ease. "I know you don't really know me, and quite frankly I am surprised that I am offering to do this, but I promise she will be okay. Miss Angie and I will take good care of her."

At the mention of Miss Angie's name, Pastor smiled at her. He forgot that Miss Angie worked for Mrs. Scott. Miss Angie was a long-standing member of his church and he trusted her wholeheartedly. "Wait right here while I get two brothers to go with you," Pastor Pallen told Mrs. Scott, and went outside to see which men were still there.

He returned shortly with two church brothers who gladly agreed to go with Mrs. Scott to get Aunt Madge. They also promised to follow Mrs. Scott to her house and help her get Aunt Madge situated in her temporary home. As Mrs. Scott drove off with the men following her, she wondered what she had done.

For the life of her she could not understand why she volunteered to take care of Aunt Madge. She did like the lady, but to have her living in her house was another story. However, she knew in her heart she was doing the right thing and if she must admit it to herself, she was looking forward to it. Mrs. Scott never knew it then, but she was being used by the Lord to help His children. When push came to shove, she would fully understand the will and power of the Almighty God.

Back at the police station a riot was about to begin. Many of the people who left the hospital, instead of going home to pray as pastor had asked, they joined those who were already at the police station. As the crowd grew larger and more boisterous, the police officers inside prepared for the worst.

Deacon Livingston lay on the cold, dirty tile floor, whimpering in pain and fright. As he listened to the angry voices outside, he knew they wanted to kill him and he could not blame them. He had ruined his life and that of his family. He wished he could turn back the hands of time but it was too late. He had already sold his soul to the devil.

Chapter Nineteen

Mrs. Scott parked her car, got out, and waited for the church brothers to do the same. The moon's pale glow faintly shimmered off the unruly bushes sandwiched between huge cedar and pine trees, casting eerie shadows over the rocky, narrow track. As they cautiously fumbled their way through the darkness of the night, their hollow footsteps reflected their dismal moods.

"Sister Madge, it's Mrs. Scott. Please don't be alarmed, we are coming in!"

As they entered the semi-dark room lit by a small kerosene oil lamp, Mrs. Scott saw the tears running down Aunt Madge's face. She assumed something was wrong since it was late and Dupree hadn't been there to care for her.

Mrs. Scott quickly informed Aunt Madge about Dupree as she held her trembling hand. "Dupree was attacked and badly beaten but she is alive. She is alive." She wanted to offer Aunt Madge some hope, if at all possible. "Your church brothers are here to help me take you to my house. You are going to stay with me for a while and when Dupree gets out of the hospital, she will also stay with us until she is fully recovered."

Mrs. Scott quickly went around the house, gathering clothes and other personal belongings for Aunt Madge. She saw her medication sitting on the crooked stool by her bed and she packed that as well.

Mrs. Scott took a sheet and wrapped it around Aunt Madge before the church brothers lifted her off the bed. Mrs. Scott noticed that she was well taken of. Her hair was clean and neatly plaited, her nightgown was clean, and she smelled fresh and looked well fed. Dupree had done a really great job taking care of her aunt.

With one church brother holding Aunt Madge's upper body and the other her legs, the church brothers followed Mrs. Scott up the rugged lane track as she led the way with the flashlight. The task took great effort from everyone involved, but finally they got to the main road and managed to place Aunt Madge in the back seat of Mrs. Scott's car. Mrs. Scott drove slowly to her house and the men followed her to help get Aunt Madge inside.

Miss Angie rushed out when she saw her new guest and helped the men get Aunt Madge into her room. They placed the grieving woman on the bed and covered her up. Aunt Madge's eyes were closed in pain and the tears were still running down her face. The only sound from her mouth was gibberish, but Miss Angie knew that tears were a language that God understood.

An exhausted and depressed Officer Gregg got home around four in the morning. He felt like the world was on his shoulders as he dragged his tired body into his bedroom. He thought his wife, Beverly, was asleep, but she was sitting up in bed waiting for him. As he got closer to her he noticed her eyes were red and puffy; she had been crying. He knew that the news about what happened earlier had spread all over the community, and beyond a doubt his wife had heard it as well. Mrs. Gregg knew Aunt Madge and Dupree because they attended the same church and from the days when Aunt Madge used to sell in the market before she got sick.

Officer Gregg sat beside his wife and reached over to hug her but she jumped off the bed and started to bawl. "Don't touch me!" Beverly screamed. Officer Gregg was puzzled by his wife's behavior. "How much longer are we going to keep this secret?" Beverly asked her husband as the tears rolled down her face.

"What . . . what secret?" Officer Gregg stuttered in alarm. "What are you talking about?"

"Oh, come on, Anthony, you know what I am talking about. You and I are going to hell for what we did to Dupree."

Officer Gregg was stunned. He looked at Beverly in shock with his mouth opened wide but his tongue could not form words to speak. His wife knew about his sin and the daughter who resulted from it. But for sixteen years she stayed with him and had never uttered a word. He was happy when Tiny left town and thought he had gotten away with what he had done, but suddenly he remembered the saying "everything that is done in the dark must come to light."

"How long have you known?"

"For too long," she answered solemnly. "She came to see me before she left town." Officer Gregg looked at his wife with shocked, pained eyes. "She wanted me to know that you were the father of her child and you had threatened to kill her and her aunt if she told anyone. She pleaded with me to talk to you in helping the baby but I ran her away. I told her to take her bastard child and get lost and if she ever spread any rumors about my husband, I would have her killed," Beverly confessed.

"What was I supposed to do? We just had a newborn baby ourselves and our reputation and that of our family was on the line. I felt hurt and betrayed but I still loved you and knew you could also go to jail for having sex with that child. I could never allow my son to grow up with his father in jail, so I decided not to say a word and keep my family together instead."

Beverly fell to the carpeted floor on her knees and cried as guilt washed over her. "I covered up your crime for my own selfish reasons and denied that little girl a chance at a better life. May God have mercy on our souls!" she cried.

Officer Gregg lay down beside her and tried to take her in his arms but she shouted, "Stay away from me!"

"I'm sorry, baby. I'm so sorry. Please, please forgive me. I'll do anything. Please don't leave me, baby, please. I'm begging you," he cried. But Beverly ignored his pleas and only cried harder as she curled herself in a ball on the floor with her husband facing her.

As the distraught couple lay on the floor, wrapped up in their misery that held them in a tight, choking embrace, they failed to notice their son standing at the bedroom door with his mouth wide open in shock.

Chapter Twenty

Tony's body slid to the floor like a heavy bag of lead. He wanted to run away and wish this night had never happened, but he stayed and listened to the conversation that would change his life forever.

"It can't be. There must be some mistake," he muttered to himself softly. His father was a pedophile and his mother was a liar who covered up his crime. But now he knew what the special bond between him and Dupree was: she was his sister!

Tony was hurt and confused. In a few hours his life had changed so much, and not for the better. He had no idea what he was going to do but he knew he wasn't staying in that house with those two traitors. So he went back outside, got in his car, and headed to his paternal grandparents' house, which was only six miles away. He had his own key and his room was always ready for when he visited. He also knew they were already in bed so he could avoid all the questions for a while. He just needed somewhere to stay while he figured out his life and what he was going to do about it.

A rainbow of flowers, teddy bears, fruit baskets, and postcards covered every nook and cranny of Dupree's hospital room. The room rivaled any florist's as everyone wanted to convey their love and support.

Her eyes blinked once, then twice, then more rapidly, before the right eyelid slowly rolled away for a peek. Like a laser gun, her eye sluggishly swept the room. It was so dark in there, Dupree thought, slightly moving her left arm away from the bed. Suddenly her body went numb with a sharp intake of breath as waves of pain flooded her being.

Where am I? Why does it hurt so much? What happened to me? Dupree pondered. Her body felt as if it had been run over by a big-wheeler truck.

Then like a ghost, he appeared. Two small balls of fire drilled holes in her already broken body as thick slobber dripped from the sides of the lopsided mouth covered with the Joker grin. Her heart galloped like a race horse at Caymanas Park, her pupils expanding like helium balloons as the fear fiercely grabbed on to her trachea. Dupree screamed but only a small squeak squeezed through. Her legs in competition with her arms cartwheeled wildly in the air, her body convulsed in agony as she tried desperately to escape the devil. But she was immobile and he just kept right on coming!

The machines beeped uncontrollably when Dupree pulled out the tubes and this alerted the nurse. Upon entering Dupree's room, she quickly pressed the emergency button requesting assistance. She grabbed Dupree by the arms, pinning her down to the bed, but Dupree continued to kick, her head thrashing about like a raging bull.

A few seconds later, another nurse burst through the room, followed by a heavy-breathing doctor. The nurses each grabbed a leg, while the doctor quickly jabbed a needle into Dupree's arm. Like a racing car over the winning line, they all watched anxiously as her movements slowed down then ceased completely before her exhausted body slipped into the world of unconsciousness.

The doctor hurriedly took her vitals and increased the pain medicine, while the nurses scurried around reconnecting the machines, cleaning the bleeding wounds, and changing her bandages. Lying eagle-like on the bed, face up, Dupree's arms and legs were restrained to prevent her from hurting herself again. Finally, they all stood around the bed and watched the troubled girl as sleep temporarily took her away from the demon that haunted her.

Chapter Twenty-one

Officer Gregg slowly woke up and looked around the unfamiliar room. He blinked rapidly as he wondered where he was. Then the details of the night before came rushing back to him like a hard kick to the groin. He buried his head under the pillow and screamed silently. He wondered why God didn't just let him die in his sleep so he didn't have to face the mess he had created in his life.

Last night after he and his wife were all cried out, she climbed into their bed with her back turned to him. His guilty conscience led him to the guest bedroom, where he twisted and turned until in the early morning. He had no idea what time he finally fell into a troubled sleep, but he knew it was just a few minutes ago. He was very confused about everything that was going on and he had no idea what he was going to do.

His mind flashed back to Dupree, his daughter being attacked by Deacon Livingston, the mob at the police station and his wife's confession about knowing and keeping his dirty secret all these years. So many people's lives were now changed forever because of his selfishness.

"He never came home! He is not here!" Beverly shouted as she ran into the guest room.

"Who is not home? What's going on?" Officer Gregg asked as he quickly jumped off the bed.

"Tony! Your son, remember him?" she screamed at him. "I passed by his room early this morning before sunrise and noticed he wasn't there. I waited a few hours but he is still not home. Where could he be? He would have called if he was going to spend the night over at Bobby's."

Officer Gregg felt his heart drop. Where was his son? Was he hurt somewhere? Were his sins finally catching up with his children?

He ran past his wife and rushed into his son's room and noticed that his bed was still neatly made. His son had not slept in it because Tony never made his own bed. He took a deep breath before he turned to face his wife, who had followed him into the room. He suddenly noticed she was dressed for work and remembered it was Thursday morning, a workday for both of them. His wife was the only dentist in town and she had patients relying on her. He was a sergeant and was scheduled for work as well but he would have to call in that day as he needed to find Tony first.

He noticed that her red, puffy eyes looked haunted and had bags under them, evidence that she too had not gotten any sleep. As he looked at her he realized that his wife seemed to have aged since last night and it was all because of him. A deep sense of remorse hit him in the gut and he reached for her but she stepped away from him.

"Please don't. Please," she said. "There is just too much going on right now. I already felt as if I was going crazy and now my son is missing as well. I'm not sure how much more I can take. It's just too much." She burst into tears.

"I'll find Tony, sweetheart, and I promise I will do whatever it takes to make things up to both of you."

"What about Dupree? Do you still plan on ignoring her? How will we make it up to her?"

He noticed that she said "we" and knew that his wife carried a great deal of guilt for the role she played in his deception. He wished he had an answer for her but he was just as confused as she was. He opened his mouth to reply when the house phone rang. He breathed a sigh of relief and quickly ran down the hall to answer it.

"Maybe it is Tony," he said before he anxiously grabbed the telephone.

"Can someone tell me what in heaven's name is going on over there, Anthony?" his father, Albert Gregg, demanded through the phone receiver. "Gerty and I woke up this morning and noticed Tony's car in the driveway. We went to his room and the door was closed and he refused to open it or talk to us."

Officer Gregg was relieved at first; then he got alarmed at Tony's odd behavior. "Dad, I am glad Tony is with you guys and I'm not sure what happened to him, but I will be over shortly to talk to him. Please don't let him leave the house until I get there." He heard his wife breathe a sigh of relief.

"Okay, but get here fast because I know something is wrong with my grandson. By the way, did you hear what happened to Sister Madge's girl? I can't believe that dirty, nasty bastard who called himself a man of God would resort to something so sick and disgusting. And he was a deacon at that. What a shame and disgrace to our church! Now people are going to think everyone at church is probably the same. All he did was ruin our good church name!" Mr. Gregg went on and on about his church's good reputation and never once did he express concern about Dupree, the granddaughter he was not aware of.

Officer Gregg felt a headache coming on at his father's lack of compassion for Dupree. "I'll be over as soon as I can, Dad," he responded and hung up the phone.

"I'm coming with you," his wife said with concern. "I want to know what's going on with my son."

"What about work?"

"I'll have my assistant inform all my patients that I have a family emergency and reschedule all my appointments until next Monday. I'm sure that Dr. Hugh in Coral Spring will take any emergency patients who may come in." As she turned to walk away, he gently grabbed her arm. She tried shaking his hand off, but he held on tight.

"What about us?" he asked in a small voice. "Are you going to leave me? Please, honey, just give me a chance to try to make this right. I know how much I have hurt you, but please don't give up on me. You see for yourself how much I have changed over the years. I know the Lord has forgiven me and I hope in time you will find it in your heart to do the same. I am begging you to let me try to right the wrong I have done."

"I am not promising you anything, Anthony. What you did was unthinkable but I am also guilty for keeping your secret all these years. We both have fallen into the bottom of the pit and I don't know if and how we can ever get out."

"We can get out, baby. It will be a long, hard journey, but if we turn it over to the Lord, He will get us all through this."

"I have to make a few calls," Mrs. Gregg said, "and then I want us to go and see about our son. I would also like to stop at the hospital on our way back and check on Dupree. We'll finish this conversation at another time because it is too much for me right now." She walked away to her room to call her assistant.

Officer Gregg went back into their closet and got himself some clean clothes, took a quick shower in the guest bathroom, and got ready in the guest room. He knew this was where he would be until he worked out his problems with his wife. He wasn't sure how long it would take, but he was willing to wait as long as it took. After getting dressed and calling into his job, he and his wife headed out to go see about their son.

The silence in the car was stifling. They were both caught up in their own thoughts, fighting their own demons. It was unsure what the future held for them, but one could only hope and pray for the best.

The last few hours had been real rough for Tony. He lay on his back still fully clothed with his hands behind his head, looking at the ceiling but seeing nothing. His head felt as if it were going to explode any minute. There was a deep pain inside him that he wished he could just reach in and pull out but he knew it would take more than that. He wanted to cry but he was all cried out. If only he could just die right now, that would solve all his problems. Then he remembered his friend Dupree—no, his sister, he quickly corrected in his mind—and he felt guilty for his thoughts. She came close to death last night but she fought for her life and was now in the hospital still fighting for it. No, death was not an option. He had to be strong for Dupree. She would need him now more than ever.

Tony heard the knock on his room door and ignored it. His grandparents just wouldn't leave him alone.

"Tony, open the door, sweetheart."

It was his mother's voice. How did they know he was there, he wondered, but quickly realized that his grandparents must have called them. Great, that was all he needed right now. The same people he was running from came running to him.

"Tony, Tony, it's Dad. Your mom and I are concerned about you and we would like to come in and talk to you. Please open the door, son."

"You are not my dad. You are a rapist and liar, that's what you are," Tony muttered to himself.

"Baby, please open the door for Mommy." He could hear his mom softly crying and this broke his heart.

Although he was angry at her, he hated to hear his mother cry.

Tony still could not believe his father was sexually involved with a child. He was an intelligent young man who had just graduated high school and would hopefully be attending college in a few weeks, so he knew what his father did was against the law. And he was a cop! Tony could not understand how a man who had always put his family first could have denied his very own daughter all these years in order to cover up his crime. His father was a man he deeply admired and looked up to; he was his hero, his mentor, and his friend. To say he was disappointed was an understatement.

While his parents continued knocking on his door and pleading with him to open the door, Tony contemplated his situation. He couldn't stay locked up forever and obviously they weren't going anywhere anytime soon. Should he tell them what he overheard last night? Would his father be arrested for a crime he committed so many years ago? There were so many questions but he had no answers as he slowly opened the door to his grieving parents.

"We were so worried about you, honey," his mom said as she hugged him tightly to her. "When we realized you never came home last night and you did not call, I began to think the worst." Beverly was so overjoyed at seeing her son that she failed to notice his still, unresponsive, cold demeanor.

"Why didn't you call home to let us know you were staying with your grandparents?" his father asked as he joined the group hug. "Don't you ever do anything like this again and worry your mother so much," he warned Tony.

With his face turned away from his father as he hugged him, Tony rolled his eyes in disgust. His father could burn in hell for all he cared. Who did he think he was, setting household rules, when he had broken every rule of humanity? *Talk about a hypocrite.*

"Let's go home," Tony said coldly as he untangled himself from his parents' embrace and headed to the door. He had decided at the last minute to wait until he got home to talk to his parents about what he overhead earlier this morning. He did not want to upset his grandparents and he also felt it was his father's responsibility to air his own dirty laundry.

Officer Gregg was about to reach for him but his wife looked at him and shook her head. Tony walked away; a deep frown covered his face.

Tony saw his grandparents' concerned looks as he came down the stairs and felt awful for worrying them. He quickly hugged his seventy-six-year-old grandmother, then his eighty-year-old grandfather.

"I am sorry for worrying you, Mama and Dada. I am just going through something right now, but I'll be all right. Is it okay if I come back later and stay with you for a while?"

His grandparents looked at his parents with puzzled looks on their faces. They loved their grandson and enjoyed when he visited them, but something told them his parents were not aware of his decision to do so then. The silence cut through the house like a sharp knife. If a pin had fallen it would have echoed throughout the house.

"Hmmm, why don't we talk about this when we all get home, sweetheart?" his mother finally said.

"Fine," Tony snapped. "I'll talk to you later, Mama and Dada," he said as he kissed his grandparents good-bye. He then swiftly walked outside, slamming the door behind him. Tony did not wait for his parents. He got in his car, started it, reversed out of the driveway, and sped away from the house, seething in anger.

"What in the world is going on around here?" Mother Gregg asked but got no answer. Officer Gregg and his wife looked at each other silently.

"Mom, I'm not sure what is going on with Tony, but I intend to find out when we get home. Please don't worry about anything. I'll take care of it," said Officer Gregg. His parents looked at him skeptically, but finally nodded their heads in agreement.

Officer Gregg and his wife travelled back home as silently as they came. They knew something was definitely wrong with their son because Tony had never behaved so disrespectfully to them before. What was going on in their lives? Could things get any worse?

Chapter Twenty-two

She blinked repeatedly before she slowly tried to open her eyes but they felt so heavy. Finally she managed to open one eye to a slit and quickly closed it back as the light hit her pupil. Where was she? Why couldn't she move her arms or her legs? Who was sitting on her head and why wouldn't they get off?

As Dupree slowly opened her right eye and looked around the strange room, she noticed all the flowers and stuffed animals. She looked down and noticed her legs were restrained and her right leg was in a cast. Her left arm was also in a cast; likewise her upper torso was stiffened in place. She then realized that she must have been in an accident and she was in the hospital. She tried to speak but her mouth was very dry and felt like cardboard.

Quickly feeling tired by just briefly looking around, Dupree closed her eyes in exhaustion. She did not understand why she could not remember her accident. She also wondered how long she had been in the hospital. Her thoughts suddenly flashed to Aunt Madge and her concern grew for her aunt. Who was taking care of her? Did she know that Dupree was in the hospital?

Dupree listened as the doctors and nurse slipped quietly into the room.

"How are you feeling?" Dr. David asked his patient softly above a whisper.

Why is he shouting? Dupree wondered. She slowly opened her eyes and noticed two doctors and a nurse standing by her bedside. Her throat was so dry there was no spittle in her mouth. As if she could read her mind, the nurse quickly poured water into a cup and approached her. She pressed a button and the bed elevated a little. She gently put the cup to Dupree's swollen lips and slowly fed her some water. Her throat hurt a little as the fluid went down, but it was a welcoming feeling as she drank greedily.

"What . . . what happened to me?" she stuttered just above a whisper.

Dr. David sat down on a chair by her bed and leaned over until his face was close to Dupree's. "I know you are feeling exhausted from the strong medication we are giving you and this is because we want to make you as comfortable as possible and for you to get better soon. However, I just need you to answer a few questions. Can you do that for me?"

Dupree nodded her head slowly and flinched at the pain that ran through her body.

"How many fingers am I holding up?" he asked. He held up two fingers.

"Two," she muttered softly.

"And what's your name?"

"Du . . . Du . . . Dupree."

"Yes, that's great, Dupree. Do you remember what you did yesterday?" He watched her face frown in concentration before she nodded.

"I went to Daily Vocation Bible School, then grocery shopping, and then home."

"And where did you go after you got home?"

Dupree closed her eyes as she tried to remember but she came up blank. She looked at Dr. David and he noticed her confusion.

"It's okay, Dupree. I think you are blocking the trau-matic experience from your mind, but that is common in situations like these. Eventually it will come back to you and we'll be here to help you through it. I don't want you to think about anything but getting better. You have been through a lot and have a long road to recovery ahead of you."

"Aunt Madge?"

The doctor looked at the nurse and she shrugged her shoulders helplessly. He told Dupree that he would make some inquiries about Aunt Madge and let her know soon. Dr. David then examined Dupree's wounds and checked her vitals and medication, while the nurse redressed her wounds. The doctors conversed among themselves as Dr. David wrote on Dupree's chart. They were a little concerned about her memory loss, which was not uncommon in situations like these, but should be monitored closely. By the time they were finished, their patient was sound asleep.

Miss Angie heard the sobbing as she approached the bedroom and her heart broke for the woman who was suffering behind the closed door. She was unsure of what to do as she gently opened the door and went in. Aunt Madge lay on her back with her eyes tightly closed and her face flooded with tears. Her body shook in pain as she cried for her grand-niece.

"Sister Madge, it's me, Miss Angie. I know you are going through a lot right now, but you have to trust and believe that the Lord will work it out. Remember, He won't give us more than we can bear." Aunt Madge slowly opened her eyes and looked at the pleasant face smiling at her warmly. She tried to talk, but as usual nothing that made sense came out. She closed her eyes again in frustration and wept.

Miss Angie began to sing "Amazing Grace" as she got ready to give Aunt Madge a sponge bath. Her soft voice was very soothing and gradually Aunt Madge stopped crying to listen to the words of her favorite song. She really needed something to comfort her heart. She wanted to be assured that the Lord did not forget about her or Dupree because if there was a time they needed Him, it was now.

Chapter Twenty-three

Tony entered his house raging mad. He went directly into the living room and sat on the expensive leather couch with his arms folded and his nostrils flared out like an opened parachute. He felt like he wanted to hit something or someone. Instantly, Deacon Livingston's ugly face came to mind and he wished the pervert was right there in front of him, but that, too, was just a fantasy, like his life.

His parents came in and looked at him apprehensively. They were surprised by the look on his face and slowly took a seat on the other couch opposite him. Looking down at the soft, plush carpet under his feet, Tony spoke in a quiet, controlled voice. "Both of you were my mentors. I spent my entire life looking up to you and admiring you, and for what? To find out my dad was a pedophile and my lying mom was his coconspirator! Were you going to keep this dirty little secret forever?" By now he was shouting.

His parents were in total shock. Tony saw the look of horror on his father's face as he sat with his mouth wide open. He looked as if he struggled to breathe, his body looking like he was electrocuted. His mother sat as stiff as a mannequin. Her face was made up in anguish, but her tears seemed to have taken a vacation. As she looked at her baby, Beverly saw only hatred in his eyes and the pain washed over her like a shower of rain. Their secret was no longer theirs alone and the one person she wanted to protect was about to be destroyed by it. What had she done to her son and that innocent girl, Dupree? Would Tony ever be able to forgive her, but most importantly, would God?

"Son, what, what are you talking about?" Officer Gregg squeaked, praying this nightmare would go away.

Tony angrily looked at his silent, grieving parents. "I overheard your little confession session last night, Mom and Dad," he stated sarcastically. "I came home late last night hurt and upset by what had happened to my best friend and heard screaming coming from your bedroom. I thought something was wrong and went to check it out, but nothing could have prepared me for what I heard. My new best friend who came to mean the world to me is actually my sister."

They both gasped in surprise and looked at their son like he was an alien from Mars. Tony noticed the look on their faces and chuckled sarcastically. "Yes, you heard me right. Dupree is a very close friend of mine. Do you know that we also have the same birthday? And where do you think I have been spending all my Saturdays recently? For years we have all watched her suffer while we lived in splendor and your conscience never once told you to help her." By now Tony's eyes were tearing up.

"We attended the same church with her, Dad!" Tony screamed at his father. "And you bought produce from her aunt, Mom, while she stood there, and never did either one of you ever even acknowledge her. She was your flesh and blood, Dad! Why did you desert her? To save your butt from jail, that's why," he answered his own question. "And you, Mom, were just trying to keep your perfect family together, I assume. What hypocrites you both are!"

The floodgates opened and the tears streaked down Beverly's face. Her lips trembled as she sobbed and reached for her son, but he pulled away from her.

"Please don't touch me, Mom. As you can see you are not one of my favorite people right now."

Tony was a little taken aback at first when he saw the tears running down his father's face. His father never cried! There was always a first for everything, Tony figured. He remembered what he had done and hardened his heart once again. He refused to let his father's tears affect him one bit.

"My son, I know how much I have let you down and I can just imagine the pain you are in right now. I wish I could go back and do it all over again but I can't." Officer Gregg was now sobbing loudly. Beside him, Beverly seemed to be competing with him on who could sob the loudest.

"I have hurt so many people with my selfish actions," he continued. "You are right; Dupree deserved so much more. She was just an innocent child, but I made her pay for my sins. I'm not sure how I will make this up to her, but I am going to spend the rest of my life trying. I'll also be doing the same for you and your mother, son. Please find it in your heart to give me the chance to try to make it right. Please, Tony," he begged as he looked into the eyes of his distraught son.

"Man, you don't owe me nothing," Tony said rudely.

"Yes, I do. I . . ." He stopped suddenly as Tony held up his right hand and signaled for him not to say another word.

"Forget about me for now. In fact, forget about Mom also. It's not like this is news to her anyway. If you have any decency left in you, then help Dupree. Please help my sister," he exclaimed and locked eyes with those of his father.

"I'll do anything, son. I'll do anything," Officer Gregg replied eagerly, glad to see that there was something he could do to help make amends with his children.

"I want you to pay all her hospital bills, the full cost for her rehabilitation, and all other costs associated with her recovery. I also want you to open an account and put enough money in it to help her, especially for college. And don't forget to add her to your will. She deserves that and so much more."

Officer Gregg looked at his wife and she nodded her head in agreement.

"Should I tell her that I am her father?

Tony sighed. "That's up to you. But I don't think now is a good time to spring this on her. She is already going through a lot and doesn't need this right now. I would appreciate it if you could wait until she is fully recovered before springing that news on her."

His father agreed. "I'll also wait to tell my parents."

"And my parents," Mrs. Gregg added, and they both turned to look at her. She had been so silent all this time that Tony almost forgot she was in the room. Her crying had subsided and she suddenly looked old and tired. She looked as if the life were being sucked out of her like a vacuum.

Beverly looked at Tony remorsefully. "Baby, I wish I could say I am sorry and that would make everything right. If I could take away all the pain we are causing you, I would so do in a heartbeat. You are an innocent victim of our sins. I know you hate me right now, but I thought I was doing the right thing back then. I had just given birth to you and I was hormonal and confused. I know that is no excuse, but I wanted to protect you and our family. I hope one day you and God can forgive me. And Dupree also," she said humbly.

Tony wanted so bad to give her a hug, but his anger would not allow him to.

The room grew silent as they looked at each other skeptically. The once close-knit family was now divided by lies and deceit. And as Tony looked at his parents, he wondered if they would ever be the family they once were. He informed them that he was going to spend the rest of the summer with his grandparents until he was ready to go away to college. They wanted to beg him to stay but they knew he needed that time away from them, and as much as it hurt, they had to respect his wishes.

Chapter Twenty-four

Dupree awoke feeling drowsy and a little bit disoriented. Her restraints were removed but she still felt encumbered with the cast and bandages all over her body. If she moved even slightly, everything hurt, especially her back. Therefore she tried to stay as still as possible.

As she lay there with her eyes closed, Dupree heard the door open and thought it was a nurse or doctor coming to check up on her. Her eyes remained closed until she heard a wheelchair running over the tiles on the floor. She slowly opened her eyes and saw Mrs. Scott pushing Aunt Madge in the wheelchair across the room to her. In her excitement, Dupree tried to move and pain shot through her body. She groaned slightly but was overjoyed to see her aunt. A small river flowed from her bloodshot eyes.

Aunt Madge gasped in horror as she saw her grand-niece, or what she thought was her grand-niece. She looked like a mummy with a swollen, badly bruised face. A scream rose from her throat: "Jesus!" she screamed and it ricocheted loudly in the small hospital room.

Dupree lay still in shock and Mrs. Scott stood in the middle of the room with her mouth opening and closing like a fish. Even Aunt Madge seemed astonished for a minute. The nurse heard the loud scream and came rushing through the door to tend to her patient. She saw Dupree in bed looking like she had seen a ghost, but was otherwise not in need of any urgent medical attention so she exited the room.

Dupree was shocked to hear her aunt, who hadn't spoken in years, talk; well, it was actually a scream, but it sounded like music to her ears.

Dupree looked at Mrs. Scott, who was still stunned, not sure what was going on. The perplexed look on her face showed her inability to fully accept the miracle that took place before her. Mrs. Scott pushed Aunt Madge closer to the bed and Aunt Madge gently rested her head beside her Dupree's and carefully took notice of the battered face, the busted lips, and the red, swollen eyes, before she softly kissed Dupree on her cheek.

Finally with her hands pressed firmly on the bed, Aunt Madge gently heaved herself up from the bed and slid back into her wheelchair. With her face lifted to heaven and her hands lifted above her head, she began to praise the Lord. It sounded like a child learning to talk or someone with a heavy tongue. Her voice was as coarse as sandpaper because it hadn't been used in a few years, but Dupree heard every word she said and she knew that the Lord definitely heard her as well.

Mrs. Scott's rubbery legs trembled under the weight of her body. Wearily she sank down into the visitor chair, her face screwed up in deep concentration, her mind zigzagging all over the place. She shook her head from side to side, puzzled, refusing to believe the power of the Almighty God.

As Dupree listened to her aunt praising and worshipping God, her voice reached something deep down in her soul. With her eyes tightly closed, shame and embarrassment drenched her from head to toe when she realized that since she had regained consciousness, not once had she acknowledged the Lord. Why was that? Was it because deep down inside she blamed Him for what had happened to her? But what exactly had happened? Moaning slightly in confusion, her head began to throb like a jackhammer piercing a concrete wall.

Aunt Madge, not aware of Dupree's memory loss about the incident and relishing in her verbal communication victory, leaned over the bed and spoke to her slowly and softly. Even though her words were jumbled, Dupree heard them clearly.

"Don't worry, baby, God will take care of that demon Deacon Livingston." And that's all it took; that dreadful name took Dupree straight back to hell.

A loud scream echoed throughout the hospital room, bounced off the walls, and went flying into the atmosphere. Dupree thrashed around, kicking her legs despite the pain as she waved her arms frantically in the air. The attending nurse rushed into the room and struggled to pin Dupree's flying arms to the bed. Mrs. Scott jumped up off the chair she sat in and grabbed Dupree's legs just as two more nurses and a doctor came through the door like a flash of lightning. The doctor quickly plunged a needle into her arm, while the nurses fought to hold her still. Even though she had broken bones in so many places, remembering the horrifying details of her ordeal gave Dupree the strength of an ox as she once again fought to escape the devil. Finally the medication took over and won the fight, and just as quickly as it started, it ended. Dupree slowly slipped into a deep, well-deserved sleep.

The concerned doctor went over and knelt down beside the wheelchair as Aunt Madge sobbed loudly.

"She is all right now," he assured her, taking the shaking hands into his own. "She is now resting comfortably and we will be watching her closely. Why don't you go home now and come back tomorrow?"

"O . . . o . . . okay," Aunt Madge stuttered, using the back of her hand to wipe tears from her blurred vision. "Prr . . . pray?" Aunt Madge said as if asking the doctor permission. The doctor nodded his head and gave her an encouraging smile before he bowed his head.

The nurses also closed their eyes, their heads lowered respectfully. Mrs. Scott did the same only out of respect for Aunt Madge.

After the prayer, Mrs. Scott quickly pushed the wheelchair out of the room, down the corridor, and into the waiting room. When they got there, Mother Sassy and some other members of the church were waiting. Everyone was excited to see Aunt Madge and hugged and kissed her joyfully.

"Prr . . . praise Lord," Aunt Madge forced out in a small, shaky voice.

Mother Sassy suddenly caught the Spirit when she heard Aunt Madge speak. Her wig went flying off her head as she went tumbling to the floor. Luckily, a quick-thinking brother caught her just in time to break her fall as she kicked her legs wildly and waved her arms frantically in the air. Some nurses heard the commotion and rushed out to offer medical assistance, but Mrs. Scott informed them dryly that this one was spiritual and not medical. In her mind Mother Sassy needed psychological help, not physical.

Chapter Twenty-five

After the exhausting, emotional discussion with his parents, Tony went to his room to shower and change his clothes. He then quickly packed some clothes and other personal items to take to his grandparents' house. When he got back downstairs he noticed his parents sitting in the same place he had left them earlier, looking beat down and depressed. Tony gave them a brief look before he went through the door without saying good-bye. As he sat in his car and started the engine, he looked back at the house he had lived in all his life and wondered if it would ever be home again.

Moments later, Tony pulled up to his grandparents' house and went inside to his room. He had stopped by the hospital but was told that Dupree was not receiving any visitors that day. The doctors were pleased with her progress but wanted her to get some rest.

Lying on his back on the bed with his hands pillowing his head, Tony gazed at the ceiling as he thought about college. Even though his maternal grandparents lived in New York and he visited often, he wasn't really fond of the place enough to live there. He preferred to go on vacation, shop, have a good time, and come back home to Jamaica. He also never wanted to go so far away from his parents.

He was glad that his friend, Bobby, had forced him to apply to NYU. If he got accepted, that would be the perfect opportunity to get away for a while. Suddenly his heartbeat quickened at the thought and he shot up in the bed like a jack-in-the-box.

"I can't leave Dupree by herself! All hell is going to break loose when she finds out who her father is. She is going to be so distraught."

Tony got off the bed and walked over to the open window overlooking the backyard. The beautiful green Jamaican landscape immediately captured his attention. Tall mango, grapefruit, and coconut trees rocked gently in the breeze; the bright sun rays flickered off their dancing leaves. As he listened to the familiar song of the humming birds, his eyes widened excitedly as a light went off in his head.

Dupree could also apply to NYU for next year. Also, he figured by then she would be fully recovered and his father could pay her tuition. He was going to make sure of that if it was the last thing he did.

Chapter Twenty-six

Over the next two weeks, Dupree's hospital room was like a revolving door at the mall.

That morning Dupree looked up when her room door opened and her eyes lit up as Officer Gregg entered the room. He was there for his daily visit. She watched him as he came and sat in the chair by her bed.

"How are you feeling today, my dear?" Officer Gregg asked as he stared at his daughter.

"Not too bad, sir," Dupree responded softly, smiling. "I think I'm getting better each day."

Officer Gregg felt like someone had kicked him in the gut. Looking at his daughter, he saw so many of his features staring right back at him. The big brown eyes and button nose were all his. And when she smiled, she resembled Tony so much it was almost eerie.

"Are you okay?" Dupree asked as Officer Gregg stared at her. "Why are you staring at me like that? What's wrong?"

"Oh, I'm . . . I'm fine," Officer Gregg stuttered. "My mind just went for a quick walk, that's all."

"Are you sure?" Dupree asked with a puzzled look on her face.

Officer Gregg nodded his head in response.

Dupree looked at the kind policeman who had introduced himself as Officer Gregg. She found out that not only was he Tony's father, but he was also one of the police officers who was first to arrive on the scene on the night she was attacked. He was also the one who took her to the hospital and Dupree knew she would be forever grateful to him and had told him so.

"I'm glad I was there to help," Officer Gregg had responded. "I wish I had done more for you."

"You did all you could, sir, and the Lord did the rest," Dupree assured him. "A man can only do so much, you know."

Officer Gregg struggled to keep the tears at bay as he looked at his well-spoken, articulate, highly educated daughter and knew he had contributed nothing to her upbringing. He knew he had no right, but he was as proud as a peacock of the wonderful young lady Dupree turned out to be. He again made a pledge to himself to be there for her from now on. He also prayed that when she found out he was her father, she would be able to forgive him and allow him into her life. It seemed a little farfetched, but with Christ, all things were possible.

Dupree's recovery was nothing short of a miracle. It was four weeks since the attack. Her face was now back to normal, the swelling and bruises had just about disappeared, and the cuts from the broken glass were healed with scars slowly fading. Her legs and arm were still in casts and the body cast was still on her back, but the last X-ray taken showed that everything was healing nicely. The doctors were very pleased with her diagnosis and she was scheduled to leave the hospital the next day.

"You are going to stay with me for as long as necessary," Mrs. Scott had informed Dupree a few days ago.

"Thank you very much, Mrs. Scott," Dupree replied, overwhelmed with emotion. "You have already opened up your home to Aunt Madge, and now me. We are both very grateful for the kindness you are showing us."

On the day of her release, Dupree sat in the back seat of Tony's car and looked up at the huge hospital building that had been her home for the last few weeks. She silently thanked God for His healing mercies and for everyone who had worked so hard to save her life and made it possible for her to be leaving.

"Ready?" Tony asked as he smiled at Dupree. She nodded her head and he drove off to Mrs. Scott's house.

"Wow. This is so beautiful," Dupree said as Tony pulled his car into Mrs. Scott's driveway. With her head hanging out the car window, she looked at the big, beautiful house in awe.

As Tony pushed the wheelchair inside, Dupree was at a loss for words. To say the place was beautiful had been an understatement. She turned and looked at Mrs. Scott, who walked beside her with a happy look on her face.

"Thank you again for doing this for me, Mrs. Scott," Dupree said.

Mrs. Scott nodded her head and blushed in embarrassment. "I am very pleased to see how happy you are, my dear. I am really looking forward to having you join Aunt Madge and me."

After Dupree went and greeted Aunt Madge, with Tony maneuvering the wheelchair, Mrs. Scott showed a wide-eyed Dupree around the house. A few minutes later Dupree yawned, her eyes drooping in exhaustion. The excitement of the day had finally caught up with her.

"Okay, I think we have covered almost everything. The rest can stay for another day," Mrs. Scott told Dupree. "It's time for you to get some rest, young lady."

Tony wheeled her to the guest room that was all ready for her. Dupree smiled as she looked around the beautifully decorated room. She had never had her own room before.

"I love it," she said to Mrs. Scott when she stepped into the room.

"It's close to Aunt Madge's room as well," Mrs. Scott informed her. "Both rooms are separated by the bathroom that the both of you will share."

After Tony helped Dupree into bed, she accepted kisses from him, Aunt Madge, Miss Angie, and Mrs. Scott.

"I love you all," Dupree mumbled, her heavy eyelids giving up the fight as she fell into a deep, restful sleep.

Chapter Twenty-seven

"I am very pleased with your progress, Dupree," the home-care nurse said as she changed her bandages. She'd now been staying with Mrs. Scott for almost a week. "I think you are healing nicely."

Dupree forced a tight smile to her lips and nodded her head politely. *Then why am I hurting so much inside? Why do I feel as if I am going to lose my mind sometimes? Why am I still having nightmares of that dreadful night?* she questioned in her mind. But of course she kept silent. This was her own cross to bear and nobody else's, she thought.

Pastor Pallen visited Dupree frequently. He knew that even though Dupree was healing physically, she was still psychologically wounded.

"We'll get through this, Dupree," he told her that morning during their counseling session. "I know that in time the Lord will wipe those ugly memories from your mind and replace them with more beautiful ones."

"I feel so tired. I can hardly sleep at night. When I do doze off, he is always there, hurting me all over again." Dupree rested her head in her lap and wept deep, heart-felt sobs that shook her small body.

Pastor Pallen stood up and walked over to her. Down on his knees, he pulled her into his arms and held her as she cried. "Don't give up now, my dear," he whispered softly in Dupree's ear. "The Lord did not save you to leave you now."

His words brought some comfort to Dupree's heart and she slowly lifted her head and smiled at him.

"We'll get through this," Pastor Pallen said, returning her smile. "Remember, we are not alone and will win this battle."

"Yes, I'll try to remember. Thank you, Pastor Pallen." Dupree looked up toward heaven, her wet eyes filled with hope and longing.

"I love you, Lord, and I lift my voice to worship . . ." Mrs. Scott stood still in the middle of her bedroom, frozen to the spot where she stood. Glancing around the room skeptically, her mind tried to comprehend what had just happened.

"That sounded like my voice. No, I know that was my voice. But why would I be singing a praise song?" she said aloud. "I haven't sung that song in decades. What the heck is going on?"

Deeply confused, she fled from the room in alarm. She went downstairs and discovered the usual.

Every morning, like clockwork, Dupree, Aunt Madge, and Miss Angie held a prayer meeting in the den. There they spent a few hours praying, singing hymns, reading the Bible, and praising the Almighty God. Dupree loved these sessions because they were like spiritual food to her soul. They gave her the strength to fight the demon haunting her and drew her closer to the Lord.

As the women worshipped, Mrs. Scott stood behind the door listening to the shouts and praises. She was no longer as angry as she was before and she tried to convince herself that she was just being a good hostess. But what Mrs. Scott didn't know was that there was a stronger force at work here. She felt stupid hiding and listening to the worship sessions and swore every time that she would stop, but for some mysterious reason she went back every morning.

"And if I'm not careful, I'll get caught up in all that religious rubbish too," she muttered as she walked away from the den just as she'd done from God.

"Hello, Officer Gregg." Dupree smiled as she greeted the friendly police officer as he came up the top of the stairs to the veranda.

"Hi, Dupree. How are you doing today?" Officer Gregg smiled as he approached his daughter, his hands filled with a huge gift basket.

"I'm getting better each day. Thank you," Dupree replied, her eyes lit up like firecrackers.

"Good. This is for you," Officer Gregg said. "I'll rest it right here on the table for you."

"No, please put it here," Dupree told him, patting her lap excitedly. "I want to see what you got me this time."

Officer Gregg was still one of Dupree's regular visitors. He would stop by every so often bearing gifts such as flowers, stuffed animals, novels, fruit baskets, snacks, and even chocolate. Dupree thought that was very nice of him and felt he had gotten attached to her because he had been one of the first people to see her immediately after her horrific ordeal. He had also helped to save her life and this had bonded him to her and vice versa. Yes, she had grown very fond of the wonderful police officer, her best friend's father.

A few days later, Officer Gregg came for another visit and this time his wife was with him. This was the first time Dupree was meeting Beverly and she was excited because Tony had spoken so much of her, although he hadn't done so in a while. In fact, Tony hadn't mentioned anything about his parents since she came out of the hospital and that was unusual. He simply adored his parents and would have some story to share with her every time she saw him. Dupree briefly wondered if something was wrong as she remembered an incident that occurred some days before.

"I just love me some mango," Dupree said, her teeth sinking into the big, juicy East Indian mango. The thick juice leaked down the sides of her mouth.

"Yup," Tony replied, his mouth full of the sweet fruit. "I could easily eat a dozen of these or even more."

Their laughter rang out in the garden, where they sat enjoying each other's company.

"Hey guys!" They both looked up as Officer Gregg entered the garden from the side of the house. "Dupree, I'm not sure if you are eating that mango or if it's eating you," he joked, his laughter mingling with Dupree's.

"Yeah, I know I look a mess, but I have no shame right now." Dupree grinned. "Right, Tony?"

"I have to go," Tony replied, his hard voice laced with anger. "Dupree, I'll see you soon."

"Where are you going?" Dupree asked. Her brows knitted in confusion.

"I have to run some errands for Mama and Dada."

With his face twisted as if he was sucking on a lime, Dupree watched in surprise as he brushed past his father and walked away without another word. Officer Gregg hung his head in embarrassment.

"What is wrong with him?" Dupree asked. "Was it something I said or did?"

"No. It's me," Officer Gregg said as he looked at his daughter. "He is upset with his mother and me right now," he added. "You know how thickheaded you teenagers can be sometimes."

Dupree noticed his smile did not reach his worried eyes and decided to let it go.

Now as she looked at the couple, she wasn't so sure she should have done that. If something was going on with her best friend and his parents, she wanted to help him. She would remind Tony how fortunate he was to have his parents, especially his father. She had never known hers and would have loved to have someone like Officer Gregg as her dad. Yes, Tony was very lucky indeed.

"So how are you feeling, my dear?" Beverly asked and recaptured Dupree's attention.

"I am doing very well, ma'am, thank you for asking. It has been six weeks since I left the hospital and tomorrow I go back to get all my casts off. I still have a long way to go, but I have passed the worst. I give God thanks for His healing mercies toward me."

Beverly sat and looked at the younger, female version of her husband, who strongly resembled their son. She was surprised no one had noticed before, or maybe because it seemed too implausible for someone to even consider. While Tony was light skinned, Dupree was dark and that was because Tony had her complexion and Dupree her dad's, but everything else was the same. She had avoided visiting Dupree in the hospital because she still felt guilty about what had happened to her and took some blame for it. She knew she had a lot to make up to Dupree and also to Tony. She had been praying every day for guidance on how to go about doing so.

"Your husband has been very nice to me and I really appreciate everything he has done for me," Dupree said. "I'm also sure you are aware by now that your son is also my best friend. Thank you for sharing your men with me. I feel as if I am actually a member of your family," Dupree told Beverly jokingly and smiled.

If only you knew how true your words are, Beverly thought.

"Dupree," Officer Gregg, who had been silent this entire time, said and took Dupree's right hand in his. "My wife and I would like to make you an offer. We hope you and Aunt Madge will accept. We would like to pay your entire hospital bill and also cover the cost for your physical therapy."

No one spoke. Aunt Madge and Dupree looked at the Greggs, then at each other and back to the Greggs. Officer Gregg and Beverly waited anxiously for Dupree's response. It was very important to them for her to accept their offer. This was one of the first steps to seek some redemption for all the wrong they had done to her. They knew they had a long way to go, but this would be a nice start in the right direction.

"Why?" Dupree asked the million dollar question. She had finally addressed the elephant that was in the room. Beverly gasped in surprise and Officer Gregg sat unmoving. They were both caught off-guard.

"Um, I would like to do this for you because I love you and would like to help you," Officer Gregg said sincerely as he looked at Dupree through misted eyes. And this was the truth. Over the last few weeks, Officer Gregg had grown to love his daughter. He now realized how much he had lost by denying his own flesh and blood. If only he had known then what he knew now.

"You love me?" Dupree asked as she stared at him, puzzled. "But . . . but why?"

"I know we haven't really known each other long, but I love the wonderful young lady you are." Officer Gregg's voice trembled with emotion. "I love your drive to overcome your troubles. I love the love you have for the Lord and I just love the person you are."

Dupree lost the battle and the tears came bursting through the floodgates. It was ironic that one man she loved like a father violated her and the one she now wished was her father was helping her. Again, Dupree accepted the generous offer. Sometimes when it rains, it pours.

Chapter Twenty-eight

"I'm here!" Tony yelled as he entered Mrs. Scott's living room. "Who is ready to go to the hospital to take her body armor off?"

"That would be me!" Dupree squealed, her eyes twinkled with happiness.

"Today your cast comes off. What a blessing!" Miss Angie said to Dupree. "You were able to use those crutches when the back allowed, but I know you need a break from that wheelchair."

"And you won't have to constantly use the hairdryer to blow cool air into my cast to relieve the itching! Thank you, Lord!" Dupree exclaimed.

"No, not anymore, baby." Miss Angie's voice trembled with emotion. "After today they will be gone."

"To God be the glory!" Aunt Madge mumbled as she rocked from side to side in her wheelchair, her eyes closed in reverence and praise.

Dupree grinned happily as she looked at the faces beaming down on her. Today would be a milestone in her recovery and a testament to her victory.

As Tony pushed the wheelchair down the long, busy hospital corridor, weaving around solemn, hurried bodies, unshed tears blurred Dupree's eyes as the familiar disinfectant smell welcomed her back to the place she spent a few agonizing weeks fighting for her life.

The next few minutes seemed like hours to Dupree, but finally all the casts were gone. With her eyes closed, she prayed silently as Dr. David examined her.

"I am very pleased with what I saw, my dear," he concluded. He then gave Dupree further instructions necessary for her continued progress.

She thanked him and Tony came and helped her out to the car.

On the way home from the hospital, Dupree noticed that Tony seemed awfully quiet. She decided to find out what it was today. "Tony, you know I'm your friend, right?"

"Yup."

"So please tell me what is bothering you. Let me try to help you and pray for you."

Tony did not respond to her. He just kept his eyes focused on the road.

Dupree turned and stared at him as he stared straight ahead and ignored her. Her eyes burned into the side of his head but he refused to look at her. Dupree frowned, her mind puzzled at Tony's behavior. "I'm waiting, Anthony," she said, this time in a very stern voice.

Tony chuckled. "Okay. Why don't I take you to the post office and get your mail, after which we can go over to Water Square and talk?"

"I hope you are not playing with me, because we are going to talk about what's going on with you today," she warned him as she pointed her finger at him.

"Look at you pointing fingers and acting all bad now that your casts are gone," Tony teased her and they both burst out laughing.

When they got to the post office, Tony pulled up and left the car running while he rushed inside and got Dupree's mail. A few minutes later he returned and dropped a mountain of envelopes on Dupree's lap.

"I have never received so much mail in my life!" she exclaimed. "I think it's mostly get-well cards and letters." Tears came to her eyes as she opened and read some of them aloud to Tony.

As Tony pulled into a small, clean park, Dupree noticed it was away from the main road and would afford them the privacy they needed for their talk. It was also an enchanting place with magnificently colored trees and shrubs, well-groomed green grass and beautiful exotic flowers.

Dupree slowly raised herself up as Tony gripped her upper arm and helped her out of the car. With his arm held tightly around her waist, Dupree leaned on him as he led her over to a bench under the shade of a giant cotton tree. She noticed his steps were hesitant and unhurried.

"Okay, start talking," she demanded after they were both seated.

"You know you are bossy, right?" he joked uncomfortably.

"Anthony!" That was his cue to start spilling the beans and that he better start doing so fast.

"Okay, okay. I am just going through some stuff with my parents right now. I am very upset about something that they did and I am very angry with them. I am also staying with my grandparents because I can't bear to be around them now."

She looked at him intently, her pointed stare fixed on him. "You moved out?"

"Well, not exactly, or maybe I did, but whatever it is, I am staying with Mama and Dada for a while."

"What did they do that was so bad?" Suspicion crept into her voice. "I am finding this very strange. Why do I think something more is going on?"

Dupree saw Tony's eyes broaden in horror. He hung his head down and stared at his lap without speaking.

An uncomfortable silence quickly crept in and held them hostage.

"They do not want me to go college," Tony finally lied. "My dad wants me to go to the police academy instead. We have three generation of police officers in our family and he would like me to continue this legacy." He felt bad for lying to Dupree, but he was doing it to protect her.

"But you should get to decide what you want to do with your life. Surely if you talk to them, they would understand this. Do you want me to talk to them for you?"

"No, no, no! Please don't do that." Tony began to panic. If Dupree talked to his parents, they would probably refute what he had said and then Dupree would find out that he had lied to her. He could not afford to let this happen.

"Please don't talk to them about this," he repeated. "I am telling you this because I trust you."

"Fine, I won't say anything to them, but I think you should talk to them again. They seem like pretty understanding people to me. Please promise me you will talk to them again."

"I will," Tony lied again. "Now let's eat."

After lunch, Tony suggested that Dupree read some more of her mail before they headed back home and she agreed enthusiastically. She picked up the first letter on top and gasped loudly. This was not a get-well card; it was a letter from the University of Technology. Dupree felt her hand tremble, and had Tony not removed the letter from her shaking hand, it would have fallen.

"What's this?" he asked as he looked at the letter. Then he realized what it was and he too got nervous. He knew how much Dupree wanted to attend the university like he did. Only he wouldn't be going there anymore if he got accepted by New York University. He still hadn't told Dupree about his college plans; he would just wait and see if he got accepted first.

"Do you want me to read it for you?" Tony asked.

Dupree nodded her head, too nervous to speak. She had thought about college a lot while she was in the hospital, but she didn't know if it would have been possible for her to attend this September due to her attack. But she had recovered faster than she thought and thankfully she had no spinal injury to complicate things. She knew she had to do physical therapy and use her crutches for a while, but it was just the beginning of August and her prognosis was looking good. Now if she could only get one of the scholarships or grants that she had applied for, maybe she could make it to college after all?

They marinated in the deep silence that followed after Tony finished reading her acceptance letter to the University of Technology. Dupree sat with her mouth open wide in stunned silence by the good news she had just received. Tony looked from Dupree to the letter and back to Dupree. Then a loud scream echoed throughout the park and Tony could have sworn he saw all the birds taking flight. He lifted her in the air and they both screamed aloud together.

"I'm so happy and proud of you, Pree." Tony choked up. "You are so deserving of this and it couldn't come at a better time for you." The siblings shared a heartfelt hug before they made their way back to the car and headed home to share the good news with everyone.

"We have to celebrate your acceptance to college tonight, Dupree," Mrs. Scott said excitedly.

"Will she be able to attend in September?" Miss Angie asked as she stepped out of the house and joined everyone on the veranda. "She is still not well and she needs physical therapy for her back. We don't want her to overdo it and injure herself again. God forbid."

"I have an old friend in Kingston where she can continue her physical therapy. Also she is going to stay on campus and won't have to travel far for her classes. She will need the crutches for a while but she will be all right. Dupree is a very strong girl and I don't think she should wait another year to start college. Don't get me wrong, I am going to miss her, but I want what is best for her. No one deserves it more," said Mrs. Scott.

As Mrs. Scott and Miss Angie spoke, Dupree's mind was far away. She was really happy she got accepted into the college of her choice but she knew it was not possible for her to go for two reasons, one of which was she couldn't afford to go. She had gone through the rest of her mail and there was nothing about the scholarships or grants she had applied for. Secondly, it would soon be time for her and Aunt Madge to go home. They had imposed on Mrs. Scott long enough. She would take a year to fully recuperate and reapply to some local colleges nearby. Going away to college right now just didn't seem realistic.

"Hello, Dupree. Are you okay?" Tony asked her with concern. He had asked her the question twice.

Dupree was deep in thought with a distant look on her face. Everyone was now looking at her with concern.

"Sorry. I am fine. Did you say something?" Dupree asked Tony.

"Forget about what I said and tell us what is wrong. You were so happy a few minutes ago. What's going on?"

"I'm not going to the University of Technology," Dupree confessed.

Mrs. Scott gasped in horror, Aunt Madge began to speak incoherently, and Tony just stared at her.

"But why not? Are you afraid you won't be well enough?" Mrs. Scott asked her. "I know you have to use the crutches, but everyone has accidents all the time. That is nothing to be ashamed of, honey."

"It's not that. I can't afford to go. I still haven't received any responses to the scholarships and grants I applied for."

"Sweetheart, I will help you with that," Mrs. Scott said and went to stand in front of Dupree. "I will pay all your expenses for school."

No, no," Dupree said, shaking her head. "I can't let you do that. You have already done so much for us."

"Please don't think like that, Dupree. Quite frankly, I will never live long enough to spend all the money I have," Mrs. Scott replied. "Hupert and I never had children any but . . ." Mrs. Scott paused, too choked up to continue.

Dupree reached out and hugged the older woman to her. Everyone looked on in silence.

"I love you like a daughter," Mrs. Scott whispered in her ear. "Please let me do this for you."

"And what about Aunt Madge," Dupree said as she pulled back and looked over at her aunt. "I just can't leave Aunt Madge right now. Who will take care of her? We can't stay with you forever. As soon as I feel better we are going home and she will need me. I think it's best if I take a year off and apply to some local colleges nearby for next year."

"No way are you going to do that!" Mrs. Scott exclaimed. "You are going away to college and Aunt Madge is going to stay right here with us. Miss Angie and I are the only people who live in this big house; there is plenty of room as you can see. Also, you guys are the closest I have for family and I love having Aunt Madge with me. Please let me continue to help."

Dupree looked at Mrs. Scott and saw the sincerity in her eyes. They were almost pleading with Dupree to say yes. She then looked over at Aunt Madge and she nodded her head in agreement. She also wanted to stay with Mrs. Scott and Miss Angie.

"Are you sure? You are going to send me to college and keep Aunt Madge here with you?" Dupree asked Mrs. Scott, still in awe of her generosity.

Mrs. Scott smiled and nodded. "Yes, my dear."

"You are truly an angel. I have prayed for the Lord to send someone to help us and He sent you. How can I ever repay you for all the kindness you have shown to both of us? You will always be in my heart, thoughts, and prayers, forever." Dupree and Mrs. Scott hugged each other tightly, while Miss Angie and Tony applauded.

Aunt Madge just smiled happily. She was thrilled that her current living arrangement would be a permanent one. She loved her little board house and it would always be her home, but due to the stroke she suffered, living with Mrs. Scott and Miss Angie was a much better accommodation for her.

"I'll have friends to interact with daily, and now that I'm closer to town, I'll be able to attend church again," Aunt Madge told Dupree through her slurred speech. "I'm also easier to reach, so many of my church sisters and brothers visit me frequently and pray with me."

Dupree nodded her head in understanding and hugged her aunt. There was also no denying the pleasure of having all the amenities that came with Aunt Madge staying with Miss Scott.

"It feels great to have electricity, doesn't it?" Dupree whispered to Aunt Madge and she nodded her head happily. "You get to watch television and listen to the radio. And let's not talk about how it feels to have a long bath, with water running from the pipe."

Aunt Madge's lips quivered.

"You worked very hard for everything you had and the Lord has blessed you abundantly. It is Him who is making all this possible," Dupree told her aunt as she held her in her arms. "You have certain needs that are being met by Mrs. Scott."

Dupree quietly reflected on Philippians 4:19.

But my God shall supply all your needs according to his riches in glory by Christ Jesus.

"Amen to that." Dupree smiled as her options for college were starting to get brighter.

Chapter Twenty-nine

Deacon Livingston lay curled up on the cold concrete floor of his prison cell, shivering, as cold sweat drenched his battered, bloodied body. With every labored breath, excruciating pain washed over him from head to toe. Moaning and groaning, he tried to sneak a peek through his bloodshot eyes, but they were swollen shut. He was in a deep, dark hell and there was no escape.

A few weeks earlier . . .

After the attack on Dupree, Deacon Livingston was checked out at the hospital before being placed in a holding cell at the Runaway Bay Police Station. He was kept in isolation for his own safety. News of the brutal attack had spread like wildfire throughout all fourteen parishes and the Jamaican people were outraged. Many wanted Deacon Livingston's head on a platter.

"Let's go!" the police officer shouted the next morning as he opened the holding cell. "Put your hands behind your back."

The officer stepped inside the cell and roughly twisted Deacon Livingston's hands behind him, before he snapped on the handcuffs. He then knelt down and chained his feet as well.

"It's time to face the music now, you little scumbag," the officer said and shoved Deacon Livingston out of the cell. He lost his balance and fell over his chained feet, landing face down on the dirty floor.

Loud laughter rang out all over the police station. The unsympathetic police officers and staff were enjoying Deacon Livingston's humiliation.

"You haven't seen anything yet," someone said. "Wait until they get their hands on you at Spanish Town." He was referring to the maximum security St. Catherine's Adult Correctional Centre, which contained the only death row on the island.

Deacon Livingston was hauled up off the floor and led outside and into a small white van parked in front of the police station. He was then transported to Spanish Town Courthouse for a court hearing.

"Your Honor, my client is an outstanding businessman in his community. He has no criminal record. Therefore, I would like to request that he be granted bail," Deacon Livingston's high-priced lawyer implored the stone-faced judge later that morning.

"Objection!" the prosecutor exclaimed. "Your Honor, this man brutally attacked an innocent young girl who is now fighting for her life in the hospital. He has a considerable amount of wealth and is a flight risk. He should not be allowed bail."

The judge agreed and Deacon Livingston was denied bail.

He was then taken to the St. Catherine Correctional Centre, where he would be remanded until his trial. The old, sprawling brick penitentiary was desperately overcrowded. It was boiling hot by day, and frequently cold and damp by night. A typical cell was six feet by eight feet, and often held up to seven or more prisoners.

Deacon Livingston sat huddled up in a corner, his pounding head resting on his bent knees. His fearful eyes constantly stole quick glances at the other hard-looking prisoners, who were watching his every move.

As night fell, Deacon Livingston struggled to stay awake but soon exhaustion overtook him. He slept on the cold concrete floor, in front of the rancid, hole-in-the-ground toilet, as all the tiny bunks were occupied.

Later that night, Deacon Livingston's eyes popped opened when a large hand was clasped over his mouth. He tried to scream but it was muffled. He tried to get up, but his body was pinned down by solid, smelly bodies.

"You like to rape babies, huh?" the cold voice whispered in his ears, the bad breath tickling his nostrils. "You know I have a daughter her age?"

The first firm fist slammed into Deacon Livingston's left eye, snapping his head farther into the ground. Stars and a variety of colors danced before his right eye, and then quickly disappeared by the next blow that followed. He felt like his intestines shifted when a strong kick was delivered to his stomach. Punches and kicks rained down on him from every angle to every part of his body. His blood decorated the wall and floor around him. Pain like he had never felt before exploded all over his body. Deacon Livingston silently prayed for death. And then he felt nothing as his body shut down and he lost consciousness.

Deacon Livingston was taken to the Spanish Town Hospital. Luckily he suffered no internal damage. He was patched up and given some pain medication before he was returned to prison.

"What happened to you last night?" the warden asked Deacon Livingston. He was sitting behind a desk in his office with Deacon Livingston sitting across from him, bandaged up from head to toe.

"I fell," Deacon Livingston whispered through his swollen, busted lips.

"You fell? Man, what kind of fall did that kind of damage to you?" the warden persisted, even though he knew his efforts were futile. The code of the prison system was "snitching results in stitching." Not that Deacon Livingston needed any more stitches.

"That's my story," Deacon Livingston insisted as his red, engorged eyes held those of the warden in a silent battle.

"Okay. Cool. Just so you know I can't protect you if you don't talk to me," the warden said. "Just try not to 'fall' again," he added sarcastically.

But he did or so he said. Night after night, Deacon Livingston was beaten. His lawyer went to court and tried to get him isolated from the general prison population but his plea was denied. Without Deacon Livingston's attestation, there was not much that could have been done.

"Why are you doing this?" Deacon Livingston's lawyer asked him one day when he visited his client. "They are going to kill you in here."

Deacon Livingston shrugged his shoulders and stared back blankly at his lawyer. That was when the lawyer figured it out.

"That's what you want!" his lawyer shouted. "You want them to kill you, don't you?"

Deacon Livingston did not respond. But the lawyer was right. Deacon Livingston felt this was his punishment for what he had done to Dupree and the embarrassment and hurt he caused his family. He really wanted the other prisoners to kill him. Then he dropped another bomb on his lawyer.

"I'm going to plead guilty."

Silence arrested the visitor's room as the wide-eyed lawyer stared at Deacon Livingston. "Now I'm convinced that you have lost your mind. I am going to file an insanity plea for you," the lawyer said.

"You will do no such thing." Deacon Livingston's voice was stern. "This is my decision and I'm not crazy."

"But, but . . ." The lawyer was perplexed. "Why?" he asked Deacon Livingston.

"It's the right thing to do," Deacon Livingston told him. "I will not put Dupree or my family through a trial. I've already hurt them enough."

"At least let me try to get you a deal," the lawyer replied. "Please let me do the job you are paying me to do."

"No," Deacon Livingston said. "I'll take whatever punishment the Lord sees fit."

The lawyer's pleas fell on deaf ears. Deacon Livingston was adamant about his decision and no one could change his mind. So a few weeks later, against his lawyer's advice, Deacon Livingston pled guilty to the assault on Dupree. He was sentenced to fifteen years in prison.

Mrs. Livingston saw her husband's demise on the television news that evening. Tears ran down her face as she watched them lead Deacon Livingston from the court in handcuffs and chains.

"Why, God?" she sobbed. "What did my children and I do to deserve this?"

After the incident, Mrs. Livingston and her children went to stay with her brother in St. Mary. A few weeks later she decided to make the move a permanent one and bought a house of her own. She sold the house with all the evil memories in Trelawny and the businesses, in hope of making a fresh start for her family. But the pain that consumed the entire family just refused to dissipate.

"I don't know what else to do," Mrs. Livingston continued to cry.

"Yes, you do," Aunt Cleaver said as she stepped farther into the room. "We are going to rely on God to get us through this tribulation."

Aunt Cleaver went and sat beside her sister on the couch. She pulled Mrs. Livingston into her arms and rocked her gently, as one would a child.

Aunt Cleaver had come to stay with her sister and nieces to help them through this dark moment in their lives. She was a strong support to the family.

"It will take some time but you and the girls are going to be okay," Aunt Cleaver said. "Psalms 27:14 says, 'Wait on the Lord, be of good courage, and he shall strengthen thine heart: wait, I say, on the Lord.'"

Aunt Cleaver proceeded to pray aloud while Mrs. Livingston embraced every word close to her heart as she waited for the day that the pain would eventually go away.

Chapter Thirty

After leaving Mrs. Scott's house, Tony decided to stop by his parents' house to check his mail. He was now anxious to see if he had received any response from the colleges he had applied to. He knew his parents should be at work; therefore, he did not have to worry about seeing them.

Tony took out his keys, opened the front door, and slowly entered the house. His soft steps sounded unusually loud to his ears as he walked to his bedroom, closing the door behind him. Sitting on top of his dresser was a pile of mail. His heartbeat quickened and he gingerly rubbed his sweaty palms together before he took up the mail and made his way over to his bed.

As he sat on the edge of the bed, Tony anxiously sorted through the mail, quickly tossing the ones he was not interested in on the bed beside him before reaching for another. Finally he held the small white envelope in his trembling hand and stared at the New York University seal. Taking a deep breath, he closed his eyes as his right index finger slit the envelope open.

Removing the letter, he began to read, his grin getting bigger and bigger. Tony would have sworn that it was the same letter Dupree got earlier; the only difference was the name of the university.

"I am in!" he screamed and jumped off the bed, pumping his fists wildly in the air. "This must be a sign from God!"

Laughing uncontrollably, he waved the letter in the air proudly. "I think this is God's way of telling me where I should go," Tony spoke aloud in the empty room. "I can't wait to tell Dupree and share my plans for her to apply to NYU for next year."

Excitedly, Tony ran around the room, grabbing some more clothes to take with him to his grandparents' house. Quickly stuffing everything into his backpack, he took the stairs down two at a time.

As he passed the kitchen Tony paused and sniffed. His mouth watered instantly and he licked his lips hungrily when the smell of sweet potato pudding filled his nostrils. This was his favorite and his mom always made it for him from scratch. His father and the housekeeper would have a slice every now and then but Tony would eat a whole pudding in a day if possible.

Stepping quickly into the kitchen, Tony saw a big sweet potato pudding on the kitchen counter. Licking his lips, he grabbed a slicing knife from the wooden knife block, cut off a huge slice of pudding, and bit into it. Instantly he closed his eyes in pleasure and groaned as the sweet dessert slid down his throat.

"Ahem."

Startled by the sound of someone clearing her throat, Tony's eyes popped wide open and the remaining piece of pudding fell from his hand as he glanced up at his mother's amused face.

"Sorry, sweetheart. I didn't mean to scare you."

Tony swallowed uncomfortably and nodded his head, his eyes flittering around the room, refusing to meet his mother's stare. Beverly reached down and pick up the pudding off the floor, then walked over to the garbage bin and threw it in.

"I couldn't sleep last night just thinking about you and how much I miss you, so I decided to make your favorite thing in the whole wide world," Beverly said as she came and stood in front of Tony, reaching out to hug him.

Tony quickly stepped away and walked over to the open window, his back turned to his mother. Unshed tears filled his eyes, making the big breadfruit tree in the backyard blurred.

"I was going to call Mama to tell you to come and get the pudding," his mother continued, her voice laced with pain. "Baby, it hurts my heart that I can't even call you anymore because you are not speaking to me." Undeterred, she walked over to him and wrapped her arms around his waist; her head rested on his back.

"Tony, I have messed up, baby, but I am still your mother and I will love you until the day I die. Please find it in your heart to forgive me and your dad. We are doing everything we can to help your sister, although that could never be enough. But we can't change the past, so we just have to deal with the present and focus on the future."

The tears spilled over and ran down Tony's cheeks. His heart ached as he felt his mother's tears soak through his shirt; her petite body quivered from her pain.

"Your dad and I are sorry for hurting you, but you are a good Christian and I am sure you will one day find it in your heart to forgive us, just as I hope the Lord has done."

"I can't do this now," Tony replied, pulling out of the mother's arms, her hands falling to her sides in defeat. "I have to go." He glanced around for his backpack and saw it by the door. Walking rapidly over to it, he picked it up and took a step before being halted by this mother's voice.

"Wait!" She sniffed and wiped her wet face with the back of her hand. "Please, let me wrap up the rest of your pudding for you." She quickly reached up into the cupboard for the roll of foil paper.

Tony stood as still as a statue as his mother approached with the wrapped pudding in her outstretched hand, his glassy eyes fixated on the shiny wooden floor. "Here, baby. Enjoy your pudding and please don't eat it all in one day. You know you'll get an upset stomach if you try to."

Slowly he raised his head, and, for the first time, looked into his mother's teary eyes. The tender love that shone through briefly softened his heart, and he gave her a tight smile before he quickly took the pudding from her hand and exited the house in distress.

Tony rested his head on the steering wheel of his car and wept. His deep, loud sobs filled the small, confined space of the parked car in his parents' driveway. "I miss you so much, Mom," he muttered, snot running down his face. "And I miss my dad too, but I just can't seem to let go of this anger I have toward the both of you. How can I ask God to forgive my sins when I am unable to do the same for my own parents? What kind of Christian am I?"

All cried out, Tony slowly lifted his head and grimaced as a sharp pain exploded in his skull. He started the car and pulled away, his shoulders slumped in agony.

Chapter Thirty-one

Standing on tippy toes, Mrs. Scott peeped through the small basement window, her eyes lit up in fascination as she watched Dupree worshipping the Lord. After a few moments she felt her right hand lift up and the most astonishing words left her mouth.

"I just want to praise you, Lord." Her eyes widened in shock as her feet gave way under her, sending her on her bottom in the grass.

Where did that come from? she asked herself, too shocked to care about the stumble. Her singing praise songs had been happening a lot lately and she didn't know why. What was going on?

Dupree heard a shuffle at the window and suddenly stopped singing, looking around, confused. "Is someone there? Mrs. Scott, is that you?" She did not get a response.

Using her crutches, Dupree slowly made her way up the steps. She was doing her physical therapy every other day and her back, though very sore, was feeling much better. Her arm and leg were also progressing nicely.

Finally she made her way outside and glanced around for Mrs. Scott, but she was nowhere to be seen. Not to be deterred, Dupree wobbled into the garden and stopped short when she saw Mrs. Scott sitting at the patio set, her head resting in her hands on top of the table. She slowly made her way over and sat beside her, unmoving, the silence embracing them both.

"I would have liked for you to join me earlier in the basement. In fact, that would have been perfect because where two or more are gathered, He is in the midst to bless them."

Mrs. Scott hung her head in embarrassment. "I am sorry for watching you like that. It—"

But Dupree stopped her before she could finish. "No. No. Please don't apologize. In fact, I should be the one apologizing."

Mrs. Scott looked at her, puzzled.

"I should have invited you to join me, but I was afraid of offending you in your own home. But I still should have because I have a responsibility to share the Lord with you."

"No, thank you. I don't want anything to do with all that God stuff."

Dupree stared at her in shock. "Why? Why would you say that?" Dupree finally asked after she had regained her composure somewhat.

Mrs. Scott was silent for a moment. "I've never talked to anyone about my Hupert," she began, feeling the need to explain herself after seeing the look on Dupree's face. Her voice trembled with emotion. "I still see it every day as if it happened just yesterday." Mrs. Scott proceeded to share with Dupree about her Hupert.

"Honey, let's go before we are late. You know how congested traffic is now because it's rush hour," Hupert called out to his wife.

"I'm coming, darling. Go and start the car and I'll be right there," Mrs. Scott responded. *After they had gotten married, they bought a beautiful mini mansion in Beverley Hills, St. Andrew. It was one of the wealthiest areas in Jamaica where only the rich and the famous could afford to live. Hupert was a successful attorney and Mrs. Scott was a controller at one of the biggest*

accounting firms in the parish of Kingston. They had a great life. They had love, money, and everything their hearts desired. What more was there to life?

Mrs. Scott hurried to the waiting car and got in. She looked at her husband and saw him jokingly pouting, and lovingly reached across the seat and gave him a big kiss. He laughed and kissed her back, and then he drove off. Thirty-five minutes later, he dropped her off in Half Way Tree, where her office was located, before heading to his office in Cross Roads.

It was almost time for lunch and she was hungry. Mrs. Scott decided to take a break from the spreadsheet she had been laboring over since morning when the phone on her desk beeped. It was her secretary and she knew it must be important because she had informed her when she got in that morning that she was not to be disturbed.

"Yes?" Mrs. Scott said.

"There is Nurse Bailey on the line for you, Mrs. Scott. She said she was calling from the hospital and it is about your husband."

"Please put her through," she whispered hurriedly. Her heart felt like it was about to jump out of her chest. She started to sweat profusely and her body began to shake. She got so nervous that the phone fell from her hand but she quickly reached for it and was glad that Nurse Bailey did not get disconnected.

"This is Mrs. Scott. May I help you?"

"Mrs. Scott, I am calling to inform you that your husband is here at University Hospital. Please don't panic, he will be fine. How soon can you get here?"

She sat unmoving as she stared at the wall in front of her. She thought she must have been dreaming because there was no way this could be real. Her husband had just dropped her off at work that morning. This was probably one of those jealous women who had been after her husband for years trying to play a trick on her.

"Now listen to me, you jezebel, and you listen very well because I am only going to say this once. I don't know who you are or what you want, but if you think this is funny, you have a poor sense of humor. Now get off my phone so that I can call my husband right now!"

"No, no, please don't hang up, Mrs. Scott. I know this is a shock, but this is no game. Hold on and I'll let you speak to your husband's partner, Mr. Levy."

At the mention of Mr. Levy's name, Mrs. Scott started to cry. She knew that the call was authentic and this wasn't a game.

"I'm on my way," Mrs. Scott said and hurriedly hung up the telephone before Mr. Levy came on.

Grabbing her handbag, Mrs. Scott ran out of her office. "I'll be right back!" she shouted to her secretary as she sprinted past her desk to the exit door.

Once outside, Mrs. Scott waved her hand frantically as she tried to hail a cab. A few seconds later, one screeched to a stop at her feet and Mrs. Scott jumped into the back seat.

"University Hospital," she informed the driver. "Make it fast, please. This is an emergency."

The driver took one look at her frightened face through his rearview mirror before he sped off at a rapid speed, Horn honking and tires squealing, he maneuvered through the busy streets of Kingston. In record time, he squealed to a stop in front of the hospital's emergency room. An appreciative Mrs. Scott handed him a wad of money before she opened the car door and dashed inside.

"Where is my husband, Hupert?" Mrs. Scott shouted hysterically.

"Are you Mrs. Scott?" a warm voice asked.

Mrs. Scott turned to see a very pleasant-looking nurse headed toward her. "Yes, and I got here as fast as I could. Are you Nurse Bailey? Is my husband all right? What's going on?" she asked rapidly.

"*Please calm down, Mrs. Scott. Your husband had a heart attack and had to be rushed into surgery when he got here. From what I understand, an artery was blocked and had to be opened up immediately. A doctor will be out soon to update you on his condition. In fact, here comes Dr. Davis as we speak.*"

A tired-looking doctor dressed in green scrubs walked out into the waiting room. Mrs. Scott rushed to Dr. Davis and quickly asked him how her husband was doing.

"*The surgery was successful and he is resting now. You can go in and see him in a few minutes, but please come with me to my office so I can explain your husband's condition to you.*"

In Dr. Davis's office she paced the floored nervously. He offered her a seat but she was too agitated to sit. She needed to know what was going on with her husband right now.

"*Your husband has coronary artery disease,*" he began. "*CAD is the buildup over time of hard cholesterol substances, known as plaque, on the inner walls of the coronary arteries. Eventually, a section of plaque can break open, causing a blood clot to form. If the clot becomes large enough to cut off most or all of the blood flow through the artery, then a heart attack occurs. This was what happened to your husband.*"

Mrs. Scott finally sat down in the seat offered earlier. Her feet were unable to hold her up any longer. She couldn't believe what she was hearing. Her husband was only forty-five years old. He exercised, ate healthy, and led a very active life.

"*Please continue,*" she asked Dr. Davis.

"*We performed a coronary artery bypass grafting to provide a new route for blood to flow to the heart muscle. Everything went perfect and in a few days you will be able to take your husband home.*"

"So he is going to be all right?" she asked.

"I am going to give him some medicines to take daily and will recommend cardiac rehabilitation. He will have to change his diet, and maybe increase his physical activity to lower his chances of having another heart attack, but we will talk about that some more."

She felt as if the world were resting on her shoulders as she left Dr. Davis's office. There were so many things going through her mind she felt like she was going crazy. As she dragged her feet and entered the hospital room, she was rendered shocked once again when she saw her husband. He was hooked up to machines with cords going in every direction. His eyes were closed and his breathing was shallow. He looked so helpless and alone. Tears came to her eyes again as she looked at the man she loved more than life itself. They had been married for over twenty-three years and she could not imagine her life without him. He had to get better, he just had to.

Mrs. Scott knelt by her husband's bedside and put her hand on his. It was cold and lifeless to her touch, but she knew in heart that this would be changing soon. She bowed her head and began to pray for his recovery.

Two weeks later, Hupert Scott was released from the hospital to go home and recuperate but instead of getting better, he got worse. The medicine and the rehabilitation just didn't seem to be working. Mrs. Scott quit her job to take care of her husband full time. She took him to different doctors all over Jamaica but no one seemed to be of any more help. Her pastor and other church members came by and prayed, but Hupert was still not getting better. She finally decided that maybe they needed a change of scenery. She contacted her lawyer and her husband's business partner to take care of his business and bought a house in Arcadia, Trelawny. It was the same size as the house in Beverly Hills for much lower price. In a matter of weeks, the Scotts moved from St. Andrew to Trelawny.

As Hupert grew weaker and sicker, Mrs. Scott prayed and fasted more. She found a nice Baptist church close to home and began to worship there. She got a live-in helper and attended church almost every day and night. She doubled her tithes and contributed to every program the church had. She knew she was doing her part as a good Christian; now it was the Lord's turn to do His. If He raised Lazarus from the dead, surely He could heal her Hupert. If He had forgiven that old thief on the cross and accepted him into heaven, then He must heal her Hupert because he was a good Christian and had never hurt a soul in his life. So she continued to pray and fast and waited for Hupert's healing, but it never came. Hupert Scott passed away six months later.

Mrs. Scott was devastated and many people were concerned about her. They feared she would have a nervous breakdown or something, but this never happened. She had too much anger and bitterness toward God to get ill. She just could not understand why after she gave God so much that He did not make her Hupert better. She knew in the Bible He said He cared about her and would supply all her needs, but He was a liar. And He was a hypocrite, too, because He said lying was a sin but He himself was a liar. She was so angry with God she made a vow that she would never ask Him for anything again. Who needed someone who would not help you when you needed it?

"From this moment on it's me, myself, and I. Away with you, God!" she shouted one day as she looked to the sky, with her fists lifted up to the heavens. "I will never enter a church again and you will not get another red cent from me. Got that?"

And after twenty years, Mrs. Scott, now sixty years old, had kept that promise.

"He didn't heal him!" Mrs. Scott yelled and Dupree looked at her through tear-filled eyes. "Can't you see He lied to me and He is lying to you now?" By now Mrs. Scott was practically screaming. She had gotten to her feet and was pacing the floor angrily like a rabid dog.

Dupree sat quietly and listened to her as she vented. Then it was her turn. "I'm sorry," Dupree said. "I don't know why God did not heal your husband but He knows best. We just have to continue to trust Him."

"But look at what happened to you. You were violated by a man who was supposedly saved. Why would God allow that to happen to you and you are saved? Why didn't He help you?"

Dupree smiled as she looked out into the beautiful garden. She inwardly asked the Lord to give her the right words to use in order to help His daughter. "But He did help me."

"What? Well He certainly helped you get beaten and a broken back, leg, and arm. I guess He helped after all," Mrs. Scott replied sarcastically, but Dupree did not take offense.

"But God saved my life. He led Mr. Bunny and John to me just before that monster raped and killed me. He is a merciful God and for that I will always give Him thanks and praise."

Mrs. Scott slowly came back and sat down beside Dupree. She looked at this young girl, young enough to be her granddaughter, but was much older than her in the Lord. "Do you think my Hupert is in heaven?" Mrs. Scott asked in a meek voice as her eyes grew misty from the unshed tears.

"That's a question I can't answer, but he had the opportunity to repent and only God knew his heart."

Mrs. Scott rested her head on the table and wept. Over twenty years of pain and hurt came pouring out like water from a broken dam. Dupree put her good arm around her and comforted her. Mrs. Scott was filled with guilt and shame. All these years she had been blaming the Lord for her husband's death but not once had she thanked Him for the wonderful years they had together. Some people waited a lifetime and would never find a love like she had in Hupert. She should have thanked the Lord, not cursed Him. She should have run to Him, not away from Him. She should have used Hupert's death to draw her closer to Him, not push her away from Him.

Mrs. Scott was devastated. She asked to be excused and went into her room and succumbed to all the emotional baggage she had been carrying around all these years.

Dupree watched her leave and knew the Holy Spirit was at work. She bowed her head and prayed for the hurting woman who had been so good to her and Aunt Madge.

The next day, instead of peeping through the window, Mrs. Scott joined Dupree in the basement.

"I'm so glad you came!" Dupree exclaimed as she hugged her.

"I'm . . . I'm just here to keep you company," Mrs. Scott stuttered, her face flushed with embarrassment. "I'll just sit here," she said and took a seat on a sofa in the corner of the room.

"Okay!" Dupree replied, her grin stretching from one ear to another. The fact that Mrs. Scott was there was a step in the right direction.

Over the next few days, Mrs. Scott joined Dupree in the basement for worship without actually taking part. However, she always listened intently as Dupree shared scriptures from the Bible. It thrilled Dupree's heart even more when she asked questions.

The next morning at devotion, Dupree watched the door anxiously for Mrs. Scott. Last night Mrs. Scott had stayed in her room and never came down to have dinner with her, Aunt Madge, and Miss Angie.

As the heated devotion got under way and the women reveled in the power of the Holy Spirit, Mrs. Scott silently slipped into the room, unbeknown to anyone. She had been giving herself excuses for not going, but it was as if her feet had a life of their own, and before she knew it, there she was. But it was not by chance that she was there. She was there for a purpose.

As Miss Angie began to sing "Nearer My God to Thee," Mrs. Scott felt it. It was like an electric current passing through her body, from the crown of her head to the soles of her feet. She jumped to her feet and began to shout praises to the Almighty God. The force was so strong she was unable to stay in one place, so she danced and skipped from one corner of the room to the other, singing and shouting. The other women rejoiced with her as they watched the Holy Spirit at work. It took some time for everyone to settle down and simmer in the afterglow of the Spirit.

Dupree prayed aloud, after which Miss Angie asked Mrs. Scott if she would like to officially give her life to the Lord, and she did not hesitate. Mrs. Scott fell to her knees, anxious to accept His gift of salvation by believing in Jesus Christ and repenting her sins. She was more than ready to turn the rest of her life over to Him and Miss Angie led her into the sinners' prayer.

It was a private celebration that day at Mrs. Scott's house. Miss Angie prepared a feast fit for a king, and Mrs. Scott retrieved her old gospel records, and the voice of Pastor Shirley Caesar bellowing "He'll Do It Again" resonated throughout the house.

Yes, He had indeed.

Mrs. Scott was now a child of God.

Chapter Thirty-two

She was running as fast as she could but it seemed to be gaining on her. Her leg and back were hurting like crazy but she knew she couldn't stop; her life depended on it. The trees zipped by and bushes slapped her face as she stumbled over some rocks. Frantically glancing over her shoulder, she stared into the blackness of the woods and saw the small red glare of its eyes. She felt a chill run down her spine and she trembled in fear. It was close. Too close.

There was no one to save her so she ran as fast as her legs allowed, screaming in horror, her voice echoing in the stillness of the night.

"Help me! Someone, please help me!"

Then she fell flat on her face and was unable to get up. Groaning, she slowly rolled over on her aching back in defeat. She looked up to see it standing over her, ready to pounce on her. She screamed again, louder this time.

"Dupree! Dupree!"

Someone was calling her name from afar, and then she felt hands on her. Dupree woke up drenched in sweat, her heart pounding in her chest, her breathing irregular.

"It's okay, darling, you were just having a nightmare," Mrs. Scott said as she rocked Dupree in her arms.

She had been heading toward the kitchen when she heard the screams coming from Dupree's room and knew that she must have been having another nightmare. They were getting fewer and farther apart, but she still got them periodically and Mrs. Scott hoped that eventually they would go away forever. Mrs. Scott looked down at the young lady who had brought her to Christ, now curled up in her arms like a child, vulnerable and defenseless. She still got angry when she thought of that old, dirty scoundrel. She hoped he'd rot in jail.

She stayed with Dupree until she fell back into a restless sleep.

Later that afternoon, after parking his car in the driveway, Tony noticed Dupree reading in the garden and he went to join her. She was very happy to see him and jumped to her feet to give him a big hug as she flashed her pearly whites at him. Tony returned the hug and smiled as he stared at her. He still couldn't get over how much she looked like him, especially when she smiled.

"I have some news to share with you," Tony said to Dupree.

"Okay, shoot!" Dupree exclaimed excitedly.

"I got accepted to a great college and I have decided to attend."

"Yes, yes! That's what I'm talking about! You are coming to UTech with me!"

"No, I will be attending New York University."

Silence filled the air. Dupree looked at him as if he had lost his mind and Tony stared back at her sadly. Tony saw her eyes tearing up and quickly informed her of the rest of his plans.

"But you can come with me. Well, not this year, but next year, and I will be coming home for Christmas and spring break until you come. I promise I'll also call you often."

There, it was confirmed, the boy had officially lost his mind, Dupree thought.

Tony saw her expression and explained his plan. "Come on. Don't look at me like that, because I know my plan will work. This is what we are going to do: you go to the University of Technology this fall and apply now to New York University, NYU, for next fall. After you get accepted—and I know you will because you are much brighter than I am—you can transfer the credits you have earned to NYU. See, it's that easy."

Dupree just stood there, looking at him.

"And when you come, we can get an apartment together off campus. What do you think?" Tony asked enthusiastically.

Dupree looked in Tony's eyes shimmering with excitement and hated to burst his bubble, but she had to explain a few things to him. "Tony, I know you mean well and I wish that were possible, but you are forgetting a major problem."

"But Aunt Madge will be staying here with Mrs. Scott, remember?"

"It's not that. I can't afford to go to NYU. Thank God Mrs. Scott is going to pay my tuition at UTech."

"You don't have to worry about it. Our dad—I mean, my dad—will pay your tuition for you to go to NYU."

Dupree never paid any attention to the slip-up. "What? I can't ask your father to do that. Both he and your mother have already done so much for me. There is no way I could ask them to take on such a huge financial responsibility just because I am your best friend. They have no obligation to me at all!"

"If only you knew," Tony mumbled under his breath.

"What was that? I didn't hear you."

"My father already agreed to do so."

"What? What? What?" Dupree knew she sounded like a parrot but she was just too flabbergasted. "You already asked him? Why would he do that for me?"

These were the types of questions Tony wished he could have avoided, but he knew they were coming and already he had his answers ready to go. "Both my father and mother have grown to love you very much and want what's best for you. Especially my dad, who has a special bond with you, and he really wants to do this for you. Also, they can afford to do so. Please don't say no. If you talked to them they will confirm what I just said." Well, he didn't exactly lie, Tony told himself. If you really looked at it, everything he said was the truth. He just had to make sure he spoke to his parents as soon as possible because they weren't aware of his decision to attend NYU that fall and his wish for his sister to join him a year later. But he would dare his father to deny Dupree that opportunity because he owed her this and much, much more.

Dupree found it hard to digest everything Tony had told her. *Why would Officer Gregg and Mrs. Gregg want to do that for me?* she thought. She knew they were wealthy and were very kind to her, but this just seemed a little too much. Was she missing something?

Dupree voiced her thoughts. "Tony, all that sounds great and it would be such a wonderful opportunity for me, but I need to think about it and get back to you."

Tony was a little disappointed but he understood her need to wait awhile before she made a decision. At least she never said no, and was thinking about it. There was still hope after all.

Tony stayed for a while, and then left for home.

Dupree went and shared with Aunt Madge everything Tony had said and carefully watched her expression. She was happy to see Aunt Madge smile and knew she liked the idea.

"It will be a wonderful opportunity for you, baby," Aunt Madge said softly in her slow, childlike voice. Her speech still was not too clear but she was gradually getting better. Dupree didn't care one bit; she was just glad that she could hear her aunt's voice again. "God knows I will miss you, but I want you to spread your wings and fly. I want you to have a very happy and prosperous life, my dear, because no one deserves it more."

Dupree listened intently to the woman who knew her better than any other and the wisdom she bestowed on her. Aunt Madge was happy her daughter would get the chance to enhance her life, thus her future, and Dupree was happy her aunt gave her blessings. Aunt Madge's opinion meant the world to her.

"Pray, my chile; seek God's face for His guidance," Aunt Madge implored Dupree.

The future was looking real bright for Dupree but there was an unknown storm brewing.

Chapter Thirty-three

As Tony pulled up in the yard, he noticed his parents' vehicles parked in the open garage and knew both of them were home. *Great,* he thought sarcastically. It would have been nice if he'd had just one parent to deal with but no such luck. He parked his car and went up the steps leading to the veranda. When he reached the front door he thought about using his key to get in but rang the doorbell instead. He felt like a visitor stopping by.

He stood waiting until he heard soft footsteps approaching. His mother opened the door, puzzled at first when she opened the door and saw him standing outside. Joy quickly spread across her face. Without thinking, she rushed to him, and hugged him so tight he almost felt suffocated. Tony stood as stiff as a board and did not return her hug. Beverly noticed his distant attitude and stepped away from him. A look of disappointment crossed her face and Tony almost felt sorry for her, but then remembered she wasn't as innocent as she wanted everyone to believe.

"Why didn't you use your key?" she asked.

Tony shrugged his shoulder in response.

"Well, I am glad to see you, baby. I miss you very much. Please come in; this is your home, you know."

Tony stepped inside and followed his mom as she led him into the living room.

Officer Gregg made his way down the stairs. He saw his son sitting uncomfortably on the couch and drank in the sight of him. He wanted so much to give him a hug, but the look on Tony's face told him not to even think about it. It was pretty obvious that Tony wasn't anywhere close to forgiving him, which made his heart sink.

"Hello, son," Officer Gregg said cautiously.

In his now-nonchalant manner, Tony nodded his head in response. "I need to talk to both of you about something important."

"Okay. Anthony, why don't you sit down right here beside me," Beverly said to her husband. Officer Gregg went and sat down next to her. "What is it, baby?" she asked Tony nervously.

"It's about college. I got accepted to New York University for the fall and I have decided to attend."

"What? When did you apply? Why didn't you tell us you were interested in going there? Why are you going so far away?" Officer Gregg jumped to his feet in bewilderment, firing one question after another. Tony just sat there, looking at his father all worked up, but said nothing. Beverly, realizing the situation had the potential to get out of control, stood up and went to her husband and took a hold of his hand, guiding him back to his seat.

"Okay. Let's all just settle down and talk about this rationally," Beverly said. "Sweetheart, I know you are upset with your father, but please don't do this," she said to Tony as she pled with him through water-filled eyes. Tony sat with his arms folded and a cold look on his face. He knew his mind was made up and nothing they said could change that.

"I thought you wanted to attend the University of Technology, son," Officer Gregg said. "I know you had your mind set on going there. Please, Tony, I know I hurt you, and if you only give me a chance I promise to try to make it up to you. But don't run away to another country just to get away from us. I know your grandparents are in New York, but I would really like you to consider staying here in Jamaica." Officer Gregg's voice broke as he took deep breaths to control his aching heart. He wanted to just break down and weep, but he had to be strong for his wife and son.

"Ba . . . ba . . . baby, why don't you . . . you think about it some more?" Beverly stammered in between sobs.

"I've already made up my mind, Mom. In fact, I would like Dupree to come next year as well."

"What? What? What?" That seemed to be the only word in Officer Gregg's vocabulary then. Quite frankly, no other words came to mind. He was too shocked to say any more. Again, he jumped to his feet and began to pace the floor.

"Give me strength, oh Lord. Please, God, do not forsake me now. Please, please. I am begging you to just show me what to do, Lord," Beverly chanted as she rocked from side to side.

Tony tried to remain tough and distance himself from his parents' distress, but something broke in him as he looked at his mom quivering in anguish. He walked over to her and knelt before her. Beverly quickly wrapped her arms around her only child as she wept on his shoulders.

Officer Gregg felt as if his head was about to explode like dynamite. It was hurting so bad, he wished he could take it off and throw it away. He didn't know what to do. He was about to lose not only his son, but his daughter as well. It looked as if his sins had indeed finally caught up with him. *So much for being a new creature in Christ, huh?* He thought his sins were washed away when he gave his life to the Lord, but he guessed not, or why would all these things be happening to his family?

"Dad, could you please come back over here please?" Tony said in a more courteous manner.

Officer Gregg, who was standing by the window looking out into the vastness of the sky, slowly walked over and retook his seat. He felt a little bit more optimistic by the change of tone in his son's voice, especially when he saw him actually cuddling with his mother.

Tony gently broke away from his mother and got up off his knee to take a seat beside her. "Mom, Dad, I would really like to do this. I originally applied because Bobby was bugging me about it. He will be going there and he wanted me to go with him. Then after I found out what you guys had done, it seemed like the perfect solution to my problem. But now that I have decided to go, even if it was for another reason, I really think this would be good for me. NYU is a great school, and, Mom, you know that. Don't get me wrong, I still can't forget what happened and I doubt I ever will, but I hope as time goes by I'll be able to deal with it better."

No one spoke and the stillness of the night coated the entire house, wall to wall. It was a very awkward moment for everyone involved: a family divided by secrets, lies, and deception. There was so much to say, so many questions that needed to be answered, but each was afraid to say the wrong thing, so no one spoke for a while. Tony finally decided to continue discussing his plans for his sister and himself.

"It will also be great for Dupree. She has never been outside this country. Just think how exciting it would be for her. This will be an investment in her future and you owe her this, Dad. She deserves this and much more and you both know it!" Tony exclaimed as he began to get agitated again talking about his sister. He quickly excused himself and went to the kitchen for a glass of water. His mouth felt as dry as sandpaper.

He grabbed a glass, filled it with water straight from the tap, and gobbled it down in one long drink. He began to wonder if he was going crazy. One minute he was consumed by anger for his parents and another minute he almost empathized with them. He was confused and did not know what to do.

In the living room, Officer Gregg held his wife in his arms and listened as she sniffled and hiccupped. If he only knew what to do in order to make things better. He didn't want his children to go so far away, not when he hadn't patched things up with his son and when he was just getting to know his daughter.

"Maybe we should let them go," Beverly said so softly he wasn't sure he'd heard her correctly.

"What did you say, babe?"

"I said we should let them go. God knows I'll miss Tony and Dupree too but this could be great for them."

"But I am just getting to know Dupree and she still doesn't know I am her father."

"She wouldn't be leaving until next year. I guess Tony just told her to apply as well, so you still have some more time with her."

"But she will be going to UTech in a few weeks, all the way in Kingston," Officer Gregg whined.

"Anthony, please. We can go to Kingston every week and see her, but for heaven's sake stop thinking about you for once," Beverly said angrily. This shut up Officer Gregg real fast. His wife was like a snake: quiet until she got riled up; then she would sting where it hurt. He also knew what she had said was right and he really appreciated her sticking by him through this ordeal he had caused.

Tony, now a little calmer, returned to the living room and joined his parents. He wanted to finish the discussion because he was feeling drained and desperately needed to get some rest. His father looked at him and then his mother, and finally back at him.

"Your mom and I have talked about this briefly and we realized although we would prefer both you and Dupree to attend college here in Jamaica for our own selfish reasons. We want what's best for the both of you and going away to NYU would be good for you."

Tony looked at them in astonishment.

"But we want you to promise us something; and when the time comes, I'll ask Dupree as well," Officer Gregg said.

Tony knew it was too good to be true.

"I want you to call home at least once a week and to come back home for Christmas and spring break, more often if you have the time. I don't care if it's only for the weekend. I'll buy your ticket whenever you want to come home. So what do you say?"

"I say you have yourself a deal," Tony said with a slight smile. "I can do that."

"And I want you to do something for me as well," Beverly informed Tony. He looked at his mom, skeptical, and almost held his breath as he waited to hear what she had to say.

"Before you leave for college I want you to go with us to see Bishop Chude in Thompson Town, in Clarendon, for some family counseling. I hate the way things are between us. I know our problem won't go away overnight, but I think if we talk to someone who can help us work through it, then we would be on our way to healing. So will you do that for me, baby?"

"I'm not sure, Mom. I don't think I like the idea of talking to a stranger about what happened. This is not something I want a lot of people to know, especially a pastor."

"Tony, a pastor will be the best person to talk to from a spiritual and mental point of view. This is very important to me."

"Okay," Tony said reluctantly. "I'll go but I'm not making any promises."

"That's all I ask, my dear," Beverly said, the relief apparent in her voice. "Please keep an open mind because this means a lot to me and your father."

They had accomplished a lot that night but there was still a 1,000-pound gorilla sitting in the room.

"What about Dupree? Will you tell her truth anytime soon?" Tony asked.

"I wanted to for a long time and I was thinking of doing so before she leaves for UTech, but now that there is a possibility she would be going away to study abroad next year, I am not sure if the time is right. I would hate to disrupt her education," Officer Gregg replied. "Also, she is still healing physically from her attack and has a long way to go mentally. I don't want to add to her fragile state of mind."

Everyone agreed to wait before telling Dupree about her father. Tony left that night feeling better than he had in a long time. He hoped in his heart that everything would go as planned.

Chapter Thirty-four

As Dupree sat under the shaded area of the big mango tree reading her novel, she looked up to see a car coming up the driveway. She watched anxiously as Officer Gregg parked his car and made his way to her.

"Hi there, Dupree, how are you feeling?" Officer Gregg asked as he embraced her with an affectionate kiss on her right cheek.

"I'm doing very well, thank you, Officer Gregg."

Inwardly he flinched when she called him Officer Gregg. It was moments like this he really wanted her to know that he was her father, but he knew the time wasn't right. Hopefully one day soon he'd be hearing "Daddy." He took a seat beside Dupree.

"Well, you are looking better. I hope you are taking it easy on your leg and back. And don't forget your arm, too. They are healing nicely and we would like it to remain so," he added in a concerned voice.

"I am, sir. I think I'll be able to use a cane more than the crutches when I leave for college. I'll also be continuing the physical therapy for my back."

"Speaking of college, I think there is something we need to speak about," he said as he looked straight in her eyes.

Dupree quickly averted her eyes and stared at the concrete ground as if it were suddenly an exquisite piece of art.

"No, please look at me, my dear." Officer Gregg reached over and touched Dupree lightly on the arm. "Tony spoke to my wife and me about your plan to maybe study at NYU with him next year. He loves you very much and is really attached to you and wants what's best for you. Beverly and I feel the same way and we would like it very much if you would accept our offer to pay your tuition and other personal expenses."

Dupree stared at him in amazement without saying a word. Officer Gregg misinterpreted her expression and thought she was about to refuse their offer. It was very important to him that she allow him to do this, but how could he convince her without revealing too much?

"I know you are wondering why we would do this for you, but please believe me when I say it's because we love you. You mean a lot to me, Dupree, and one day you will understand how much. For now, please let me do this for you." He was a little surprised when tears began to fill his eyes. He really needed to get himself under control. He didn't want her to get suspicious or start asking too many questions.

"It's just that you have been through so much and I know in my heart this is what the Lord would want me to do," he quickly redeemed himself.

"But both of you have already done so much already and I know this will be a huge financial expense for you."

"We have been very blessed, Dupree, and we would like to share our blessings with you. We have more than enough for us and Tony. I just want you to have a secured future and there is no better way to do that than getting a good education."

"Oh, thank you so much, Officer Gregg. This almost seems like a dream to me. I have already talked to Aunt Madge and prayed about it and I'll accept your generous offer. Please express my heartfelt gratitude to Mrs. Gregg. I promise I won't let you down!"

Dupree wasn't sure what she had done to find such favor in God's sight, but she was humbled by His bountiful blessings. She hugged the man who was giving her a chance of a lifetime and, unbeknownst to her, the man who also gave her life.

"I love you very much," Dupree whispered from her heart and that was all it took.

The floodgates came wide open and the salty water charged from Officer Gregg's eyes. To have heard his daughter tell him that she loved him was something he would cherish forever. He knew she was telling Officer Gregg the Good Samaritan, and not her father, but right then it was all he had and he would take it. And at that wonderful moment an even stronger bond formed between father and daughter. But how long would this last?

After Officer Gregg left, an exhausted Dupree went to rest her back. She would wait until Mrs. Scott and Aunt Madge came back before sharing the wonderful news with Miss Angie.

Later that afternoon, they all sat around the dining table chitchatting after a delicious dinner when Dupree decided to break the news while they were all full and content.

"Mrs. Scott, Miss Angie, I have something I would like to tell you," she began in a meek voice. The chatting instantaneously ceased and three pairs of eyes turned toward her. Aunt Madge was already aware of what was going on.

"What's going on?" Mrs. Scott asked nervously. She hoped Dupree wasn't going to tell her that she had changed her mind about going away to the University of Technology.

Dupree relayed the plan for her to attend New York University the next year. By the time she was finished with her story, all three women were choked up, but in a good way.

"Oh, thank you, Jesus!" Aunt Madge exclaimed as loud as her small voice allowed.

Mrs. Scott jumped up from her chair and enfolded Dupree in her arms. She wanted what was best for Dupree and knew this was an investment on a successful future.

Miss Angie was next in line to receive her hug. She too was elated about Dupree's plans. She would miss her dearly but she felt Dupree needed to explore every good opportunity that came her way.

They all laughed joyously and spent some time talking some more about Dupree's exciting future. But would it be everything they hoped for?

Chapter Thirty-five

Tony drove to his parents' house, and parked his car in the driveway. They had all agreed that Tony would meet them at the house when they got off work and would all travel together to Thompson Town to go see Bishop Chude.

"I'm glad you came, baby." Beverly hugged him affectionately and he returned the warm embrace. His father came down the stairs and they did the "manly" embrace where they bumped shoulder to shoulder. *So far, so good*. Beverly opened the door and walked outside to the car, with her two men following close behind.

Tony watched as his father pulled up into the parking lot of a huge church. They all got out and were stretching their legs when the door opened and Bishop Chude stepped out to greet them. He was an elderly, overweight man of short stature with the biggest and warmest smile Tony had ever seen on a man. He hugged both his father and mother, and then turned soft, gentle eyes on Tony.

"So this is Tony. Mr. Soon To Be Going To College," he joked as he pulled Tony in for a warm embrace.

Instantly Tony felt comfortable with him. Bishop Chude invited them inside and they followed him down a long, narrow corridor to his office.

Bishop Chude asked Tony to pull over the La-Z-Boy chair for his mom and then he and Officer Gregg took the two remaining chairs. They all looked at Bishop Chude as he sat in his large chair facing them. It was getting a little uncomfortable in the office but Bishop Chude's eyes sparkled as he flashed his warm smile at them.

"First, let's pray before we begin. We need the presence of the Holy Spirit to guide us right now," Bishop Chude said. They all bowed their head and Bishop Chude began to pray.

"Okay, let us begin," Bishop Chude said in his gentle voice after ending the prayer. "I want everyone to know that everything said in this room remains in this room. I am not here to judge anyone, just to help you sort things out. So Brother Gregg, senior Gregg that is, I would like you to start by telling me what's going on."

Officer Gregg looked like a deer caught in a bright light and Tony snickered quietly. He thought it was funny that the one who created all the problems was now speechless. But Bishop Chude waited patiently until Officer Gregg finally found his voice and began to speak slowly.

"I . . . I . . . ahem . . . I would like to first apologize to my wife for my betrayal," he stuttered, looking deep into his wife's eyes. "And to my son for all the pain my behavior has caused them both." He looked over at Tony, who was fixated on something on the ceiling.

"It started out when I offered this young girl a ride home one night." His voice grew stronger as he looked at Bishop Chude with remorse. "Bishop, it was dark out and too late for her to be by herself. I can assure you I had no ulterior motive." His voice broke and he began to sob softly.

"Please, go on, son," Bishop Chude urged him gently.

"But she developed a crush on me and began to pursue me," he continued. "I knew it was wrong but I was unable to stop myself. God help me but I really tried."

Officer Gregg spoke of the sexual encounters at the high school and Beverly began sobbing, while Tony looked at his father in anger.

"Are you okay, my sister?" Bishop Chude asked Beverly, his eyes filled with compassion. She shook her head and he nodded to Officer Gregg to continue with his story.

It broke Officer Gregg's heart to see his wife crying and he could feel the steam pouring out of his son but he knew he had to finish what he started. They were there to get help and he would not start out by lying. He recalled Tiny's news that she was pregnant and how he threatened her into silence.

Tony jumped to his feet and began to pace the office in a heated rage. "I can't believe this rubbish!" Tony screamed, his right fist pounding into his open left hand.

"Son! Tony! Baby!" All three adults spoke at the same time. Beverly rose from her seat with her arms out to Tony but Bishop Chude shook his head and she sat back down.

"This couldn't be my father," he cried as angry tears drenched his face. "My father would never have done something like that!"

Tony walked over to the closed window, rested his head against the glass pane, and had a much-needed cry. He cried for the little lost girl who went looking for love in the wrong place, only to be betrayed by the hero she thought would have saved her. Tony cried for Tiny.

Bishop Chude got up and went to Tony. He wrapped his arms around him, and Tony, who was a few inches taller than the bishop, bent slightly and returned the comforting embrace while across the room Officer Gregg held Beverly in his arms. He whispered softly in her ear as she cried, consumed by the pain caused by her husband's ultimate betrayal. It wasn't as if this was the first time she was learning of his infidelity that resulted in a child, because she had known for years, but to actually listen to all the graphic details was too much for her.

It took awhile for Bishop Chude to get Tony to calm down, after which he led him back to his chair. He then went to a small refrigerator that was concealed behind one of the large plants and took out four bottles of water. Tony gratefully accepted the bottled water and drank thirstily. Beverly, who was still crying softly, and Officer Gregg gratefully drank their water. Bishop Chude handed out Kleenex and went back to his seat behind the desk. His eyes held so much compassion Tony felt like crying again, but he fought against it.

"It breaks my heart to see my brothers and sister in so much pain, but I take comfort in the fact that there is no problem that the Lord cannot fix. It might take awhile but you can rest assured it will be done," Bishop Chude told the Greggs. "Sister Gregg, I know this is very hard but, believe me, this is the hardest part; and for you too, Tony. So when you are ready, I would like the both of you to tell your side of the story. Sister Gregg, let's start with you."

It was a long, drawn-out, painful exercise but after they had all relayed their side of the story, Bishop Chude took over.

"As painful as that was for everyone, believe me, it was necessary. I wanted each of you to explain your actions and to express how you felt about what happened. You have to acknowledge that you did something wrong, Brother and Sister Gregg, before you can move on. But one important thing I would like to point out is that this happened before both of you got saved and turned your lives over to the Lord. When you repented your sins, the Lord forgave them all. You became new creatures, old things were passed away, and everything became new. Therefore, please remember you have already been pardoned for what you did and you must move on. Jesus wiped the slate clean!" Bishop Chude paused and looked pointedly at each of them before he continued. "On that note I would like to have some sessions with just Brother and Sister Gregg."

Both Officer Gregg and Beverly anxiously agreed. They knew those private sessions would make a big difference in their struggling marriage.

"Any questions so far?" Bishop Chude looked from one face to another. "No? Okay, we will continue," Bishop Chude said and broke the silence that had descended on the room. "Tony, my boy, I can only imagine what you are going through, but I know I would never fully understand because he who feels it, knows it. It must have been hard to find out that your best friend was actually your biological sister, and that your hero, your mentor, had done such a despicable act. And on top of that, your favorite woman in the whole world, who you have idolized since birth, was also guilty by her deception of covering it up.

"The Lord has forgiven them and He would want you to do the same. It won't happen overnight, but as a young Christian yourself, you know He admonished us to always forgive. I will share with you ways by which you can start on this journey and I can't emphasize too much how important it is for you to fast and pray. You have to seek God's guidance or you will be lost to your parents and them to you and we will not allow that to happen. 1 Peter 5:8 says, 'Be sober, be vigilant, because your adversary the devil, as a roaring lion, walketh about, seeking whom he may devour.'"

They had a few more successful counseling sessions with Bishop Chude and Tony planned on continuing his sessions until he left for college. His parents also informed him that they too would continue seeing the bishop as they worked through the darkness in their marriage. He was happy for them because he would really hate for them to separate now after everything they have been through together. Only time would tell.

Chapter Thirty-six

Dupree was excited as she got dressed that morning. Tony would bet here soon and she still wasn't ready. She slowly walked over to her closet and, being careful with her old injured arm, took down the new halter-top maxi dress that Beverly had bought her a few days ago. It was a multicolor light blue dress, with white and yellow flower patterns all over. It was a perfect fit and molded itself to her slim, shapely figure. Next she slipped on the comfortable pair of white sandals and grabbed her large white handbag. Taking one final look in the mirror before leaving, her flawless face was bare of makeup, except some lip gloss. Her straightened hair fell lustrously down her back.

Mrs. Scott and Miss Angie oohed and aahed when Dupree joined them on the veranda, and Aunt Madge simply stared at the stunning young lady she raised. Her baby was all grown up and in a few days she would be off on her own, attending college.

"You are absolutely beautiful, baby," Mrs. Angie said to her.

"I agree. I think I should go and borrow my dad's gun to take with us," joked Tony.

Dupree turned around and smiled at him. She was so caught up with the women lavishing her with compliments that she hadn't even seen him drive up.

"Thank you, everyone." Dupree blushed, embarrassed. "Are you ready to go, Tony? We have a long ride ahead of us."

"Your chariot awaits, madam," Tony replied and flashed his hand in the direction of his car sitting in the driveway.

The ladies laughed out loud and Dupree playfully punched him on the arm. She carried her walking cane in her right hand while Tony held her left arm as he helped her to the car. Dupree rarely used her crutches anymore and her back was responding great to the physical therapy. There were times when she even forgot that she was ever injured because she felt so great. However, Aunt Madge insisted that Dupree take her crutches with them and Tony placed them in the back seat of the car.

They were headed to the University of Technology in Kingston, St. Andrew. Dupree had already accepted their offer of admission and had submitted the enrollment contract by the said deadline. She had also returned her housing application, seeking on-campus residence. Today was orientation and registration day and she would be touring the campus, meeting with her advisor, paying her tuition and fees, meeting fellow students, and registering for classes.

Dupree was really hyped about the trip, not just to see her college but she was also very anxious to visit the big city of Kingston. For a country girl like herself, this was an absolute treat and as they headed out on their two-hour trip, she was fascinated by everything she saw.

As they entered Kingston the traffic thickened. Kingston is the capital of Jamaica and the largest city. It is at the core of Jamaica's economy as a majority of economic activity takes place within Kingston.

As Tony slowly made his way through Half Way Tree, it felt as if he was literally fighting to stay on the road. The taxis and buses seemed to come out of nowhere, cutting him off at every turn he took. Frustrated and impatient drivers had their hands on the horns as if they were actually playing a piano. People dodged in front of the car, trying to cross the street, not the least bit interested in the stoplights. He found himself pulling up so often to avoid hitting someone, his seat belt was probably groaning in protest. Vendors literally stood in the street trying to sell their wares and carts burdened down with goods darted in and out of traffic; it was man competing with machine. It was boisterous and Dupree loved it!

Wiping the perspiration from his face, Tony crept along Old Hope Road in the direction of the college. Finally he made a left turn onto the college campus. He parked in the visitors' parking lot and Dupree got out of the car, as fast as her back allowed, in great anticipation. Tony, however, took a minute to calm his nerves and to breathe a quick word of prayer.

They followed the signs that led them to the auditorium, where a chirpy assistant whose name tag read MERRY met them at the door. "Helloooo, how are you this beautiful morning? Welcome to UTech! We are glad to have youuuu!"

Tony wished she could share with him some of what she had for breakfast that morning. Her name really said it all. They introduced themselves and she checked her list before leading them inside to meet Dupree's advisor.

Dupree's advisor was Mrs. Samantha Barr, an attractive, friendly young lady who looked as if she should be a student herself. Dupree liked her immediately. After her registration was completed, they were taken on a tour of the beautiful campus.

"Wow, I think I'm going to really love it here," Dupree said to Tony enthusiastically. "This is the beginning of my dream to become a certified public accountant one day."

It was late afternoon when Tony and Dupree left the college, satisfied that they had accomplished everything they came to do. They headed back to Falmouth, "cheesing" all the way. Life was good, wasn't it?

Chapter Thirty-seven

Two days before Tony left for New York, and a little over a week before Dupree left for Kingston, Mrs. Scott decided to have a send-off party at her house for the both of them. It was amazing that a woman who once lived in seclusion would be opening up her home to strangers for such a festive occasion. What a difference it made having Jesus in her life.

Mrs. Scott contracted with Jimmy's Restaurant to do the catering. Mr. Jim and his wife, Shauna, who were huge fans of Dupree, gave her a big discount despite her protest.

Later that afternoon the food arrived and took up most of the kitchen space. There was enough food to feed an army and the tantalizing aroma teased the entire household. There were thick, rich stew peas with chunks of salted pig's tail, steamed parrot and king fish sandwiched between boiled okra, spicy jerked chicken, tender curried goat, gungo peas and rice, steamed cabbage, callaloo and popchoy and goat head soup, called mannish water. There were also two large cakes, Dupree's favorite, a red velvet cake and Tony's favorite, a black forest cake. There was a lot of lemonade, D&G soft drinks, ginger ale, Ting, and nonalcoholic wines.

By sunset the invitees were all in attendance and were having a blast. It was a buffet style dinner and people helped themselves to the wide spread of delicious food. The guests were talking and eating, laughing and dancing and having a jolly old time. The honored guests, Tony and Dupree, went around and spent some time with everyone. They were very happy with all the people who came out to offer their well wishes to them before they went off to college.

Later that night Mrs. Scott moved everyone into the living room for the toasts, opening of gifts, and prayer. Dupree and Tony went and sat in their designated chairs with big grins on their faces and Officer Gregg captured everything with his camera. He got teary-eyed as he looked at how happy his two children were. It was really a Kodak moment for him.

There were some heartfelt toasts and then it was time for the prayer before Dupree and Tony opened their gifts. Mother Sassy stepped forward and a few church members silently groaned. Mother Sassy was known for her long, drawn-out, unusual prayers and it only got longer when she caught the Spirit.

"Thank God we had something to eat or we would all die from hunger," Sister Nadine whispered to Sister Carol.

Everyone bowed their heads in reverence as Mother Sassy wobbled over to Dupree and Tony. She stood before Dupree and grabbed a hold of her head. Miss Angie took a few steps closer to Dupree. Even with their heads bowed, a few people had one eye open as they watched Mother Sassy intently.

"Papa Jesus, this is me, Mother Sassy, your honey-bunch, your little sugar plum, calling on your precious name, sweetie. I want you to cover this here chile under your blood. Praise Him! Wash her and make her pure. Halleluiah! Let her run far away from them forced ripe boys. Glory! Let her keep herself like a young lady. Blessed be His name! Let her do her schoolwork. Praise ye the Lord! Let her not go to that there Sodom and Gomorrah place and stray. Bless the Lord, oh my soul!"

By now Mother Sassy was in the Spirit and was shaking Dupree's head so hard, Miss Angie stepped forward and tried to free Dupree's head from her grip but Mother Sassy held on. Miss Angie was surprised that such a small, elderly woman could be so strong, and she firmly but gently managed to finally free Dupree's head. Forgetting about bowing their heads and closing their eyes, everyone was now looking in amazement.

"Hmmm, well, it's time to open the gifts," Mrs. Scott said loudly, trying to bring everyone's attention back to Dupree and Tony.

Dupree was shocked when she saw the large pile of gifts for her. She felt on top of the world! Officer Gregg gave her a CD player and she squealed in delight. She got a small color television from Beverly, and Mrs. Patty gave her an entire new wardrobe consisting of jeans, blouses, and shoes. She also received household items such as pots, a blender, and a mini microwave.

Mother Sassy was the last one to give Dupree her gift. Everyone held their breath as Mother Sassy opened the black plastic bag and slowly and dramatically pulled out the first item and held it up in the air for all to see. Someone gasped, a few opened their mouths in surprise, some were speechless, and others blushed in embarrassment.

Mother Sassy held up in the air a big, bright floral panty with frills all around it! It was at least three times Dupree's size. She smiled proudly and handed it to Dupree. "I asked Sister Imogene to sew this here 'drawers' especially for you. It is of good quality and very sexy. I bought the material myself. These are going to last you for years," Mother Sassy stated proudly.

"They certainly will, because she won't be wearing them," Miss Angie muttered to the amusement of those standing close to her. Beverly put her hand over her mouth to stifle her laugh.

Then Mother Sassy reached in the plastic bag again and pulled out the twin for the first panty. This one was purple and black with white frills.

"Oh, Lord, she made a funeral one, too," Sister Carol said under her breath.

"And it's pretty obvious Sister Imogene's eyesight has gotten worse." This was from Sister Nadine.

"Now I want you to wear these here drawers with pride and remember no man sees these except your husband," Mother Sassy said and Dupree blushed. "These are something for you to always remember your dear Mother Sassy."

"I'm sure she will," Sister Nadine whispered.

Holding the panties in her hand, Dupree plastered her biggest smile on her face and stuttered her thanks. Tony, unable to hold it back anymore, burst out in laughter. Mother Sassy gave him the evil eye but it was too late. This created a chain reaction and laughter washed over the room by the ones unable to control themselves. Tony laughed so hard he had tears running down his face. Dupree bit her lips to keep a straight face and went and gave Mother Sassy a bear hug.

It was a wonderful night, one Dupree would never forget, in more ways than one.

Chapter Thirty-eight

The next day Dupree got a call from her college advisor, Mrs. Samantha Barr, informing her that there had been some mix-up with her housing application. There were no more rooms available. Dupree was crushed. Everything was going so well and now this. Where was she going to live in Kingston? Would she still be able to attend college?

As if she were reading her mind, Mrs. Barr quickly answered both questions. "Unfortunately, there are a few students affected by this incident. However, there are some houses close to campus available for rent. I have another student, Amanda Gray, who was lucky enough to get a furnished two-bedroom apartment to rent in Mona Heights. She is from St. Mary and now she is looking for a roommate, which is why I called you."

Dupree was silent as she listened to Mrs. Barr. She had her mind set on living on campus but now it wouldn't be happening.

"Dupree, this is a very nice neighborhood and it is within walking distance of UTech. It will only be you and Amanda sharing the apartment. You will have your own bedroom; there is a nice living room, a kitchen, and a huge bathroom. There is also a telephone and cable television. It's a great apartment. I know because I went with Amanda and her parents to look at it. Also, the rent is not that much more than what you would be paying on campus. So what do you think?"

Theresa A. Campbell

"I would like to speak to my aunt about it first. Is it okay if I call you back in a few minutes?"

"Sure, but please get back to me soon. Amanda has other students interested in the apartment but I told her to wait until I spoke to you."

"Thank you, Mrs. Barr. I really appreciate you looking out for me. I'll call you back shortly."

Aunt Madge and Mrs. Scott were sitting on the veranda enjoying the beautiful day when Dupree came and sat across from them. They took one look at her face and knew that the phone call she'd just gotten had upset her deeply.

"What's wrong, baby?" Aunt Madge asked with concern and Dupree told her everything Mrs. Barr had told her. Both women were silent for a while before Mrs. Scott spoke.

"Okay, let's be optimistic about this. The Lord works in mysterious ways and I believe nothing happens without a reason. I knew Mona Heights very well and it was a good neighborhood. It has been a few years but I doubt that has changed. Also, Mrs. Barr had confirmed that it still is. It is close to campus and you will have your privacy. Personally, it sounds like a winner to me, Dupree. What do you think, Aunt Madge?"

"I think I would have preferred for her to be on campus with security being there and all. But on the other hand if this apartment is close by I guess it's not too bad. Also, both you and her advisor said it was a good neighborhood so I am not too worried. I have placed my daughter in the hands of the Lord and I know He will cover her under His blood," Aunt Madge responded.

Dupree listened to what her aunt and Mrs. Scott had to say and agreed. This might actually be a blessing in disguise. She could definitely make herself at home there. Also, if she got accepted by New York University she would only be there for a year anyway. She told the women she would be back and quickly went to call Mrs. Barr and told her she would be Amanda's roommate.

The next morning Tony came by before leaving for New York that afternoon. The two best friends looked at each through misty eyes. Tony also reminded his sister that he would be home for Christmas in a few weeks and this calmed Dupree somewhat. After saying good-bye to his sister, he went and hugged and kissed Aunt Madge, Mrs. Scott, and Miss Angie. They prayed for him and made him promise to keep in touch.

Over the next few days Dupree got ready to leave for college. She had a lot of stuff to pack but Mrs. Scott and Miss Angie helped her.

The morning of her departure, they had devotion in the den. All four ladies spent the time crying and praying for Dupree. But as Dupree hugged her aunt, she reminded Aunt Madge that she wouldn't be alone because the Lord was with her always. Still saddened by her grand-niece leaving, Aunt Madge finally let her go. After loading up the trunk and the back seat of Mrs. Scott's car, they were off.

The trip with Mrs. Scott was very pleasant. They talked all the way into Kingston and before they knew it they were in Mona Heights. Mrs. Scott pulled up into the apartment complex and parked. Dupree got out and looked around in curiosity. The neighborhood seemed very quiet and the grounds were well kept. They found the apartment and luckily it was on the ground floor because Dupree was still recuperating from her injuries. Mrs. Scott took two bags from the car and Dupree had one in her good arm, and her walking cane in the other. They approached the apartment and before they could ring the doorbell, the door flew opened and a beautiful young lady greeted them.

"Hello. You must be Dupree. I am Amanda."

"Hi, Amanda, yes, I am Dupree. Nice meeting you." Dupree then introduced Mrs. Scott and Amanda invited them in. She took them on a tour of the apartment and they were both impressed. The place was beautiful and sparkling clean. Dupree's room was large with a full-sized bed, two bedside lamps, a dresser, a large closet, a desk, and a chair. She loved it!

With Amanda's help, they made a few trips to the car to get the rest of Dupree's stuff and eventually everything was placed in the apartment. Mrs. Scott told Dupree to rest her back and she would unpack the stuff but she wouldn't hear of it. However, she promised to rest if it started to hurt. Dupree then explained to Amanda that she was in an accident and had broken her back, leg, and arm. She mentioned nothing of the attack. Amanda was surprised Dupree looked so well after being hurt that bad.

"It's the power of the Lord," Mrs. Scott answered after Amanda voiced her thoughts aloud. "Just one touch from Him is all you need."

With the three women working together, they got everything unpacked faster than they thought. Finally it was time for Mrs. Scott to leave; she had a long trip back to Falmouth. She took Dupree into her bedroom and hugged her for a long time. Fighting back tears, she made her promise to call if she ever needed anything and then she was off.

That night she and Amanda stayed up and chatted into the wee hours of the morning. Dupree liked Amanda; she seemed like such a wonderful person.

A very excited Dupree started college that Monday morning. Dupree had two classes that day and she liked her professors. She also met some new friends and already joined a study group. College life was going to be good. Dupree could already tell.

Chapter Thirty-nine

The next few days went by very fast as Dupree got busy with school. She had a lot of assignments to be completed, approaching deadlines for numerous projects and research papers, and many exams to study for. Dupree also had physical therapy with Mrs. Scott's friend Mario three days per week, and Officer Gregg sent him a check every month for his services.

With their busy schedule, Dupree and Amanda mostly saw each other at night. Dupree tried speaking to her a few times but noticed she wasn't as friendly as before. However, she passed this off as stress because she knew they both had a lot on their plates.

One afternoon after school, Dupree came home tired and hungry. As she entered the living room she heard sounds coming from Amanda's room. She grew concerned and walked toward the room. She had her hand poised at the door to knock when Amanda screamed out, followed by a deep masculine voice. Dupree was shocked; she suddenly realized what was going on beyond the closed door. She blushed embarrassedly and quickly went to her room. They had never talked about religion but she had assumed Amanda was a Christian as well, but obviously not. She was appalled at what she found out and decided to speak to her about it later.

A few hours later, as she completed an assignment, she heard the front door open and then close. She looked through her window and saw a man leaving. She waited a few minutes before going in search of Amanda and found her lying on the couch in the living room.

"Mandy, can I talk to you for a minute?"

Amanda stared at her without responding.

"I came home earlier and heard you and your company in your room. Then a few minutes ago I saw a man leaving our apartment."

"So what's the problem? It's no big deal," Amanda responded testily.

"But it is a big deal, Mandy. What you did was wrong. You are fornicating and that is a sin in the sight of God. Your body is the temple of the Lord."

"Yeah, sure, Miss Goody Two-shoes. Whatever."

Dupree was astonished at how rude Amanda had become. Where was the happy, friendly girl? "I just want to help you, Mandy. You are worth so much more than what you are settling for."

"If and when I need your help, I'll ask for it. Now stay out of my business!" Amanda then jumped up off the couch in anger, stormed into her room, and slammed the door.

Dupree was perplexed. She went to her room and did the one thing she knew: she prayed.

It was two days later before Dupree saw Amanda again. Dupree was in the living room watching television when she heard Amanda's room door open and she came into the living room. For a minute Dupree couldn't speak. She closed her eyes and opened them again but her eyes weren't deceiving her. Amanda was naked except for the small thong panties she wore!

"What are you doing, Mandy?" Dupree finally found her voice. "Walking around the house like this is so very inappropriate. Please do not do so again."

"I have nothing to hide and I'm gonna do whatever I please," Amanda replied in a condescending tone.

And things only got worse from that point on.

The next night Dupree was in the kitchen when the doorbell rang. She was about to get the door when Mandy came out of her room in a sexy red negligee and glided over to the door and pulled it open. A tall man stepped inside and lifted her in the air, his large hands gripping her buttocks real tight. They both kissed passionately before he lowered her to the ground and she turned around to lead him to her room. The man slapped her lightly on the butt as he walked behind her and they both laughed. Then the room door was slammed shut, leaving a horrified Dupree still staring at it in dismay.

Minutes later the sex sounds, as Dupree referred to them, quickly filled the apartment. Losing her appetite, Dupree threw the dinner she had just prepared in the garbage and went to her room. She felt the tears stinging her eyes but she refused to cry. So Dupree got on her knees and prayed. She asked the Lord to give her the strength to cope with her situation until He got her out of it. She also prayed for Amanda and her very low self-esteem.

But before things got better, they only got worse. Amanda used pots and plates and left them in the kitchen sink for days without washing them. Uneaten food was left on the stove until it began to rot. The bathroom was always dirty because as soon as Dupree cleaned it, Amanda messed it up. There was loose hair in the sink and the bathtub; dirty panties were on the floor and toothpaste was on the sink and the mirror. Dupree was real grossed out; she hated a dirty and untidy house. One of the things she had learned since she was a child was that cleanliness was next to godliness. Speaking to Amanda did not help. In fact, Dupree was convinced she took pleasure in what she was doing, but she decided to hang in there. She stayed locked up in her room for the most part and tried to avoid Amanda at all cost.

One afternoon Dupree went to the neighborhood pharmacy. As she browsed through items on the shelf, she heard a deep "Barry White" voice say hello from behind her. Every nerve in her body came alive and she slowly turned around to see the most handsome guy she had ever seen in her life. He smiled and the dimples in his cheeks winked at her. He had the most beautiful eyes and Dupree felt herself falling into them. He wore his hair in short dreads and she thought it was so cute. He was well dressed in his baggy blue jeans and white T-shirt with a new pair of white Adidas sneakers on his feet. He had a large diamond chain around his neck and a Rolex on his left wrist.

"Hello, I'm Suave."

"Hi," Dupree said in a squeaky voice. Feeling slightly embarrassed, she tried again. "Hi. My name is Dupree. Pleasure meeting you, Suave." *Much better,* she told herself.

"No, the pleasure is all mine, lovely lady. Has anyone ever told you that you have a very beautiful smile? You literally lit up the room when you smiled."

Dupree blushed and looked down at the floor shyly.

"So do you go to school around here?"

"Yes, I go to UTech."

"Cool, that's my old school. I graduated last year," Suave said.

Dupree asked him what he was doing now and he told her he did pharmaceutical sales. Dupree was impressed with the handsome, educated brother. He followed her to the cashier.

"Let me get those for you," Suave said as he pulled out his wallet.

"No, thank you. It's fine," Dupree responded.

"Cool, I respect that," Suave replied, nodding his head. "Most of the women I know only want something from me. So how about I give you a ride home?"

"Hmmm, you seem like a nice guy but I just met you," Dupree told him, shaking her head. "But thanks for offering."

"Okay. No problem," Suave said. "But at least take my number so we can keep in touch."

Dupree took a pen out of her handbag and jotted down the telephone number Suave told her on the back of the receipt.

"Got it," Dupree said with a big smile on her face. "I have to go now."

"Good night, beautiful." Suave grinned and winked at her. "Call me soon."

Dupree laughed and waved good-bye. She hastily exited the store and walked home in a daze.

When Dupree arrived home, the apartment was in total darkness. After turning on the light in the living room she headed toward her bedroom. She noticed Amanda's room door was wide open and briefly glanced inside as she passed by, and it was empty. *It is just as good*, she thought, *Amanda isn't home as yet.* But as she approached her bedroom she heard the sex sounds coming from inside. In a fit of anger she grabbed the doorknob and turned, but the door was locked. She began pounding on the door, screaming for Amanda to get out of her room, but she was ignored. In fact, Amanda took the sounds to a higher level for dramatic effect. Dupree wanted to cry so badly, but she was too mad.

She went into the living room and sat on the couch with her head laid back and her eyes closed. Her back began to throb and she knew it was the stress adding to her discomfort. She had a long day at school and just wanted to take a shower and get something to eat. So Dupree sat there and waited and waited.

Finally she heard her bedroom door open and Amanda came out as naked as a jaybird with a huge man following behind. This one was new, just like all the others. She ignored Dupree as she passed by with a smirk on her face and the man gave her a mocking wink. After closing the front door behind her exiting lover, Amanda still ignoring Dupree, went into her own room, and slammed the door shut. Dupree closed her eyes and took deep breaths, inhaling and exhaling. She did this a few times to calm her nerves.

"Help me, God. Please let this anger pass from me, Lord."

Feeling a little calmer she went into her room and felt nauseated. The room smelled disgusting and her sheet lay ruffled on the unmade bed. As she cautiously entered the room, she stepped on something real gross and shrieked out in fright. She looked down and realized it was a used condom on the floor. This was just too much for her. The tears won the fight and came rushing out in victory. Standing in the middle of the room, Dupree cried as she looked at the mess. This was her own personal space and her privacy was violated in the worst way. With the tears still running down her face, she went into the kitchen and got a pair of plastic gloves and went to work. She took off the soiled sheets and dumped them in the garbage bin. She used a piece of tissue to pick up the used condom and disposed of it. But as she searched for the air freshener, something snapped in Dupree's head.

She stormed out of her room and headed to Amanda's, where she kicked the door wide open. The door slammed loudly against the wall and Amanda, who was lying on her back still in the nude, jumped up in fear. She cowered in the corner of the bed and looked at Dupree with wide, frightened eyes. She had never seen her like that before but a person could take only so much and no more.

"Don't you ever disrespect me like that again," Dupree said through clenched teeth as she stepped closer to the bed. "That was my room and I am paying for it. You have violated my privacy for the last time. Do not ever do that again! Ever!" She screamed so loud, Amanda yelped in fear. "You have very low self-esteem and you are pathetic! You need help!" Dupree stormed back into her room and slammed the door so hard the apartment literally shook.

Still seething in anger, Dupree went and got some disinfectant and cleaned her room from top to bottom. Finally she lit one of the scented candles she got at her send-off party, and the lilac scent quickly covered the entire room in its sweet fragrance.

Amanda avoided Dupree like a plague over the next few days and stayed away from her room. It seemed as if the "little chat" Dupree had with her had worked, to some extent. Her bedroom was still a very busy place, with strange men in and out at all hours of the night.

Dupree waited anxiously for the fall semester to end so that she could go home and get some peace of mind for a little while.

Chapter Forty

Dupree was going home for Christmas break today. *Thank you, Lord!* She had already packed all her stuff and was standing outside, anxiously waiting for Mrs. Scott to come and get her.

The sound of an approaching car made Dupree's heart leap in her chest; her mouth opened wide. "No, it couldn't be," she said to herself and watched as the car came to a complete stop beside her and her best friend stepped out grinning like the Cheshire cat.

"Oh my gosh! Tony!" She screamed in delight and jumped into his waiting arms.

They hugged each other for a while without saying anything, just enjoying their reunion. Dupree felt herself tearing up as she hugged Tony. After everything she had been through, it was great to be going home to the people who loved her more than anything in the world.

"Well, well, well. Look at my little college coed," Tony teased as he gently pulled away, his eyes scanning Dupree from head to toe. "I miss you so much, sis."

"I miss you, too!" Dupree squealed, dismissing the slip-up Tony made as a term of endearment. "I am so glad to see you. Why didn't you tell me you were coming for me?" She punched him softly on the arm. Tony screamed as if in pain and the siblings laughed in contentment.

"I got home last night but I wanted to surprise you," Tony told Dupree. He helped her in the car before putting her bags in the trunk.

"I got the address from Mrs. Scott and came for you myself," he said as he maneuvered the car down Liguanea Road, headed home to Falmouth.

The siblings joked and laughed as they caught up on each other's lives. Well, on most things, anyway, because Dupree refused to tell anyone about what she was going through with Amanda. She wanted to take care of the situation herself and not to worry her family.

A few hours later Tony pulled up into Mrs. Scott's driveway and Dupree shrieked when she saw the group of people waiting outside for them. She flung the car door open once it slowed to a stop. She then hurried over to Aunt Madge, who was jiggling around excitedly in her wheelchair.

Dupree fell to her knees and engulfed her aunt into her arms. As she inhaled the familiar scent she had been missing all this time, her eyes filled with tears. "I miss you so much, Aunt Madge," Dupree said.

"Me . . . me too, baby," Aunt Madge whispered, her arms wrapped tightly around Dupree.

Finally freeing herself from Aunt Madge, Dupree went over and hugged Mrs. Scott, followed by Miss Angie. She felt a small tap on her shoulder and turned around to Officer Gregg standing with his arms wide open.

"Oooh! My God! I didn't see you," Dupree said as she hugged the man who had come to mean so much to her. She was so focused on getting to Aunt Madge that she had failed to notice Officer Gregg and Beverly waiting for her.

"Ahem," Beverly said in an attempt to get Dupree's attention.

"Mrs. Gregg! What a lovely surprise!" She went into the older woman's arms. "It's good to be home!" Dupree shouted with her arms above her head and her face lifted in the air. Everyone laughed.

***

Dupree enjoyed every minute of her Christmas break. She took part in everything at church; Bible Studies, prayer meetings, choir practice; and she sang in the choir for the Christmas program. It felt like old times and she loved it.

Dupree and Tony also spent a lot of time together.

"I'm so glad you are staying with your parents for Christmas," Dupree told him one afternoon. They sat Indian style on the lush green grass in the park having lunch.

"Me too," Tony replied, his eyes fixed on his corned beef sandwich.

"And you guys are not going out of town today, so you can come to prayer meeting later."

Tony nodded in agreement and took a sip of his Ting drink. There were a few afternoons when he had informed Dupree that he and his parents were going out of town for a few hours. But what Dupree didn't know was that they went to Thompson Town to see Bishop Chude for family counseling and it was slowly bringing the family back together.

Finally it was time for Tony to return to New York, and the night before he left, Dupree was invited to dinner at the Greggs' house. It was the first time she was going to their home and she was excited when Tony came and got her.

As they drove up the long driveway and the house came into view, Dupree gawked when she saw it. It was huge and very beautiful.

"You have a very nice home, Mrs. Gregg," Dupree complimented her while getting a tour of the house.

"Thank you, my dear," Beverly responded.

"I can't imagine what it was like for Tony growing up here. He is very lucky." Silence sashayed into the room. Not getting a response, Dupree turned away from the antique cabinet she was admiring in the dining room and looked at Beverly. Her brows knitted in confusion when she met the woman's watery stare.

"I'm sorry. I didn't mean to upset you," Dupree said as she nervously twisted her hands together. "Please—"

"No, no," Beverly replied. "It's okay. I'm just sorry that you never had all you deserved when you were growing up."

"I had all I needed." Dupree smiled. A tender look covered her face and her eyes sparkled with happiness. "I too have been very blessed in my own way."

"I'm so sorry," Beverly said just above a whisper. "Please forgive me."

"Sorry for what?" Dupree asked, puzzled. "There is nothing to forgive. Is there?"

"Dupree, there—"

"Mom!" Tony's voice interposed from the dining room. "I am hungry!"

"I swear that boy's belly has no bottom." Beverly chuckled nervously, and relief filled her voice. "Come on, let's go and have dinner." She reached for Dupree's hand and took a step but she pulled back slightly, forcing her to stop.

"Just a minute. You were saying something before Tony interrupted you. What were you saying?"

"Oh, it . . . it . . . it was nothing," Beverly stuttered. "Really." And she fled into the dining room with Dupree looking after her in confusion.

As all four sat down to dinner, Officer Gregg looked at his family having dinner alone together for the first time. It felt good to have his son, daughter, and wife with him in this wonderful setting. It was times like those he wished Dupree knew about their kinship and he knew in his heart the time would be coming soon.

***

That Saturday afternoon Tony returned to college, and Dupree the following day. As she and Mrs. Scott entered the dark apartment, Dupree flicked the light switch on, paused expectantly, and then breathed a sigh of relief at the silence that greeted her.

"Is something wrong?" Mrs. Scott asked from the doorway, her hands filled with two heavy bags.

"No, ma'am. I was just wondering if Mandy was home. Please come in," Dupree answered.

They spent a few minutes unpacking her stuff, which was mostly food this time, before Mrs. Scott left to return to Falmouth.

Monday afternoon, as Dupree left campus to head home, she stopped short when she saw Suave leaning up against the outside gate. She was surprised and blushed with embarrassment because she had never called him. But Suave didn't seem to have any grudges; he flashed his signature smile as she walked up to him.

"Well, hello, pretty lady. I had to camp out by your school just to say hi."

"I'm sorry that I didn't call. The last few weeks have been real crazy for me."

"That's an even better reason to call me, baby. I am here if you ever need someone to talk to or to just get away for a while." Suave was putting on the charm real heavy and Dupree was taking it all in, hook, line, and sinker.

"So how about having a drink with me by Sovereign?"

"I don't drink, sorry," Dupree responded, a frown on her face.

"Yeah, they do have nonalcoholic drinks. I just want to spend a few minutes with you. You know, get to know you some more." He flashed those dimples again and the butterflies returned to Dupree's tummy. She blushed and nodded her head in agreement. Suave led her over to a Mercedes-Benz SL500 and opened the door for her to get in. He was such a gentleman, Dupree thought as she leaned back into the soft leather seats and looked around the luxury car, impressed. Suave got in the car and asked her if she was okay. She told him yes and they were off to Sovereign.

They actually went to a small restaurant that Suave recommended after they decided to have dinner as well. It was a cozy, homely place and only had a few patrons inside. Suave led Dupree to a table in back so that they could have all the privacy they needed to chat. Still being the perfect gentleman, Suave pulled out her chair for her.

Dupree enjoyed her dinner but more so the conversation she shared with Suave.

"I've never been married and have no children," Suave said. "A brother has also never been in trouble with the law and is a law-abiding citizen." His dimples twinkled in his handsome face and Dupree gazed at him dreamily, in total adoration.

"I am proud to be a Christian and I attend church frequently," Suave continued. "I'm also trusting the Lord to help me open up my own pharmacy soon."

Dupree was impressed with Suave's ambition. As the words spilled from Suave's mouth like Liquid-Plumr down a drain, Dupree sucked it up like a dry sponge.

That night, after she got home, Dupree called Suave and they talked until the wee hours of the morning. With a big smile on her face, she fell asleep dreaming of Suave.

Over the next few weeks Dupree spent a lot of time with Suave and they talked on the phone every day. He was the first person she spoke to in the morning and the last one at night. He took her out to dinner at least once per week. He brought her flowers, chocolates, and stuffed animals. He wrote her love letters and poems. Needless to say, Dupree was in love.

"So we are still on for Saturday, right? I already made plans for us," Suave informed Dupree that Wednesday afternoon when he picked her up from school. That Saturday, January 25, 1996, was Dupree's and Tony's eighteenth birthday. Her loved ones wanted her to come home but she really wanted to spend the day with Suave. So Dupree informed them that she had plans with friends and surprisingly enough they understood, even though they were disappointed. However, Mrs. Scott promised to take her birthday gifts to her the following weekend.

Dupree felt like she was in a fairy tale. This was the best birthday ever! Suave came and picked her up early that morning in his sparkling-clean Mercedes-Benz. He had informed her the night before that they would be spending the day at the Pegasus Hotel in New Kingston but quickly added that he had gotten them separate rooms. Dupree was relieved because even though she loved Suave, she had no intention of crossing the line with him. She was a Christian and she would not allow herself to heed to temptation. But she knew she had nothing to worry about because Suave was a Christian himself and he understood.

They had the most delicious breakfast in the hotel's restaurant, after which they took off to the day spa for facials and body massages. After being pampered from head to toe, Dupree was so relaxed she wanted a nap. Suave escorted her up to her royal one-bedroom suite and told her he would be back for her in three hours to take her downstairs to dinner.

The suite was breathtaking but the king-sized bed was the best feature and Dupree took advantage of it. With a big smile on her face, she was asleep before her head hit the pillow.

A couple hours later the ringing of the telephone woke Dupree from a deep sleep. It was Suave telling her he would be there in about forty-five minutes to take her to dinner. She got up and had a shower, before she got dressed. Suave was right on time and whistled when she opened the door for him. Dupree blushed, very flattered by the attention. She wore a simple red dress that fell a little bit above the knees and fit perfectly to her slim body. The color also complemented her flawless ebony skin. She wore a pair of low-heeled black strappy sandals, and her thick hair was pulled back in a bun, highlighting her high cheekbones. The only jewelry she wore was a pair of gold knob earrings that Suave had given her last week after he took her to get her ears pierced. This was something Dupree would have never thought of doing, but Suave liked it, so she did it for him.

They had a romantic candlelight dinner overlooking the pool, after which Suave suggested they go back to her suite and talk for a while before bidding her good night.

As they sat on the couch, Dupree rested her head on his shoulder and he had his arm around her. With her eyes closed, she listened to his sexy voice as he whispered loving words in her ear. She felt relaxed and comfortable as they chatted about everything. Then she felt his mouth on hers and jumped up in shock, accidentally hitting him in the face with her hand. Dupree ran into the bathroom and closed the door. She was embarrassed by her childish behavior. She was eighteen years old and was behaving like an eight-year-old child. She could just imagine what Suave thought of her now. For heaven's sake, it was only a kiss. It wasn't as if she was committing fornication or anything like that. It was just an innocent kiss between two people who cared about each other. What was the harm in that?

There was a knock on the door. "Dupree, it's me," Suave said from behind the door. "Can I talk to you for a minute, please?"

Taking a deep breath, Dupree opened the door to see Suave standing there with a sad look on his face.

"I'm really sorry for what I did, sweetheart. It's just that we had such a romantic day and I just wanted to tell you how much I care about you. Please forgive me." His sad puppy eyes met hers pleadingly.

Dupree felt worse than before. The man she felt safe to say she was falling in love with after only a month was just showing his love for her and she messed up.

"No, I'm the one who is sorry. I was just surprised when you kissed me because I have never done anything like that before. Thank you for the best birthday I have ever had. I care about you too, very much."

Suave took her in his arms and told her everything was okay. He gave her a light kiss on the cheek, wished her a happy birthday again, and bid her good night.

Chapter Forty-one

Dupree got home around noon the next day still feeling as if she were floating on air. The phone rang when she got in her room.

"Helloooo," Dupree sang into the phone.

"Hello, sweetheart," Suave said melodiously. "I miss you already."

"I miss you, too," Dupree said with a big smile on her face.

"Listen, baby. I need to tell you something," Suave said in a serious tone.

Dupree's hand gripped the phone receiver tighter. Her heart leaped in her chest. "Yes?" she said nervously.

"Dupree, I have fallen in love with you," Suave said softly. "I love you, girl."

Dupree squealed in delight. "I love you too."

"And, baby, I just want you to know how much I respect you for not having sex with me," Suave replied happily. "Again, I'm sorry if I made you uncomfortable."

"It's okay." Dupree replied, her voice laced with adoration. "I'm just so happy to have such a wonderful boyfriend like you."

The couple laughed and talked some more, then made plans to see each other that night. It looked as if Dupree had finally found her Prince Charming.

A few days later Dupree was working on a project for school when the phone rang. It was Aunt Madge.

"Hi, baa . . . baby, how you doin'?"

"I'm doing great, Aunt Madge. School is going great."

"That's go . . . goo . . . good to hear, sweetheart," Aunt Madge replied in her childlike voice. Her words were very slow and sometimes she stuttered but her speech continued to improve every day and Dupree understood her well.

"Over the last few days you have been on my mind more than ever, but I have been praying for you as always," Aunt Madge continued. "Remember there are some wolves out there in sheep's clothing. I have taught you to pray and to study the word of God because it is food for our spiritual growth. Honey, don't ever lose sight of the Lord, okay?"

Dupree hung her head in shame and was glad Aunt Madge couldn't see her face. She hadn't prayed in days, something that she used to do a few times a day. And as for reading her Bible, she wasn't even sure where it was. This was the beginning of Dupree's spiritual demise and she didn't even know it.

One day Mrs. Scott called Dupree to let her know a Miss Bulgaria had called for her from New York University. She didn't want to leave a message, so Mrs. Scott gave her Dupree's telephone number at the apartment. Dupree was nervous. Miss Bulgaria probably didn't want to leave a message of bad news. Dupree hung up the phone with a dreaded feeling in her gut. Within seconds almost the phone rang. It was Miss Bulgaria.

"Hello, may I please speak to Dupree?" a woman said in a thick American accent.

"This is she."

"Dupree, my name is Miss Bulgaria, calling from the admissions office of New York University. We would like to thank you for your interest in studying with us here at NYU. However . . ."

Here it comes, Dupree thought and tears welled up in her eyes. She was really looking forward to attending New York University with Tony.

"We are not accepting any more international students for this fall semester as you have requested," Miss Bulgaria continued.

Dupree swallowed the lump in her throat as she choked up. With tears running down her face, Dupree mustered up enough strength to respond. "Okay. I am very disappointed, but thank you for letting me know. Good-bye."

"No, no, Dupree, please don't hang up the phone. I am not finished yet. While you weren't accepted for this fall, you were accepted for next spring. I'm calling to see if this would be okay with you. We have a lot of international students on standby; therefore, every vacancy counts."

Dupree started the fall semester at UTech in September of 1995. She wanted to attend to NYU for the fall of 1996 but was instead accepted for next spring, which would begin late January of 1997.

Dupree was in shock. "So instead of starting this September, I would start January of next year?" she asked Miss Bulgaria.

"That's right," Miss Bulgaria replied.

"Yes! Yes! It is fine with me, Miss Bulgaria. Thank you so much!"

"Great. I am going to make a note of it and I'll be sending you an enrollment package that covers everything needed to complete your admission to NYU. Do you have any questions for me?"

"Not at this time."

"Well, let me give you my telephone number. If you do later, please feel free to call me. I'll speak to you soon."

"Thank you again, Miss Bulgaria."

Dupree took Miss Bulgaria's number, and then hung up the phone. She screamed out in glee in the empty apartment and danced from one room to the next.

Dupree called all her loved ones and shared the great news. Her final call was to Officer Gregg.

"Congratulations, my dear," Officer Gregg said to Dupree on her acceptance to NYU. "Please remember our agreement still stands. Beverly and I will be footing the bill for you to study in New York."

"Thank you, sir," Dupree replied ecstatically.

Dupree needed a summer job. The school term would end late May and she would be in Jamaica for that summer. She'd also be doing an additional fall semester at UTech that September as she wouldn't be going to New York until next year January.

She had applied for summer jobs at a few accounting firms, including BDO Jamaica, Deloitte & Touche Jamaica, and PricewaterhouseCoopers Jamaica. If she didn't get a job, she would have to go back home to Falmouth for the summer and she didn't want to leave Suave.

Dupree had developed a love for Suave. So she waited and prayed that the phone call offering her a job would come soon.

Chapter Forty-two

Today was an important day for Dupree because it was her beau's birthday and she was cooking him dinner. It was Friday, April 3, and Suave would be twenty-three years old.

That afternoon he was running late. As he pulled up to Dupree's apartment and parked, he quickly gave himself a pep talk to play it cool with Dupree. He did, though, eventually want to close the deal on Dupree. It had taken a few months longer than he thought but he could tell she would be worth the wait. He had visited her at the apartment a few times and they had gotten past the kissing stage. Dupree was now more than comfortable with it because Suave had convinced her that it wasn't a sin and nothing was wrong with it. In fact, she had gotten to love it so much she was now the one who initiated the passionate kisses they shared. A few times things got real heated, but she always managed to stop before anything happened.

Suave and Dupree had a great candlelight dinner that she had prepared. He had to admit, the girl could really cook. If ever he was ready to settle down, Dupree would be a likely candidate.

After dinner Suave and Dupree cuddled on the couch enjoying a glass of Moët champagne. This was something that Suave had also introduced Dupree to. The first time he offered it to her she was reluctant and told him she didn't think Christians should drink alcoholic beverages, but Suave reminded her that Jesus turned water into wine, and she could read it for herself in St. John 2:1–11. He knew Dupree would protest when he bought it, but thanks to his religious-fanatic sister he actually remembered that story and used it to convinced Dupree. At first she didn't like the taste, but over time it grew on her and now having a glass of wine after dinner was a natural thing for her.

They had the entire apartment to themselves because Amanda hadn't been home in two days and Dupree was happy for the privacy. As she sipped her wine, she felt more relaxed and mellow. She loved the tantalizing sensation it ignited in her and as soon as she finished her first glass, Suave quickly refilled it. Dupree was about to stop him because one glass was her limit, but tonight was a special night, so she would make an exception; after all, it was her beau's birthday. The second glass led to a third and by then Dupree was more than tipsy. Suave looked at her anxiously. He began to kiss Dupree and she reciprocated willingly. She loved the way she was feeling and fed on Suave's mouth hungrily. Dupree was so caught up in the moment she didn't protest the fact that Suave had taken her into the bedroom, and in no time at all she was naked.

The only light in the room was the moonlight shining through the glass-paned windows and as Suave looked at Dupree's body, he licked his lips in anticipation. His months of hard work and patience was about to pay off big time. He quickly went and closed the window blinds for privacy and illuminated the room with the bedside lamp. Then in record time he took off his clothes and joined Dupree on the bed. Through glazed eyes, Dupree saw Suave coming toward her and wondered why he was naked, but before she could say anything, Suave was kissing her and she became caught up in the moment once again. They were just kissing as they always did, Dupree thought groggily; there was no harm in it. In fact, Suave knew how she felt about premarital sex and they had both agreed to wait until they got married.

Dupree was experiencing feelings she had never felt before but nothing had prepared her for the sharp pain that flashed through her body. It was enough to sober her up and she looked up at Suave with wide eyes.

"No, no, no," she mumbled, her eyes widened in shocked. With as much force as she could muster, Dupree shoved Suave off of her, almost knocking him off the bed.

This angered him. He got off the bed and looked down at her with an evil grin on his face. "Hey, listen, baby, the deed is already done so you might as well just let us enjoy the rest of our night. After all, it is still my birthday," he said mockingly.

"How could you, Suave? I trusted you," Dupree cried, tears running down her face.

"Baby, it was bound to happen sooner than later. It was much later than I wanted, but better late than never, right?"

"Get out! Get out now!" Dupree screamed in anger. "I hate you!"

Suave looked at her and laughed before slowly putting on his clothes. He looked at Dupree crying on the bed and felt no remorse for her. In fact, he was pissed off that he didn't get to show her a few things he had planned for her. But he would give her some time to get herself together.

Without another glance at Dupree, a now fully dressed Suave left the apartment, slamming the door shut on his way out.

Dupree was crying so hard her entire body shook. As a result of the wine she had consumed earlier and her disgust with what had happened, Dupree literally felt sick to her stomach and threw up all over herself, too weak to make it off the bed. She wished she could open her eyes and realize she was having a nightmare, but her body reminded her it was all too real. She reached over and turned off the bedside lamp, flooding the room in darkness.

Dupree awoke the next morning feeling as if she had gotten run over by a big truck. She had cried until the wee hours of the morning but now she only felt worse. *How could I have been so stupid?* she asked herself as she stared into the darkened room. She had not only let her family and friends down, but she had let down the Lord. What she did last night was unforgivable because she had defiled her body in the worst way.

Later that afternoon, all cried out, a puffy-eyed Dupree reluctantly got up to use the bathroom. She hadn't been outside the room since last night and she looked and smelled awful. She slowly turned on the light and saw the evidence of her sin on the bed sheet. She felt nauseated and made it to the bathroom just in time. Sitting on the floor with her head hanging over the toilet bowl, Dupree wept. It wasn't a dream after all; she had really fallen out of grace with the Lord. She had sinned physically and mentally. The two things she had cherished all her life were gone in a second: her salvation and her virginity. But while she wasn't able to get back the latter, the first was still available to her. However, Dupree wasn't in that frame of mind. She felt unworthy of God's forgiveness because she was unable to forgive herself.

After soaking in the bath for almost an hour, Dupree went about "cleansing" her room. She took the soiled bed sheets from the bed and put them in the garbage. At the rate she was throwing away sheets, she would soon be sleeping on the bare mattress, she thought sarcastically. Next, she reached for the disinfectant, and before she knew it, all the evidence of the disastrous night had disappeared from the room, but not from her mind.

As she lay on her bed curled up in a fetal position feeling sorry for herself, the telephone rang. Dupree let it ring without answering it because she didn't want to talk to any of her loved ones or Suave. She knew she was wrong for placing all the blame on Suave because she played a part in what had happened. Maybe she was the one who led him on. Maybe she shouldn't have kissed him first. Maybe she shouldn't have worn that dress. Dupree was trying to think of every possible way to explain Suave's disgusting behavior and by doing so she was willing to take all the blame herself. She just didn't want to admit that the man she loved and trusted had betrayed her in the worst way.

The sudden ringing of the telephone later that night shattered the silence of the room and Dupree reached for it hesitantly. "Hello," she answered in a soft voice.

"Yo, waddup?"

Dupree stared at the phone in surprise; she had never heard Suave speak like that before. Where was the perfect English-speaking Suave she knew? "Suave?" She had to confirm it was really him.

"That's right, hot stuff, Smooth Suave in da house! Listen, yo, I'm on my way to your crib. We about to finish what we started last night, cool?"

"What?" Dupree was shocked.

"You heard me, baby. I'm tired of the front I've been putting on. Keeping it real; I don't do church, I don't do college, and I'm a thirty-four-year-old man with eight kids by six baby mommas."

The telephone fell from Dupree's hand onto the bed beside her. She closed her eyes as the room became a merry-go-round. Feeling queasy, she clasped a hand over her mouth, willing her flip-flopped stomach to settle down. The tears flowed as the pain of deception draped over her like a coarse acrylic sheet.

This can't be happening. Dupree took deep breaths as she struggled to breathe. Her head felt like a boiled egg in a microwave. *No, no, no. This is not real.*

It was just a few minutes later but it seemed like hours when Dupree groggily reached for the telephone, her eyes still tightly shut against the throbbing in her head. She slowly raised the receiver to her ear. Amazingly, the line was still open.

"Yo! Yo!" She heard Suave screaming into the phone. "Talk to me!"

Dupree wanted so badly to hang up the telephone but she also needed some answers. Her mind just couldn't grapple the situation.

"You said you wanted to expand your pharmacy business," Dupree whispered, her voice breaking. "And that you attended UTech." Her throat constricted as she struggled to breathe. Dupree took a deep breath in, and let a deep breath out.

"Baby, the only business I'm trying to expand is my drug empire," Suave said proudly. "And as for UTech, I do have some very loyal customers there." His mocking laughter echoed into Dupree's beating eardrum.

Dupree felt sick to her stomach. Too stunned to respond, she slowly hung up the phone and began to cry again. She had been so stupid. What was she going to do now? Her life was as good as over.

Chapter Forty-three

Dupree awoke to her tummy grumbling later that night. She knew that she had to try to get it together. She also had to call home soon before someone came looking for her. She gingerly made her way off the bed and headed for the bathroom to have her bath. After her shower, she prepared something to eat that tasted like cardboard but ate it anyway, after which she went into her room to make the dreaded call home.

As she waited for the phone to connect, Dupree mentally prepared herself to remain as calm as possible; then Aunt Madge answered the phone. Dupree greeted her in a too-chirpy voice, but the woman who had raised her since she was a baby wasn't to be fooled.

"What's wrong, baby?" Aunt Madge asked with concern.

Dupree knew she couldn't lie to her aunt but she couldn't afford to tell her the entire truth either, so she stayed somewhere in the middle. "I'm just feeling a little bit under the weather, Aunt Madge. I'll be fine." Aunt Madge paused for a while and Dupree knew she really wasn't buying what she was selling.

"Baby, please know I am always here for you. I am very proud of you and I will be until the day I die. Remember what I told you before you left for school? I said if you ever fall down, you better pick yourself up and get back on track. You have been to hell and back, yet you survived. The Lord says in St. Luke 10:19, 'Below, I give unto you power to tread on serpents and scorpions, and over all the power of the enemy: and nothing shall by any means hurt you.'"

This was just what Dupree wanted to hear as she sat on her bed, hugging her teddy bear close in her arms. She began to feel a sense of hope; maybe, just maybe, she might actually get out of this mess and forget anything ever happened between her and Suave.

"Thanks, Aunt Madge, I really needed to hear that. I love you."

"I love you too, baby. Remember that the Lord loves you as well."

Dupree was sure of her aunt's love but she still had doubt about the other.

Dupree spent the next week like a zombie for the most part. At school she went through the motions but looked lifeless and lost. A few of her classmates noticed the change in her demeanor and asked her about it. It was a complete contrast to the happy, vibrant young lady they knew. But Dupree gave the generic response to everyone who asked: "I'm fine." But that was the furthest from the truth.

Chapter Forty-four

It had been two weeks since Dupree had hung up the phone on Suave and she hadn't seen or heard from him since. But that changed one afternoon as she left school. Dupree was on the sidewalk waiting for the stoplight to change when she saw Suave coming toward her with his arms around a beautiful young girl. She got real nervous as it was the first time seeing him since that awful incident.

As he got to where Dupree stood, Suave passed by laughing and chatting to the object of his next deception without even a glance in Dupree's direction. It was as if she didn't exist. As Dupree turned around and looked at the back of the man who had once told her he loved her, only to disrespect her, she felt the tears well up in her eyes but refused to cry. However, she couldn't help feeling as low as a worm crawling on its belly.

It was days later, on a beautiful Friday evening. Dupree walked home feeling more comfortable than she had in weeks. It was over three weeks since her "fall from grace" but who was really counting?

Upon entering the apartment, Dupree heard the usual sex sounds coming from Amanda's room and rolled her eyes in disgust. Dupree had to pass by Amanda's bedroom to get to hers at the end of the hall, and as she got closer she noticed that Amanda's room door was wide open. She got a little apprehensive about passing, but, try as she might, Dupree couldn't help glancing into the bedroom, and got the shock of her life. Nothing in the world would have prepared her for what her eyes were looking at.

A naked Amanda was having sex with an equally naked man. But it just wasn't any ordinary man. Dupree placed her hand over her mouth to suppress the scream that rose in her throat as she stared straight into Suave's sardonic eyes.

Suave looked at Dupree with a smirk on his face as if it was the most natural thing in the world for him to be having sex with her roommate. Amanda laughed maliciously at the astonished look on Dupree's face and increased her sexual dramatics for more effect. Suave went right along with her. They never missed a beat or paused even once with Dupree frozen in time looking at them.

She wasn't sure what was happening, but Dupree slowly advanced in the room, a river flowing from her eyes. Her steps were slow and almost robotic as she approached the couple on the bed. Suave saw the haunted look in Dupree's eyes and jumped off Amanda in alarm, while Amanda was too scared to even move. They both thought Dupree would have run to her little room and cry her heart out, but that wasn't what happened. Suave watched her come closer and wondered if she had a gun they weren't aware of. Amanda looked on, horrified.

Dupree did something that threw them for a loop.

"I'm sorry," Dupree whispered between sobs. "I'm sorry I gave the devil so much power over me that two people I cared so much about felt it necessary to degrade themselves this way. I have failed not just myself but the both of you as well. And if someday the Lord feels I am worthy enough to be redeemed, I'll be praying your souls out of hell."

Suave looked down in embarrassment and quickly grabbed his shirt off the floor and placed it in front of him, while Amanda used the pillow to cover her nakedness.

Dupree, still sobbing, looked at them sadly before turning around and leaving the apartment. As she walked along Old Hope Road, crying, a few people stopped and stared. She had no idea where she was going until she ended up back on the school's campus. Dupree found a large tree in a dimly lit section of the campus and sat under it, crying. A few minutes later she felt someone touch her shoulder and jumped in fright. She looked up through swollen eyes to see her classmate, Jasmine, looking down at her.

Jas, as she was affectionately called, sat on the ground beside Dupree and put her arms around her. She almost felt the pain vibrating through Dupree's body and she was saddened by it. She asked Dupree what was wrong but she only shook her head and cried harder. Jas never took no for an answer. She kept asking Dupree to talk to her as she rocked her gently. Finally, Dupree gave in, and although she felt ashamed, she needed to talk to someone before she went crazy. So with her head hanging down, she told Jas everything that had happened between her and Suave. She told her about Suave and Amanda's ultimate betrayal. When she was finished she looked up at her friend to see the condemnation in her eyes, but she only saw tenderness shining through the tears rolling down her cheeks.

"You are staying at my place tonight and for as long as you want. My last roommate moved in with her boyfriend a few weeks ago, so I have an empty bed. Let's go back to the apartment and get some of your stuff," Jas told Dupree.

"No. No, Jas. I can't go back there," Dupree told her, shaking her head.

"It's okay, girlfriend. I am sure the show is over by now, and those two deserved each other. We will be in and out in no time."

Dupree finally agreed, although she hated the thought of seeing Amanda and Suave again.

As they approached the apartment, reggae music greeted them at the door. It seemed as if Suave and Amanda had used the time to regroup and were continuing their party. Jas took the key from Dupree's trembling hand and opened the door before gently pushing her inside.

Amanda was sitting on the couch topless in a skimpy bikini panty while Suave only had on a pair of tight briefs, puffing away on a marijuana spliff. Dupree looked at him in disgust. She had no idea he smoked but there were a lot of things about the creep she never knew.

Jas took her hand and they passed by them without a word and went into Dupree's room. They stopped short as they entered and saw all her clothes spread all over the bed and the floor. Her television was unplugged and was upside down on the unmade bed and her CD player was face down on the floor. Dupree looked around without saying a word and heard Jas say something under her breath. Jas liked to refer to herself as a "trying" Christian and she would inform anyone unfortunate enough to make her mad that her tongue was yet to be saved. She was a dignified young lady but she grew up in the ghetto and was a street gal through and through.

Jas stormed out into the living room and went and stood over a grinning Amanda.

"What the heck is this? Why did you do that to her stuff?" she asked Amanda angrily.

"I want that skank out of here!" Amanda shouted with her big boobs dancing erotically as she waved her hands in the air angrily.

"Skank? You are calling myyyyyyyyyyy friend skank? You have all the nerve in the world." Jas looked down at Amanda like she made her nauseated just being in the same room with her. "See, you are looking for company but I've got some news for you. My friend never has and never will be lowered to your standard. She is way above your level, Sketel!" By now an angry Jas was shouting and had stepped closer to Amanda. "Sketel" is West Indian slang for a girl who has been around the block once or twice and shows no shame, to put it mildly.

Suave laughed out as he sat back farther on the couch, obviously enjoying the show. Dupree rushed out of the room and grabbed Jas, telling her it was okay before she wiped the floor clean with Amanda.

"Oh heck to the no, it's not okay! "

"I just want to get out of here," Dupree told her.

Amanda opened her mouth to speak but one glance from Jas shut her up. She knew it was best to keep quiet before she got the whooping of her life. Amanda had thought only Dupree would be coming back to the apartment and by no means was she prepared for Hurricane Jas. With Suave high as a kite and laughing like he was crazy, she knew she didn't have much of a backup.

Jas reluctantly allowed Dupree to pull her back into the room, angrier now that she didn't get a go at Amanda.

"Okay, this is what we are going to do. I am going to call my friend Bullfrog to come and get your things. He has a van that he uses to run a little illegal taxi business but it will hold all your stuff," Jas informed Dupree, who nodded her head in agreement.

Dupree wasn't sure what should worry her more: a man named Bullfrog or the illegal taxi business he had. But luckily Bullfrog was close by, dropping off a passenger, and in less than five minutes he was ringing the doorbell.

Jas strolled out into the living room to let Bullfrog in and passed Amanda sulking on the couch, her arms crossed over her naked breasts, with Suave lying with his head in her lap, a silly grin on his face from the marijuana he had smoked. She gave them both the evil eye and opened the door for Bullfrog.

Bullfrog stepped into the apartment and looked at Amanda and Suave with disgust. While he didn't know them personally, he knew of them and it was nothing flattering. Dupree looked up from picking up her clothes off the floor when Bullfrog came into the room, and right then and there she knew where the name came from. However, whatever Bullfrog lacked in the looks department he made up for in his mannerism.

He made trips to the van carrying Dupree's television, CD player, clothes, and other personal items. With the three of them working together, in less than an hour Dupree had taken all her stuff out of the apartment. She felt Jas take her hand as she prepared to pass through the living room to leave. Amanda and Suave were spooned on the couch, with Amanda looking victorious as she watched Dupree leaving, and Suave appeared nonchalant.

Instead of hatred or anger, Dupree felt sympathy for the two misguided souls. With Jas holding her hand, she stepped out of the apartment and never looked back. And Amanda, still wanting to have the final say, ran to the door.

"I got your man!" she screamed and slammed the door so hard it echoed throughout the neighborhood.

Chapter Forty-five

Jas lived in Olympic Gardens, a community that was often divided by politics, drugs, and violence. As Bullfrog drove through the community, Dupree saw people hanging out on the streets engaged in different activities. Men were playing dominoes, smoking, and having a drink while women sat in groups laughing and talking. Little children ran around, getting in a little more fun before their bedtime.

Soon Bullfrog pulled up in front of a two-story tenement house. Outside looked as if it was in need of some repairs, and when they got inside, Dupree realized the inside needed some as well. Jas only had one bedroom and shared a bathroom and kitchen with six other people. Her room was very small with two small camp-sized beds, a dresser, and a closet, but it was clean and neat. Jas also had pictures of her family hung on the wall, giving it a homely feeling.

"I know it's not much, Dupree, and tomorrow we can start looking for better accommodations for you because I am sure you are not used to these humble dwellings."

Dupree laughed so hard Jas began to wonder if the events of the night had finally caught up with her in an unstable sort of way. "Are we okay? Do I need to get the men with the straitjackets?" Jas asked apprehensively and Dupree howled harder with laughter.

She hadn't really laughed in days and it felt real good. "Oh, Jas, if you only knew, girl," Dupree told her. "I am going to have to tell you about my life someday. I will be fine here with you until I get somewhere to live. Also, if I don't get a summer job, then I will be going back home for the summer anyway."

Dupree had too much stuff to fit in Jas's small room, so they piled everything in a corner and left most her clothes in the suitcases, taking a few necessary pieces and hanging them in the closet. After unpacking as best they could, Jas showed Dupree the rest of the house she had access to, which was just the bathroom and kitchen. Even though it was getting late into the night, the house was very noisy. Reggae music competed with televisions for the highest volume. Screams and shouts were coming from upstairs directed to someone downstairs. Pots were banging and babies were crying. It was chaotic sounding.

"How do you get to study with all this noise?" Dupree asked Jas as the girls sat on her bed chatting.

"I think I have gotten a little used to it, although it can be hard at times. That is one reason why I always stayed back at school to study."

"But why don't you live somewhere else?"

"I can't afford anywhere else. My mother lives in a two-bedroom house with nine children she is working hard to take care of without any of the seven baby daddies. I finally moved out and came here to live after I got a partial scholarship to UTech, working weekends at Tastee Bakery to make ends meet. But I am just trying to hang in there until I finish college and can get a good job."

It now became clearer to Dupree why she felt so close to Jas: they were both fighters.

The next morning Dupree woke up exhausted.
"Good morning!"

Dupree looked over and saw Jas sitting up in bed with a big grin on her well-rested face. "What's so good about the morning?" Dupree rolled her eyes in distress.

"What's wrong?" Jas asked with concern and patted the space beside her.

Dupree came over and sat, her face etched in despair. "I need to call home but I don't know what to tell my family. I don't want to lie to them but I can't tell them the truth either," she explained and became choked up.

"I think you can tell them the truth and just eliminate a few things," Jas advised. So they both got dressed and went to use the public phone by the main road, as Jas didn't have a telephone in the apartment.

"We got into an argument and she put me out of the apartment," Dupree told Mrs. Scott.

"I am coming to get you right now!" Mrs. Scott replied. "Give me the address and I'll be there in a few hours."

"Mrs. Scott, please remember that I still have school." Dupree tried to calm her down as she deposited more coins into the phone. "It's best if I stay with Jas while I am looking for a new place to live."

Mrs. Scott asked her if she needed more money but she said she had enough. Mrs. Scott had insisted that Dupree open an account at the bank, and she had deposited enough money for Dupree to buy food and pay her rent and other bills for the school year. Dupree refused to accept any more money from her. She had to get out of this predicament by herself.

Dupree finally got the ladies to calm down somewhat after assuring them she wasn't alone because she had Jas with her.

Jas and Dupree spent the entire day by the public phone calling apartments listed in the newspaper but had no luck. Most were already rented and the available ones were more than three times what she had been paying. But Dupree decided not to give up.

***

It was two weeks later and Dupree was still living with Jas, unable to find an apartment. Jas silently wondered if Dupree was going through all this because she wanted to punish herself for what had happened. She knew that, unlike her, Dupree could get help if she needed it. And Jas was correct because Dupree was battling her own personal demons. She had lost her relationship with the Lord and felt deserving of all the misfortunes going on in her life. Inside she had stopped living and was just functioning. Dupree felt unworthy of help from the people she let down, so she continued to live in misery.

"I'm so tired. I think I'm about to fall asleep on my feet," Jas grumbled as she opened the squeaky door and entered the room with Dupree lagging behind her.

"Tell me about it," Dupree replied. "It's almost midnight. I can't believe we stayed back at school so late."

Jas tossed her backpack on the floor and fell face down on her bed. "At least we got some good studying done."

"Yeah, we did."

They had end-of-term exams and Dupree found it impossible to study at the noisy tenement yard, so they stayed back and used the college library.

"Come on. Let's go and shower real quick before you fall asleep," Dupree said while tugging on Jas's arm dangling off the side of the bed.

After their shower, Dupree and Jas both tumbled into their tiny beds and fell into an exhausted sleep.

Two hours later, Dupree popped up in the bed like a jack-in-the-box and glanced around worriedly, straining her eyes to see in the semi-dark room illuminated by a small nightlight. Her heart galloped in her chest as she remained still, her labored breathing ringing in her ears. Not sure why she had woken up so suddenly, she waited, her body trembling in fear.

Then she heard a sound coming from outside the door. Dupree looked in that direction and saw the doorknob slightly turn as muffled voices leaked inside. Eyes wide in horror, Dupree tiptoed over to Jas's bed and quietly shook her awake.

"Shhhh." Dupree put a finger over her lips and Jas stared at her in fright. "Someone is trying to break in."

Jas looked toward the door and heard the lock rattle.

"Murderrrrr! Helpppp! Thief!" Jas's high-pitched voice bounced off the walls and echoed throughout the entire house. Dupree quickly joined in and began to scream her head off. They continued screaming until they heard banging on their door. Moments later they heard voices loud and clear.

"You girls okay in there?" someone asked.

"Open the door! It's Millie from upstairs," came a squeaky voice.

Jas ran over and quickly opened the door to see many of the tenants standing in the hall with various weapons in their hands.

"What happened?" Mille asked again, a big machete in her right hand.

"Someone was trying to break in on us," Jas replied shakily. "Luckily my friend woke up in time."

"What? Them try to violate the little princesses?" a dread asked in anger, a big hunting knife gripped tightly in his folded fist. "Yo, them disrespect the king palace."

Dupree stood by the bed and listened to the angry voices outside the door as her mind travelled back to her attack and she began reliving the entire ordeal. A loud screech rang out like a wounded wolf and some of the tenants jumped back in alarm and others stared wide-eyed into the room.

Jas spun around and gaped at Dupree as she kicked and swung her arms wildly, wailing hysterically. "No!

Leave me alone!" She punched at the air rowdily, her dilated pupils filled with rage.

Jas ran over and grabbed her around the waist from the back, while Millie held her arms down from the front. Dupree struggled to break away unsuccessfully.

"Dupree, it's me, Jas! Dupree! Stop it now!" Jas screamed in her ears as she held her. A few seconds later, the fight seeped out of Dupree like a punctured balloon as she fell forward in Millie's strong arms. The ladies took her over to her bed and helped her onto it. Dupree curled up in a ball on her side, her knees almost touching her chin as she stared unseeingly at the wall.

An exhausted Jas and the tenants looked at her in concern.

"I think she is having a delayed reaction to what happened earlier," Millie said to Jas and she nodded her head in agreement.

But in Dupree's mind, she knew it was her sin that had invited the devil back in her life. The guilt and shame had her in a chokehold so tight it was suffocating the life out of her.

Before long the news made its way throughout the neighborhood that the two college girls were almost attacked. Many people were upset about it and promised to find the culprits responsible.

Later that night and every one after, the girls pushed the lopsided dresser in front of the little flimsy door for extra protection. Jas also stuck an empty soda bottle in the door handle: their makeshift security alarm. But despite the security measures taken, Dupree didn't sleep a wink that night and many, many more nights to come. She continued to look for somewhere else to live because she didn't feel safe at that house anymore. But no such luck. It looked as if she was doomed.

Chapter Forty-six

It was two weeks before the school term ended and Dupree was getting depressed that she hadn't gotten a positive response to one of her numerous job applications. She needed a job for a few reasons, one of which was she would have an income to get one of those apartments she couldn't currently afford, as she refused to ask Mrs. Scott for extra money. Secondly she did not want to go home and see her loved ones, especially Aunt Madge, who seemed to be able to read her thoughts and mind.

One afternoon when they got home, there was a letter waiting for Jas from National Commercial Bank informing her that she had gotten the bank teller position she had interviewed for the week before.

"Why don't you call a few of those companies you sent your application?" Jas asked Dupree with concern.

"I called last week and got through to Mr. Chevon Brown, the human resources manager at BDO, and he promised me I would get something in the mail. I've gotten nothing." Dupree had changed her mailing address at the post office from Mona Heights to Olympic Gardens.

"Well, we are going to call him back tomorrow and the day after and the day after," Jas told her with determination. One thing about Jas, she didn't accept no from anyone.

So the next day Jas and Dupree went to the public phone, deposited some coins, and called Mr. Brown. They didn't get an answer and Dupree left a message. The next day she called again and got the same result. On the fourth day she called, Mr. Brown answered the phone and Dupree was elated.

As Chevon Brown listened to the anxious young lady on the phone, he felt something that was rare for him: compassion. He remembered Dupree because not only had she left numerous messages for him, but her name was very unique. Mr. Brown had so many applications to review that he hadn't gotten a chance to look at Dupree's.

As he listened to Dupree's pleas over the phone, Mrs. Eleanor Humphrey, the human resources director and his boss, walked into his office and he quickly finished up the conversation with Dupree.

"Well, Dupree, I do appreciate your interest in BDO but I have yet to review your application. I promise to do so very soon and get back to you. Okay, dear? Thank you for calling and have a wonderful day."

Mr. Brown hung up the phone and looked up to see Mrs. Humphrey staring at him intently and wondered if he had done something wrong. "Is something wrong, Eleanor?" he asked her nervously. They had a close working relationship and got along great, but Mr. Brown never forgot that she was his superior.

"No. I'm sorry for interrupting your call, Chevon, and it seemed to be an interesting one, too. Why don't you tell me some more about it?" Mrs. Humphrey said and smiled at him.

Mr. Brown breathed a sigh of relief and went on to tell her about his conversation with Dupree. "She is from Falmouth, Trelawny, and is currently attending UTech. She would like to work here in Kingston for the summer," he concluded. He watched as Mrs. Humphrey gazed out the window, her lips folded in deep concentration. "Eleanor?"

"Oh, sorry. My mind took a little walk. Well, she seems like an ambitious young lady and we could always use more people like her around here. Why don't you have her come in for an interview with me?" she instructed Mr. Brown. "And let's make it sooner rather than later. We need an assistant for one of our chief financial officers and this young lady might be perfect for it."

Mr. Brown had a situation. He remembered that Dupree didn't have a telephone so he would have to send her an overnight mail.

Dupree hung up the phone, feeling like a punctured tire.

"You are going to get something soon. I can feel it in my soul." Jas hugged Dupree as they leaned against the phone booth. "You can't lose faith, girlie. In fact, when we get home, we are going to pray real hard about this."

As the friends stood talking, they jumped in surprise when the public phone rang. They looked at each other in confusion before Jas stepped around a stunned Dupree and answered it. She listened for a minute before handing the phone to Dupree. "It's for you," she said with excitement in her voice.

Dupree wondered who would be calling her on a public phone. "Hello?" Dupree nearly fainted when she heard Mr. Brown on the other end of the line.

Mr. Brown was about to do the letter for Dupree when he remembered she was the last person who had called him on his straight line. He knew it was farfetched but he decided to take a chance and hit star sixty-nine on his phone and luckily Dupree and Jas had stood there talking and hadn't walked away. He asked Dupree to come in the next day for an interview with the human resources director, and she thanked him before she hung up the phone in a daze.

"Do you see how good the Lord is to you?" Jas asked with unshed tears in her eyes. "That was no coincidence. That was the power of the Almighty God and you better not say otherwise, got it?"

Dupree nodded her head in agreement but her heart was filled with doubt as she wondered, *Are you there, God? Are you really?*

The next morning Dupree arrived at BDO at nine a.m. sharp for her interview. She was escorted to Mr. Brown's office where she finally met the man she had stalked for a job. After the introductions were made, Mr. Brown led Dupree to his boss's office.

Dupree felt a lump in her throat and nervously wrung her hands together as she stepped into Mrs. Humphrey lavish office. From her conversation with Mr. Brown, she knew that this was the lady responsible for her being there that morning and the one who would decide whether she would get the job.

As Mrs. Humphrey came around her desk and walked toward her, Dupree gawked at her in surprise. She stood frozen as the young, stunningly beautiful woman came and stood in front of her. For some strange reason Dupree was expecting to meet an older woman, but that was the furthest from the truth.

Without saying a word, Mrs. Humphrey looked at Dupree for few long seconds, her eyes raking over her from head to toe. Suddenly she realized that she was staring and smiled awkwardly.

"Please forgive me for staring," Mrs. Humphrey said, her right hand outstretched. Dupree reached out and grabbed it in a firm handshake. "You are a very beautiful young lady," she added.

"Thank you," Dupree responded shyly.

"I'm Eleanor Humphrey. Please, have a seat." Mrs. Humphrey smiled and waved her arm toward the chair in front of her desk. She waited until Dupree sat before she went and took her own seat, facing Dupree.

"I love to see young ladies striving to make something of their lives, and that was one of the reasons I admired your determination to get a job," Mrs. Humphrey began the interview.

Dupree took a deep breath and felt herself relax. The interview went very well and concluded with Dupree being offered the job as an assistant to Mr. Ryan Patterson, Chief Financial Officer. She was scheduled to start working in less than one week, right after the school term ended.

Dupree started her new job with a lot of enthusiasm and after a week she knew for a fact that she loved it. "My boss and coworkers are so nice to me," she told Jas one night as they sat up in their beds talking. "I feel so accepted."

"I am enjoying my job at the bank, too." Jas smiled. "We are so blessed to find jobs that we both like."

Dupree nodded. "If only we could get somewhere safer to live now."

"I know you are not sleeping well since the attempted break-in," Jas said as she looked at her friend with concern. "You are scared it will happen again."

"I can't go through that again," Dupree whispered, unbeknown to Jas referring to the attack by Deacon Livingston. She lowered her head to hide the tears that welled up in her eyes.

The hunt for an apartment continued with the young ladies spending their weekends taking buses from one end of Kingston to the other, but they were unable to find anything in their price range.

"I know you are disappointed, but we won't stop searching," Jas assured Dupree as she held her stare. "The Lord will provide somewhere for us soon."

The next day at work, Dupree looked up from her lunch and smiled as Mrs. Humphrey made her way to her table in the lunchroom. Her eyes shone bright with adoration for her mentor. Not only was she beautiful but she carried herself with so much confidence, everyone took notice of her when she walked into the lunchroom.

"Hi, Dupree," Mrs. Humphrey greeted her, and pulled out a chair and sat down. "I'm so hungry I could eat a cow and her calf." They shared a hearty laugh.

Even though she was an executive at the company, Mrs. Humphrey was very down-to-earth and Dupree liked that a lot. They often had lunch together and Mrs. Humphrey would ask her questions about her life in Falmouth. Dupree was flattered she took such an interest in her and would share a little about herself without going into too much detail. She still found it very hard to really open up to people because her trust had been abused too many times. Once bitten, twice shy.

Chapter Forty-seven

One Thursday morning some of Dupree's coworkers invited her to a baby shower after work, and although she didn't know them that well, they had always been nice to her, so she accepted.

"I'm glad you could make it," the very pregnant co-worker greeted her at the door later that day. "Please, come in."

As Dupree entered the festive apartment, she saw some familiar faces and was introduced to unfamiliar ones. Quickly she found herself mingling, laughing and talking and actually having fun, so she stayed longer than she anticipated.

Dupree got off the bus on the main road a few minutes after ten that night. The streets were dimly lit and she had to pass a few areas where the streetlights were knocked out; obviously some privacy was required in those areas and Dupree refused to think why. She just wanted to get to the house where Jas was waiting for her.

But as she got around a dark corner passing under a big mango tree, someone grabbed her from behind and a hand immediately covered her mouth, stifling the scream that rose in her throat. Dupree felt the hard body behind her and struggled but to no avail. The person was very strong and also very dirty. A foul smell filled her nose and she felt the food she had earlier at the baby shower making its way up. But Dupree refused to be a victim again and was grateful for the three-inch stiletto heels she wore as she stomped down hard on her attacker's feet, simultaneously forcing her elbow back into his gut. The sudden move startled the creep and he momentarily released her, howling in pain. Dupree made use of this opportunity and ran down the street as fast as she could in her high heels, screaming in fear.

It took a few minutes for her to realize that she was headed the wrong way, away from her house, but she didn't stop. A few people farther down the road tried to stop her to find out what was going on but her feet just kept right on moving. Dupree glanced behind her and saw a van following her; fearing it was her attacker she ran even faster. As the van pulled up alongside her, she picked up the pace and zoomed down the narrow road.

Suddenly she felt herself flying through the air as she stumbled over a piece of log in the road. She screamed as she landed on her belly; her hands helped to break her fall. Winded, she lay still, gasping for breath before the sound of approaching tires caught her ears.

Dupree quickly rolled over and pulled herself into a sitting position as the van screeched to a stop at her feet. Ignoring the pain that shot through her banged-up body, she vaulted to her feet, looking about frantically for a weapon. Her eyes fell on a big rock close by and she grabbed it, her eyes blazing with anger as she watched the van door open.

With the rock raised above her head, Dupree stared as a man stepped out and shouted to her.

"Don't throw that thing! It's me," Bullfrog yelled at her. "What's going on?"

Bullfrog ran to her with concern on his face and Dupree began to cry hysterically.

"What's wrong?" Bullfrog asked again. "I saw you sprinting down the street like Merlene Ottey."

"I . . . I . . . I . . ." Dupree was sobbing too hard to speak. She dropped the rock and rested her face in the palms of her hands and wept.

Bullfrog stood by helplessly, unsure what to do. Restlessly he paced back and forth as he allowed Dupree some time to compose herself.

"I was attacked," Dupree finally whispered, and in between sobs she explained to Bullfrog what had happened.

"What?" Bullfrog was furious. He took out his cell phone and called a few people to let them know what had happened, so they could start searching for the culprit.

"Come on. Let me drop you home," he said and led a distraught Dupree to his van. "Don't worry, my people are on the hunt for that punk," he told Dupree as he drove off down the street; his cold voice reflected his mood. It was common knowledge that some of the men in the community disapproved of violence of any kind toward the women and children who lived there.

Shortly after, Bullfrog parked the van and helped a trembling Dupree to her door. Jas was waiting worriedly because it was later than she thought Dupree would be home. She took one look at her friend and started to cry before she had even heard what had happened. She only cried harder after hearing about the ordeal.

After having her shower, Dupree went to lie on the bed, still trembling despite the eighty-four-degree temperature. Jas held her friend in her arms until she fell into a restless sleep and knew they really couldn't stay there much longer.

The next morning Jas and Dupree, still shaken up from the night before, went to the bus stop together. They made arrangement for Jas to wait for Dupree at the last bus stop so that they could walk home together. Bullfrog had also informed them that he had a few of his men keeping an eye on them; Dupree wasn't sure whether she should be happy or horrified.

Dupree went to work and found it hard to concentrate. She walked around aimlessly, not sure what to do or where to turn. At lunchtime she sat in the back of the lunchroom at a table by herself. Mrs. Humphrey came in and invited herself to Dupree's table but Dupree's mind was miles away and she didn't realize her mentor was there.

"Dupree? Dupree?" No response. Mrs. Humphrey looked at Dupree worriedly. "Dupree?" She snapped her finger before Dupree's face and Dupree jerked back in alarm.

"Yes?" Her eyes met Mrs. Humphrey apologetically. "I'm sorry. I . . ."

"Please. No apologies are necessary; just tell me what's wrong."

With tears in her eyes Dupree relayed the incident that occurred the night before.

"You can't go back there. You have to get out now and you can stay with me until we get you a place of your own," she told Dupree in an angry voice.

"Thank you, but I can't leave Jas there by herself," Dupree replied with gratitude.

"You know what, I have to go and check on something. Please come to my office after you finish your lunch," Mrs. Humphrey instructed Dupree and marched out of the lunchroom without touching her food.

A few minutes later, Dupree left most of the food on her plate and went to Mrs. Humphrey's office. Mrs. Humphrey invited her to have a seat and it was obvious that she was still upset by what Dupree had told her.

"My husband's best friend, Edward, is a developer who builds and rents apartments all over the country. He has a few places in Norbrook Heights, Constant Spring Road, Meadowbrook, Forest Hills, Cherry Gardens, and Stony Hill to name a few."

Dupree looked at Mrs. Humphrey as if she was crazy; her eyes had grown wider with the name of each place she mentioned. These were some of the most influential communities in Kingston, maybe even Jamaica. To say they were expensive was being modest. Dupree knew Mrs. Humphrey was a wealthy woman, not just because of her high-powered job, but she knew her husband was also the chief executive officer of the Bank of Nova Scotia, one of the largest banks in Jamaica.

Mrs. Humphrey noticed Dupree's expression and quickly explained. "I know what you are thinking, but let me explain. Edward's youngest daughter, Jessica, recently got married and is now living in Miami with her new husband. However, she refused to sell or rent her Oakland apartment on Constant Spring Road, which was a gift from her dad. I told Edward what happened to you and, as a father of three daughters, he too was enraged. He is offering you and Jas the apartment to stay for as long as you want, free of charge."

Dupree didn't know she had any more left but obviously she did because the tears came rushing out her eyes, dancing crazily as they travelled down her face. Dupree, too overwhelmed, rested her head on the desk and cried.

Mrs. Humphrey quickly went around her desk, pulled up another chair beside Dupree, took her in her arms and cried with her. It took a few minutes for the women to gain some composure and Mrs. Humphrey offered Dupree some Kleenex. As she wiped her face and running nose, Dupree looked at Mrs. Humphrey with gratitude.

"Here, why don't you use my telephone and call Jas. Let her know we are coming to get her after work to go and look at the apartment."

After work, Mrs. Humphrey and Dupree drove to National Commercial Bank in Cross Roads to get Jas, who was anxiously waiting outside. She was excited to finally meet the woman her friend talked so much about. Without even knowing her, Jas had developed a lot of respect for Mrs. Humphrey and the feeling was mutual.

It was rush hour and they got caught in the bumper-to-bumper traffic and it was almost an hour later when Mrs. Humphrey pulled up to the security guard post of the apartment complex. She gave the security guard her name and he gave her a key before he opened the gate allowing them entrance. Jas gasped when she saw the magnificent apartments, and the well-manicured lawns and trees and beautiful flowers that decorated the grounds.

Both she and Dupree got out of the car as soon as it was parked in front of the apartment and looked around in awe. The place was so quiet they heard each other breathing. Mrs. Humphrey put her handbag over her shoulder and went in between both girls, taking each by the arm, and led them to the apartment entrance. She used the key she got from the security guard to open the door and Dupree covered her mouth in shock.

Plush beige carpet led them into a huge living room with floor-to-ceiling windows capturing the essence of the sunlight that poured through them. There was a huge aquarium full of exotic fish that took up an entire wall, with a sixty-inch television facing it across the room. A soft beige five-piece leather reclining sectional and storage ottoman sat in the middle of the room with walls covered with exquisite paintings. It looked like something out of the movies!

The rest of the three-bedroom apartment was just as fabulous. The bedrooms were beautifully decorated, each with a queen-sized bed, and the bathroom, which was all white, was an extravagant paradise. Dupree stared at the white antique bathtub and would have given anything for a nice warm bath, but reluctantly followed Mrs. Humphrey in a kitchen that was a cook's paradise.

Everything almost seemed too surreal for Dupree and Jas. They felt as if they would wake up anytime in the little room in Olympic Gardens, but when they saw Mrs. Humphrey smiling at them, they knew it was for real. They were about to move into a luxury apartment in one of the wealthiest neighborhood in Jamaica, free of cost!

As Mrs. Humphrey led them back into the living room, Dupree got real overwhelmed when she finally realized what was going on. She fell to her knees with hands raised to heaven and repented before the Almighty God. She realized that even though she had sinned against the Lord, He was still there for her, waiting with open arms. Tears ran down Dupree's face and, oblivious of the other two people in the room, Dupree confessed her sin and asked the Lord for forgiveness. It was the first time she had prayed since that disastrous night with Suave. So with a heart of repentance and her voice filled with praise, she reflected on Isaiah 44:22.

I have blotted out, as a thick cloud, thy transgressions, and, as a cloud, thy sins: return unto me; for I have redeemed thee.

Jas and Mrs. Humphrey joined Dupree on the floor, praising and worshipping the Lord. It was a very special moment as the Holy Spirit administered to their hearts. "Greater is He that is in me!" Dupree declared with a strong personal conviction.

Chapter Forty-eight

A few minutes later everyone was still feeling rejuvenated.

"I am going to call a moving company to get your things." Mrs. Humphrey smiled widely at Dupree and Jas. "I hope I can still get someone today. I don't care how much it costs."

"Oh, we already know someone who can move us," Dupree eagerly informed her. "He is a good friend of ours."

"Okay. Why don't you give him a call?" Mrs. Humphrey handed her cell phone to Jas.

Jas hurried placed a call to Bullfrog. After their conversation she looked at Dupree and Mrs. Humphrey. "Okay. Bullfrog is going to meet us by the lane," Jas said after hanging up the phone.

"Bullfrog?" Mrs. Humphrey asked skeptically. The girls laughed at her perplexed expression.

"That's our friend who helped me that night," Dupree told her. "He is a great guy."

"Oh, that's the guy. Well, I am looking forward to meeting him," Mrs. Humphrey said, her eyes dancing in amusement. "I have to thank him for all he has done for you girls. Come on, let's go."

"Over there!" A few minutes later Jas pointed excitedly to Bullfrog's van parked by the side of the road.

"I see him," Mrs. Humphrey said and pulled up behind the van.

Bullfrog stuck his head out the window and waved at them to follow him, before slowly driving off down the lane. Mrs. Humphrey followed closely behind, carefully maneuvering her BMW over the potholes and uneven paved road.

Soon Bullfrog pulled up to the house and parked and Mrs. Humphrey did the same behind the van. She opened the door and walked toward Bullfrog, her right hand outstretched and her face fixed with a pleasant smile.

"You must be Bullfrog," she greeted him when he shook her hand. "Thank you for everything you have done for these girls. You are a blessing to them."

"It's . . . hmmm . . . It's no problem." Bullfrog quickly released her hand and actually blushed, glancing away in embarrassment. "Let's start moving." And he walked off hurriedly toward the house. Jas and Dupree grinned and followed him with Mrs. Humphrey close behind.

As they entered the small room, Dupree glanced out the side of her eye at Mrs. Humphrey to see her reaction to where they lived, but the elegant, classy woman, rolled up the sleeves of her silk shirt and walked over to the lopsided closet. She pulled the door open and began taking clothes out.

"All right everyone, get to work," she said sternly before glancing over her shoulder and winking at Dupree. The laughter eased the tension and everyone began scurrying around the small room.

It took the four of them less than an hour to get everything to Bullfrog's van and to cram a few things in the trunk of Mrs. Humphrey's car. As they were leaving, Dupree and Jas went over to some of the tenants who sat idly on the wall by the side of the house and said their good-byes.

"I am going to miss having you girls here," Millie said as she bounced her baby over her shoulder. "But I am glad you are leaving after what happened. Take care of yourselves and stay in school."

The girls nodded and waved before walking to the waiting car. Dupree stopped and turned around to take one last look at the house before she slid in the front seat beside Mrs. Humphrey.

"Thank you, Lord," Dupree said aloud and smiled at Mrs. Humphrey through water-filled eyes. "We are leaving, Jas." She looked over in the back seat and saw the tears rolling down Jas's face. Mrs. Humphrey sniffed and hastily drove off with Bullfrog on her tail.

Back at the apartment, Bullfrog pulled some bags from the van and followed Mrs. Humphrey inside the apartment. His grin grew wider as he looked around the chic apartment in appreciation.

"So this is how you big shots are rolling now?' he teased the girls as they entered the apartment, their hands filled with bags and clothes.

"You know how we do, when we do the do," Jas replied and their laughter filled the air.

"I'm happy for you girls. Now I don't have to worry so much about you."

They worked swiftly and before long everything was transported into the apartment.

"Thank you very much," Mrs. Humphrey said to Bullfrog as she held out some money to him.

"What's that for?" He frowned, looking insulted. "I don't need to be paid to help people I care about."

"I'm so sorry," Mrs. Humphrey quickly apologized. "I didn't mean to offend you. I am just so grateful to you for everything you have done for the girls."

"No problem." Bullfrog nodded understandingly. "I'm happy I could help."

Mrs. Humphrey wrote the telephone number of the apartment on a piece of paper and handed it to him. "The phone will be back on tomorrow. Now you can always keep in touch with the girls." Bullfrog smiled and thanked her.

Jas and Dupree had a heartfelt group hug with Bullfrog as they told him how grateful they were for all his help. They walked him to the door and waved as he drove off, knowing they had found a friend for life.

"You girls better get some rest for work tomorrow," Mrs. Humphrey told them when they returned to the living room. "You can always unpack after work and over the weekend."

"Sounds good to me," Dupree said and yawned.

"That's my clue to leave now." Mrs. Humphrey laughed. "We are all exhausted."

She hugged each girl and said good-bye and jokingly waved off their thanks, before leaving to go home to her husband.

Dupree held her head back and sighed in pleasure as the cool, refreshing water caressed her body. With her eyes closed, she stood under the shower rain and reflected on where the Lord had brought her from and where she could have been.

Last night I slept in an unsafe house after being attacked, but tonight I am in a gated community with a security guard outside keeping watch. Lord, you have taken me from the bottom and put me at the top. Thank you, Lord.

And even though she was tired, Dupree twisted and turned for a while before falling asleep on the 800-thread count satin sheets.

***

It was Friday afternoon after work and Dupree had called home to spread the good news and inform the ladies of her new address.

"Did you say Oakland apartments?" Mrs. Scott asked, flabbergasted.

"Yes!" Dupree squealed over the telephone. "Mrs. Scott, you should see this place. It's absolutely fabulous!"

"Oh, I know that area very well and I totally agree with you. Thank you, Lord!" she yelled. "Hold on a second."

Dupree laughed and Jas, who had her ear pressed to the phone, giggled. "They are very happy," she mouthed to Dupree and she nodded as they listened to Mrs. Scott explain to Aunt Madge and Miss Angie that it was a beautiful place to live.

"I'm . . . so . . . so . . . happy for you, baby," Aunt Madge cried loudly over the phone when it was her turn to speak. "I knew the Lord would make a way for you. What a blessing."

"Yes, Aunt Madge, we are very blessed," Dupree agreed. "I'll talk to you tomorrow. I need to call Tony and the Greggs before Jas and I begin to unpack all this stuff. I love you."

Dupree gave them her new telephone number before hanging up, and then proceeded to call her best friend in New York.

"I can't wait to visit," Tony exclaimed when he heard the great news. "Have you spoken to our dad as yet?"

"Our dad?" Dupree asked, puzzled. This time she caught Tony's slip of tongue.

"Huh?" Tony played dumb.

"You just said 'our dad,'" Dupree pressed. "What do you mean by that?"

"Oh, did I say that? Girl, my mouth just slipped," Tony quickly replied. "I meant my dad. It has been a long day."

"Okay," Dupree said with a slight hesitation in her voice. "I am going to give your folks a quick call now."

"Great. Bye." Tony hurriedly hung up the phone.

"I'll . . ." Dupree stopped and listened to the dial tone. After hanging up the phone she gazed through the window and thought about Tony's weird behavior. "Am I missing something here?" she asked herself. Dupree stood rooted to the same spot for a few minutes with an unsettling feeling in her spirit.

Chapter Forty-nine

"Dupree! Telephone!" Jas yelled.

"Who is it?" Dupree asked as she entered the living room from her bedroom.

"Mrs. Scott," Jas replied as she handed her the phone.

"Hello, Mrs. Scott. Is everything all right?"

"Yes, my dear. I just called to let you know that a letter came for you from New York University."

"Really? I've been waiting on that letter for a while now."

"I know. We are also longing to see you so we have decided to come for a visit and bring you the letter. Why not kill two birds with one stone?"

"Yes! Yes!" Dupree pumped her fists in the air and did a little jiggle. Mrs. Scott laughed out loud at the excitement in her voice. "I hope you are staying a day or two," she told Mrs. Scott.

"Sorry. You know Miss Angie won't stay over."

Dupree shook her head. Miss Angie refused to sleep in Sodom and Gomorrah, the city of sin, as she referred to Kingston. Therefore, the three women planned on coming early the next morning to leave later that afternoon.

"We can't wait to meet Jas and we hope to possibly meet Mrs. Humphrey as well," Mrs. Scott said.

"I think you just might meet Mrs. Humphrey. She promised to come for a visit tomorrow with her husband."

"Wonderful," Mrs. Scott replied.

Dupree instructed Mrs. Scott to open the letter and give Officer Gregg all the forms from New York University that he needed to complete as her sponsor.

"I'll give him a call so he'll expect you," she informed Mrs. Scott.

Early the next morning Dupree and Jas stood outside and anxiously watched the gate for Mrs. Scott's car.

"There it is!" Dupree bellowed as the car passed the guard station and slowly drove toward the apartment. The two girls ran to the car and waited impatiently as Mrs. Scott parked.

"Hi, Mrs. Scott," Dupree said as she hugged the older woman affectionately.

"Look at you," Mrs. Scott said as she pulled back, looking Dupree up and down. "Sweetheart, you look great."

"Thanks." Dupree blushed and glanced over her shoulder to see Miss Angie and Jas embracing each other.

"Hey, Aunt Madge." Dupree slid into the back seat of the car and fell into her aunt's arms. Aunt Madge planted little kisses all over her face and hugged her as if their lives depended on it.

"You look happy, baby," she whispered in Dupree's ear. "I'm glad you are back to the place where you started."

Dupree squeezed her aunt in response, too choked up to speak.

"It's all right, baby. Just continue to take it one day at a time."

"I'm waiting for my hug," Miss Angie interrupted from outside the car. "And we need to help Sister Madge into her wheelchair."

Dupree laughed and stepped out of the car into Miss Angie's waiting arms. "Muah!" Dupree kissed the leathery right cheek. "Muah!" A loud one landed on the left cheek. Miss Angie giggled and returned the kisses.

After Dupree and Mrs. Scott helped Aunt Madge into her wheelchair, she opened her arms and Jas knelt down and lost herself in the bear hug. Her grin was so wide, Dupree knew her jaw must be hurting.

"Mrs. Humphrey and her husband will be here soon," Dupree told the women as she pushed the wheelchair into the apartment. "I wanted to surprise her, so I didn't tell her you guys were visiting,"

"That's great," Aunt Madge replied. "I can't wait to meet her."

Dupree and Jas gave them a tour of the apartment and the older women oohed and aahed as they went from one room to the other.

"I love it!" Mrs. Scott exclaimed.

"Absolutely beautiful!" said Miss Angie.

Dupree and Jas smiled proudly at each other. They loved it!

"Why don't you girls get the food out the car," Mrs. Scott suggested. "We'll wait for the Humphreys to get here, then feast on what Miss Angie stayed up late last night preparing."

Dupree and Jas sprinted to the door, the ladies' laughter following them outside. In record time, containers of food were laid out on the dining table.

"Wow, we have enough food here to feed an army." Jas's eyes expanded like an owl's. "Oh! My! Gosh! Oxtail and butterbeans!" she shouted after she peeked inside an aluminum container.

Dupree laughed at her friend's enthusiasm. Jas was a foodie like herself.

"I would like to lie down and rest a little before we eat." Aunt Madge's voice was tired. The long drive had worn her out.

Dupree quickly walked over to the wheelchair and pushed Aunt Madge down the hall and into her bedroom, with Jas following closely behind. The two girls helped Aunt Madge onto the bed and got her comfortable. Gently pulling the door closed, Jas and Dupree went back to join the other ladies in the living room.

"They are here!" Dupree screamed excitedly about forty-five minutes later, as she peeped through the window and saw a sparkling Mercedes-Benz parking beside Mrs. Scott's car.

A tall, handsome man came out of the driver's side and hurried around to open the passenger door. Mrs. Humphrey stepped out the car and walked into the tight embrace waiting for her.

"Oh, he is fine," Jas said beside Dupree as she too watched the scene outside. "You go, Mrs. Humphrey."

The other women laughed and Dupree put her index finger to her lips, signaling their silence. Dupree then ran to the front door and pulled it open, just as the doorbell rang.

"Hello, sweetheart," Mrs. Humphrey said as she hugged Dupree. After releasing Dupree, she slipped her hand into her husband's and pulled him closer to her side.

"Dupree, this is my husband, Dwight," Mrs. Humphrey said as she turned slightly to glance at her husband.

"Hello, Mr. Humphrey." Dupree flashed her bright smile, her right hand outstretched toward him. No response.

Dwight stood in silence, staring at Dupree, a weird look on his face.

"Babe?" Mrs. Humphrey lightly elbowed him in the side.

"Oh, I'm so sorry," Dwight said quickly. "Hi, Dupree. It's a pleasure to meet you." He ignored Dupree's outstretched hand and reached down and hugged her instead. "My mind just traveled for a while," he added after he let her go.

"Nice to meet you, sir," Dupree replied. "Please, come in." Dupree followed the Humphreys as they walked into the living room.

"Hello," Jas, Mrs. Scott, and Miss Angie said in sync.

Mrs. Humphrey stopped suddenly and looked at them in alarm. "What's going on?" she croaked. "I . . . I . . . I didn't know you had visitors." She turned to Dupree, panic splashed across her face.

"I wanted to surprise you," Dupree responded, a little confused.

Silence covered the room as everyone looked at each other, perplexed. One could have heard a mouse peeing on a cotton ball.

"Hmmm, well, it's certainly wonderful to meet you all," Dwight said a little too loud. He chuckled nervously as he slipped his arm around his wife's waist. "Please excuse my wife. She gets a little overwhelmed with too much attention."

"Yes," Mrs. Humphrey whispered, her eyes locked on the beige carpet. "All of this caught me off-guard." Her laugh sounded like a whooping cough.

"I hope it was okay?" Dupree asked worriedly, her eyes moving back and forth between Mrs. Humphrey and Dwight. The last thing she wanted to do was to offend her boss and her boss's husband.

"Yes, yes. It's fine," Dwight replied with a grin pulling from one ear to the other. "Why don't we all have a seat?"

"I'll be right back," Mrs. Humphrey said hastily as she pulled away from her husband and sprinted down the hall.

"Wait!" Dupree shouted at her back but Mrs. Humphrey had disappeared from sight.

Mrs. Humphrey hurriedly grabbed the first door handle her legs took her to and pulled the door open. Rushing inside, she slammed the door shut and pressed her back firmly against it. With her eyes tightly shut, she took deep breaths as she tried to get her mind and body under control.

Suddenly Mrs. Humphrey sensed another presence in the room and realized she wasn't alone. Her body began to tremble uncontrollably as she slowly opened her eyes and stared into the other all-too-familiar ones.

"Aunt Madge," Mrs. Humphrey whispered as she crumbled to the floor in distress.

"Tiny?" Aunt Madge asked in surprise. "Tiny, is that you?"

"Yes, Aunt Madge," Mrs. Eleanor Humphrey, aka Tiny, answered. "It's me."

Chapter Fifty

Pain ignited the bedroom as the past collided with the present. Mrs. Humphrey was curled up on the floor, shivering, as deep sobs shook her body. Aunt Madge lay on her side staring at the crumpled figure on the floor, her tears seeping into the pillow under the head. While Mrs. Humphrey cried tears of despair and shame, Aunt Madge cried tears of joy. The niece she had lost was now found.

"Tiny. Come here, baby," Aunt Madge said in between sobs. "Get up off that floor and come to me."

Mrs. Humphrey staggered to her feet and wobbled over to the bed. Tears and mucus ran down her face as she looked into the sorrowful eyes of the woman who had raised her.

"Oh, Aunt Madge. I'm so sorry," Mrs. Humphrey wept. "Please, please forgive me."

Aunt Madge opened her arms and Mrs. Humphrey fell on the bed beside her and tightly hugged the aged, fragile body.

"I didn't know what happened to you," Aunt Madge cried as she stroked Mrs. Humphrey's hair. "I went through hell not knowing."

"I'm so sorry," Mrs. Humphrey said again and again, her wet face pressed firmly against her aunt's neck. "Please, don't hate me, Aunt Madge."

"I could never hate you, my niece." Aunt Madge whispered. "I love you too much."

***

"So, where is Aunt Madge?" Dwight asked after he sat down on the couch facing the women.

"She is resting in Dupree's bedroom," Mrs. Scott replied.

"Oh, okay." Dwight glanced nervously down the hall where his wife had fled minutes before.

"As a matter of fact, let me go and check on Aunt Madge," Dupree said and stood to her feet. "I'll be right back."

"Hmmm, maybe you should just . . ." Dwight stood abruptly as Dupree hurried away before he finished his sentence. "Wait," he whispered under his breath as a feeling of dread filled his soul. Slowly he lowered his tall frame back into the couch, three remaining pair of eyes looking at him, puzzled.

As Dupree approached her bedroom she heard muffled voices through the door. *Great, Mrs. Humphrey already met Aunt Madge.* With a smile on her face, she gently opened the door and stepped inside. The smile instantly fell from her face. Her eyes and mouth popped wide open when she saw Aunt Madge and Mrs. Humphrey huddled on the bed, crying.

"It's going to be all right, Tiny," Aunt Madge said. "The Lord knows best."

"Tiny?" Dupree asked in bewilderment. "Did you say Tiny?"

Like a frisky, young goat, Mrs. Humphrey jumped off the bed and stood facing her daughter, trembling. The tears were still flowing down her face as her red, puffy eyes met Dupree's horrified ones.

"No, no, no. It couldn't be," Dupree muttered repeatedly, shaking her head from side to side. Her shaky hand covered her mouth as the truth from Mrs. Humphrey's expression slammed into her gut. It felt like a right uppercut. "Please, God. This can't be happening."

Dupree turned and staggered out of the bedroom as if drunk. She grunted in pain when her hip connected with doorframe. Robotically, she walked across the hall and grabbed the door handle of Jas's bedroom door and pushed it open.

"Dupree! Please wait!"

She vaguely heard her name as it seemed to be coming from a thousand miles away but her foggy mind ignored it.

"Dupree," Mrs. Humphrey shouted as she frantically grabbed Dupree's left arm, preventing her from entering the room. "Please let me explain," she begged pleadingly.

"Take your hands off me!" Dupree snarled and shook off the offensive hand. With her pounding head held straight, she stepped into the bedroom, slamming the door shut in her mother's face.

Dupree threw herself down on Jas's bed. Lying face down with her face muffled by the thick pillow, she screamed. It sounded like a growl from an angry, wounded bear.

Outside the room, Mrs. Humphrey rested her forehead on the closed door and wept deep, heart-wrenching sobs that literally shook her slender frame.

By this time, Dwight, Jas, Mrs. Scott, and Miss Angie heard the commotion and came running down the hall. Dwight quickly went to wife and pulled her into his arms. The other ladies rushed into the Dupree's bedroom to find a distraught Aunt Madge.

"What's going on?" Mrs. Scott asked as she wrapped her arms around Aunt Madge's quivering body.

"Where is Dupree?" Jas asked almost at the same time.

"Tiny," Aunt Madge whispered and pointed to Mrs. Humphrey standing outside the room door in her husband's arms.

The three women's mouths opened wide as they turned to look at Mrs. Humphrey in shock. They were all familiar with Tiny's story.

"She is Dupree's mother." Jas whispered the obvious. She quickly walked out of the room, across the hall to her bedroom door. With a quick glance at the distressed couple standing close by, she knocked on the door.

"Dupree," Jas called to her friend. "Please let me in." No response.

Dupree heard the knocking at the door and her name being called repeatedly, but she ignored it. She just wanted to be alone. With her tearstained face to the ceiling, she pondered her situation.

Mrs. Humphrey was her mother.

Fifty-one

Mrs. Humphrey was so consumed with grief that her husband decided it was best he take her home. Dwight promised Aunt Madge that she would be back in the morning when she was feeling better and more capable of dealing with things. Aunt Madge agreed. It was also decided that Mrs. Scott and Miss Angie would return to Falmouth without Aunt Madge.

"My nieces need me," Aunt Madge informed the ladies. "I can't leave them right now."

"You are right," Mrs. Scott agreed. "I'll be back tomorrow with some of your things."

"We are praying for you all," Miss Angie said as she hugged Aunt Madge good-bye. "Please tell Dupree we love her." She and Mrs. Scott left for home.

"Jas, please go and tell Dupree that everyone has left and I need to see her," Aunt Madge instructed.

Jas ran across the hall and knocked on her bedroom door. She relayed Aunt Madge's message through the closed door, then walked away into the living room to give them some privacy.

Dupree heard the message and suddenly the child in her awoke. She felt an urgent need for her grand-aunt, the only mother she had ever known.

Slowly making her way off the bed, Dupree opened the door softly. Walking at an almost ninety-degree angle, she crossed the hall and entered her bedroom where her aunt lay. Without a word, Dupree climbed on the bed and fell into Aunt Madge's waiting arms. All cried out, no words were spoken as the two women clung together, sharing each other's pain. Soon an exhausted sleep crept up on them and took them away temporarily from the misery.

"Dupree," Jas whispered as she shook her roommate by the shoulder. "Dupree, wake up."

"What?" Dupree replied foggily and rolled over onto her back. "What's the matter?" She saw the solemn look on Jas's face. She then realized Aunt Madge was no longer lying next to her.

"Where is Aunt Madge?" she asked as she jumped out of the bed.

"Aunt Madge is in the living room with her," Jas said a little above a whisper. "They have been talking for a long time and now Mrs. Humphrey wants to see you."

Dupree knew eventually she would have to face her mother again but she needed more time. "I don't want to talk to her," Dupree informed Jas. "Tell her to go away."

"Okay, I'll tell her," Jas replied and left the bedroom, subtly closing the door behind her.

Dupree paced the room, nervously wringing her hands together as she waited for Jas to return. She jumped when she heard a knock on the door.

"I'm not leaving until we talk, Dupree," Mrs. Humphrey said from the other side of the door. "We are going to talk today."

"Go away!" Dupree screamed. "Now you want to talk, huh? You are eighteen years too late!"

"Baby, please let me come in and explain." Mrs. Humphrey's voice cracked as she struggled to hold the tears at bay.

"I'm not your baby!" Dupree yelled. "You never wanted me in the first place. Get lost!" And Dupree fell on the bed and began to sob.

Mrs. Humphrey heard her crying and turned the doorknob. Stepping into the room, she walked over to her distraught daughter lying on the bed.

"I'm so sorry, sweetheart," Mrs. Humphrey said as she gently ran her fingers through her daughter's hair. Dupree flinched and turned away. "I promise if it takes the rest of my life, I'll make it up to you."

Mrs. Humphrey sat on the edge on the bed, staring helplessly at Dupree's back. Finally she stood up and sighed deeply. Maybe today wasn't the right time to speak with her daughter after all.

"Okay. I'm going to leave now, baby. But I'm ready to talk when you are. I promise I'll explain everything to you," Mrs. Humphrey said and walked toward the door.

"Wait," Dupree said.

Mrs. Humphrey stopped suddenly and turned around excitedly to her daughter. She was glad that perhaps Dupree had had a change of heart.

Dupree's crying had tapered off, and using the back of her hand, she wiped her wet face. Sluggishly pulling herself up into a sitting position on the bed, she faced her mother. "Tell me something," Dupree said.

"Anything," Mrs. Humphrey replied quickly as she sat down on the edge of the bed.

"Who is he?" Dupree asked.

"Huh?" Mrs. Humphrey's eyes bulged out of her head. "He?"

"Please don't play any more games with me," Dupree said. "You owe me that much. Who is my father?"

"Oh, sweetheart. It's so complicated," Mrs. Humphrey began. "It was such a long time ago and—"

"Who is he?" Dupree snapped angrily.

Mrs. Humphrey flinched at her daughter's tone of voice but knew her behavior was justified.

"His name is Anthony Gregg," Mrs. Humphrey whispered, her head hanging low. "Your father is Officer Anthony Gregg."

Dupree felt as if someone had thrown a bucket of ice-cold water over her head. Instead of the familiar pain, she felt numb. Her body began to shiver, the force of the deception freezing her from inside out.

"Dupree, please let—" Mrs. Humphrey halted in mid-sentence when Dupree held up a hand for her to stop.

"Please leave now," Dupree said in a very cold voice. Her arms were wrapped tightly around her body as she rocked from side to side.

Mrs. Humphrey took one look at her face and knew there would be no more conversation that day. Reluctantly she stood up, her heart breaking at the misery her daughter was going through. "I'll be back," she informed Dupree. "And I do love you." Mrs. Humphrey silently slipped out the door, pulling it closed behind her.

As if in a trance, Dupree reached for the telephone on the bedside table. With each number she dialed, the anger in her rose. By the time the call connected, Dupree was like an erupting volcano.

"Hello?" Officer Gregg answered on the second ring.

"It's me." Dupree words were chipped in ice.

"Dupree," Officer Greg's said excitedly, his face lit up at the sound of his daughter's voice. "How are you doing, my dear?" he asked Dupree.

"How do you think I'm doing, Father?" Dupree replied sarcastically. "I'm not doing too well, Daddy!" Dupree screamed into the phone.

"How did you . . . ? I mean, who? What?" Officer Gregg was flabbergasted. "How did you find out?" he finally whispered.

"Does it really matter?" Dupree spat. "Do you even care?"

"My daughter, I do—"

"I am not your daughter!" Dupree screamed. "I never have been and I never will be!"

With that Dupree slammed the phone down and just as quickly picked it back up again. Her breathing was labored as the anger was now fully in charge. She had one more call to make.

"Hello," Dupree said when Tony answered the phone. "This is your sister, Dupree, speaking."

Tony was too shocked to respond. This was the confirmation Dupree needed of his betrayal. He, too, had known all along.

"Speak to me, my darling brother!" Dupree shrieked into the phone.

Tony's mouth opened but for the life of him he couldn't get a word out.

"You, your father, and Tiny are all cowards!" Dupree yelled. "I don't need any of you!" She slammed the phone down again. Emotionally drained, Dupree lay on her bed. The anger was now giving way to that familiar ache.

"I don't need any of you," Dupree whispered again and allowed the tears to seep out of her eyes. "I have my God and He is all I need."

Dupree made it up in her mind that she wouldn't have anything to do with Tiny or Mr. Gregg. Little did she know, that might have been her plan, but it certainly wasn't God's.

Discussion Questions

1. What are your feelings about growing up without electricity or running water? Would this make a difference in your upbringing? Why? Why not?

2. Under the law, Officer Gregg committed statutory rape. Do you think he should have faced charges so many years later? What do you think about the statute of limitation for this crime?

3. Mrs. Gregg knew of her husband's infidelity that resulted in a child, yet she stayed with him. Should she have forgiven him? What would you do if you were in a similar situation?

4. Tony was devastated when he found out Dupree was his sister and was furious with his parents. Do you think he should have told Dupree the truth immediately? Should Officer Gregg have? Why? Why not?

5. Aunt Madge was a child of God and was plagued by an illness that made life more difficult for her but she never lost faith in God. If this were you, how would you feel about your faith? Would you question God's healing power?

6. Mrs. Scott blamed God after her husband died. Was this justified? Do you think she was right to turn her back on God? How do you feel about her getting saved?

7. Dupree saw Deacon Livingston as a father figure but he betrayed her trust. How do you feel about his attacks on her? Were you surprised he was the same

person who had attacked her the first time? Was justice served?

8. What do you think of Suave? Could you tell he was just playing Dupree? Should Dupree have seen through his game? How? When?

9. Dupree lost her virginity to Suave unintentionally. Was it her fault? Why? Why not? What should she have done differently to avoid that situation?

10. By committing fornication, Dupree felt her sin had separated her from the Lord. Was this true? Was she wrong in not forgiving herself? Do you think God had forgiven her?

11. How do you feel about Mandy's promiscuous behavior? What could be the reason for such behavior? Were you surprised she slept with Suave? What would be her motive?

12. Mrs. Humphrey became Dupree's mentor. Were you surprised she was Tiny, Dupree's mother? Do you think that was the reason she gave her the job and helped her with the apartment?

13. Do you think Dupree will ever forgive Mrs. Humphrey, Officer Greg, and Tony? Why? Why not?

About the Author

Theresa A. Campbell was born and raised in Jamaica, West Indies. She received her associate's degree in business administration from Bronx Community College, a bachelor's degree in business administration from Baruch College, and a master's degree in business administration from Fairleigh Dickinson University.

Theresa has had a deep passion for reading ever since she was a child. It is her desire to inspire readers with her stories by uplifting their faith in God.

UC HIS GLORY BOOK CLUB!

www.uchisglorybookclub.net

UC His Glory Book Club is the spirit-inspired brain-child of Joylynn Ross, Author and Acquisitions Editor of Urban Christian, and Kendra Norman-Bellamy, Author for Urban Christian. This is an online book club that hosts authors of Urban Christian. We welcome as members all men and women who have a passion for reading Christian-based fiction.

UC His Glory Book Club pledges our commitment to provide support, positive feedback, encouragement, and a forum whereby members can openly discuss and review the literary works of Urban Christian authors.

There is no membership fee associated with UC His Glory Book Club; however, we do ask that you support the authors through purchasing, encouraging, providing book reviews, and of course, your prayers. We also ask that you respect our beliefs and follow the guidelines of the book club. We hope to receive your valuable input, opinions, and reviews that build up, rather than tear down our authors.

What We Believe:

—We believe that Jesus is the Christ, Son of the Living God

—We believe the Bible is the true, living Word of God

—We believe all Urban Christian authors should use their God-given writing abilities to honor God and share the message of the written word God has given to each of them uniquely.

—We believe in supporting Urban Christian authors in their literary endeavors by reading, purchasing and sharing their titles with our online community.

—We believe that in everything we do in our literary arena should be done in a manner that will lead to God being glorified and honored.

We look forward to the online fellowship with you. Please visit us often at *www.uchisglorybookclub.net*.

Many Blessing to You!

Shelia E. Lipsey,
President, UC His Glory Book Club